The Summer Girl

Jenny Blackhurst lives in Shropshire where she grew up dreaming that one day she would get paid for making up stories. She is an avid reader and can mostly be found with her head in a book or hunting Pokemon with her son, otherwise you can get her on Twitter @JennyBlackhurst or Facebook. Her favourite film is Fried Green Tomatoes at the Whistle Stop Cafe, but if her children ask it's definitely Moana.

Also by Jenny Blackhurst

How I Lost You
The Foster Child
Before I Let You In
The Night She Died
The Perfect Guests
The Girl Who Left
The Hiking Trip

The
summer
girl

JENNY
BLACKHURST

San Diego, California

CANELO US

Canelo US
An imprint of Printers Row Publishing Group
9717 Pacific Heights Blvd, San Diego, CA 92121
www.canelobooksus.com

Printers Row Publishing Group is a division of Readerlink Distribution Services, LLC. Canelo US is a registered trademark of Readerlink Distribution Services, LLC.

This edition originally published in the United Kingdom in 2023 by Canelo.

Published in partnership with Canelo.

Correspondence regarding the content of this book should be sent to Canelo US, Editorial Department, at the above address. Author inquiries should be sent to Canelo, Unit 9, 5th Floor, Cargo Works, 1–2 Hatfields, London SE1 9PG, United Kingdom, www.canelo.co.

Publisher: Peter Norton • Associate Publisher: Ana Parker
Art Director: Charles McStravick
Senior Developmental Editor: April Graham
Editor: Angela Garcia
Production Team: Beno Chan, Julie Greene

Library of Congress Control Number: 2023941288

ISBN: 978-1-6672-0654-7

Printed in India

27 26 25 24 23   1 2 3 4 5

To my honorary sisters, Jo, Lorna, Sarah and Laura, who always have gum.

Prologue

She can see him watching her across the bonfire again. He's been looking her way all night, not even being subtle about it, like he doesn't care who sees. The other teenagers drink and dance and laugh, but for her there may as well be no one else there. A summer of gentle flirting, teasing, it has all come down to tonight, the last big blowout before they leave their summer homes and go back to their normal lives.

Her hair glows golden in the light of the flames, her tanned skin smelling of warmth and sunscreen. She smiles, self-conscious of his attention, but enjoying it all the same. She is everything it means to be young, beautiful and full of life. Soon, her lifeless body will be found floating face down in the marina.

She watches as he makes his way around the fire, greeting everyone as he goes. They all know who he is. He's older than her, but that hasn't seemed to matter to him and it makes it all the more thrilling as far as she's concerned. She's seen how the other girls look at him and it makes her nervous, this weight of responsibility she has to be cooler than them, to be funnier and sexier — otherwise why would he want to be with her?

She wonders if he will kiss her tonight; innocent as she is, she has no idea that he will expect — no, demand — more than a kiss when the time comes. For now, there is still a way out for her, she still has a chance to put down her drink and call for a lift home, ask her sister's advice – her sister would warn her away from boys like him and she doesn't want to be warned away.

He's closer now, and she knows that she is his final destination, after all the hollow greetings and cheek kisses, she is the one his arrow has sighted on. The thought makes her palms slick and she wipes them on her denim shorts. The gap between them closes and the air between them fizzles. Any small action might change her fate – if she decides to get her own drinks instead of taking the one he hands her, if one of the bystanders recognises the signs and calls someone to come and collect her. If it had been a different boy she had set her sights on, if anyone had ever taught him that power and influence don't entitle you to take whatever you want, or if just one of the girls before hadn't been silenced so effectively.

She is not the first summer girl whose course will be forever altered by the thousand small actions that led to them both being here tonight, and tragically she will not be the last. Maybe the next summer girl will be luckier than she is. Maybe someone will discover the truth before another life is ended.

Or maybe not.

Chapter One

Claire

The music thumped in my chest and the buzz from the alcohol I'd been drinking all evening surged through me, making it hard to focus. That last whisky on the rocks had made me feel absolutely certain that the man sitting opposite me was The One That Got Away and I was pretty adamant that he wasn't getting away tonight – although he didn't actually seem to be trying that hard.

'I'm trying to remember why we ever broke up,' I said, wagging my finger in his face in what I knew was an incredibly sexy, teasing gesture. Well, it was until I almost knocked his pint of beer into his lap.

'It was because you said I had fewer prospects than Katie Hopkins trying to win the Nobel Peace Prize,' he helpfully reminded me.

I frowned. It did sound like something I'd say.

'That doesn't sound like something I'd say,' I replied.

'It was also because he tried to sleep with your sister,' a voice from behind me said. A voice I knew very well, even over the pounding bass.

I let out a groan and turned to face my cousin and best friend, Jess, while plastering on a smile. She was standing with her hand on her hip, silently judging me. Jess was three months younger than me, but she had been trying

3

her best lately to act like my mother, as if I was a wayward teen who was coasting off the rails. For context, I was thirty years old and perfectly entitled to get drunk and sleep with an ex if I so wanted. And tonight I so wanted.

'What are you doing here?' I asked, not bothering to hide my irritation.

Jess frowned. She looked even younger when she did that. Jess somehow still managed to look like a fresh-faced teenager; she was one of those annoying natural beauties who barely wore make-up and could dress however she wanted. She was even a real blonde. 'Never mind me,' she said. 'What are *you* doing?'

'What does it look like I'm doing?'

She gave Chris a long, withering glare. 'It looks like you're pouring alcohol on an old flame.'

'Nice to see you too, Jess,' Chris retorted.

Those two had never got along. Probably because he had fewer prospects than Katie Hopkins trying to win the Nobel Peace Prize and had tried to sleep with my sister.

I raised my eyebrows. 'Did you come here just to get annoyed at me?'

'Have you spoken to your sister?' Jess demanded, ignoring my tone.

I sighed. Leaning back, I murmured to Chris that I'd call him when I could get rid of my dear cousin. I was lying. She was right, he was the same shade of loser now as he had been when I'd thrown him out for trying to sleep with my sister.

Chris nodded, and, scowling at Jess, he turned to leave.

'Which one?' I asked.

Jess frowned, *again*. I got the feeling I was irritating her. 'You only have one sister,' she pointed out.

'Yes,' I agreed. 'But she has multiple personalities.' I drained the last of my drink and put up my hand to order another, but Jess took it and pulled it down.

'Don't be an idiot. I know you're mad at her for leaving, but you're not the only one going through a tough time. This was her way of dealing with it.'

I twisted my wrist from her loose grip and put my hand back up. 'And this is mine.'

'Same again?' the barman asked.

I nodded and gestured to Jess. 'And a Virgin Mary for my virtuous best friend.'

Jess gritted her teeth. 'Holly isn't returning my calls.'

'Maybe that's her way of dealing with it.'

Jess slammed her hand down on the bar. 'Don't act like you don't care when we both know you do. I've been calling her and calling her and she isn't answering. When was the last time you spoke to her?'

I thought about it. When was it? Could I really not remember the last time I'd spoken to my sister? Whenever it was, it had ended in an argument. I remembered Holly's voice, almost pleading her big sister to be happy for her, loving life three thousand miles away, and the pain and fury I had felt at the thought of us being so far apart, her having fun and moving on, without me. I'd tried to call her since we fought – maybe this morning? But she hadn't answered. Not surprising, it probably would have been five a.m. in Massachusetts and I had been a complete bitch.

'I don't know… maybe Thursday?'

Jess took in a deep breath as though she was struggling to stay calm with me. 'I spoke to her Friday morning. And I've called her every day since. Today it just went to answerphone.'

5

I pressed my eyes closed and tried to think again, but everything felt muddled. That last Jack and Coke was probably a bad idea. Today was Tuesday, nine thirty p.m. in Hampshire, so it would be, what... I counted on my fingers. Four thirty in the afternoon in Massachusetts?

I took my phone out of my pocket and pressed Holly's name, putting it on speaker so that when my sister answered, Jess could hear her voice. The phone didn't even ring.

'You have reached the T-Mobile answering service. Please leave a message after the tone.'

Jess's eyes widened. 'I *told you* it was going straight to answerphone. What's going on?'

'Jesus, Jess, she's probably blocked my number,' I said, tiring of the conversation. I didn't like thinking about my sister. I hated being mad at her, but I *was* mad at her, and I also knew I was unreasonable for being mad at her. It hurt my head. I just wanted to drink and forget. 'We didn't exactly have the best chat the other day. You try it again.'

Jess dialled from her phone and we both heard the same answerphone message. Jess clenched her jaw and glared at me. 'It's off. I'm telling you, there's something wrong. Holly never goes this long without responding to my messages.'

'Lucky you,' I said, well aware of how sulky my voice sounded.

The bartender arrived with another JD for me and a Virgin Mary for Jess. Ouch. He clearly hadn't picked up on my sarcasm. Jess looked as though she wanted to throw the drink at me.

'What's this really about, Jess?' I asked with a sigh. 'If Holly was just ignoring your calls, you would have rung me, or texted. You wouldn't have stormed down here to

6

accost me and slam me for having a few drinks after a nine-hour shift. Why don't you just tell me what's actually going on?'

Jess and I had been thick as thieves for as long as I could remember. She was the reason I had tolerated my younger sister hanging around us as we'd grown up – Jess was an only child and had doted on Holly, who was eight years younger than us. Boy, had that been a shock for me, growing up used to having my parents' attention all to myself and then suddenly realising I was going to have to share. And when my parents had broken up not long after Holly was born, I had *known* it was all Holly's fault. I'd spent so much time resenting my little sister that if it hadn't been for Jess, we probably wouldn't have had a relationship at all. It had only been in the last few years, when Holly was around nineteen and I was in my late twenties, that we had settled into a normal sisterly friendship. Now we were further apart than ever, and not just physically.

Jess looked around and sighed. 'Tom's waiting in the car. Can we just talk about this back at mine?'

Jesus, she'd brought the cavalry.

'Why?' I asked. 'Just tell me now. She's run off and got married, right? Pregnant? What are you trying not to tell me?'

Jess pulled out her mobile and started tapping on it. She handed it to me.

'She sent me this today.'

'I thought you hadn't heard from her since…' I stopped as my brain took in what she was showing me. It was only a couple of lines of text, but I knew now what Jess was doing here. I knew what had made her so worried.

7

> Having a great time. Going away for a few days so won't have signal. Will speak to Mum when I'm back, tell her sorry I missed her call this morning. Love you all xx

'Oh shit,' I muttered. 'You got this today?'

'Right before she turned her phone off,' Jess confirmed.

'Or someone did,' I replied, getting up off the stool and grasping the bar for support. I had no idea if my legs were wobbly from the drink or from the shock. 'Because we both know Holly didn't send that text.'

Chapter Two

Claire

Tom was indeed waiting with the car. Good old loyal Tom did whatever Jess asked him to do in the hopes that one day she'd realise how much she loved him. And, actually, she might. They would make a great couple, and anyone with eyes could see that he'd been in love with her ever since he started working at Jessica's vegan bakery four years ago. *Au Natural* (I'd wanted her to call it *No Bull*) had been Jess's dream for as long as I could remember, and although my aunty Karen was paying the rent on both the unit and her flat, *and* Jess had had a hefty bank loan, she was managing to pay Tom's wages and not get her electricity cut off. I was proud of her.

When other kids were fantasising about being astronauts (me) and actresses (Holly), Jess had received an easy-bake oven for her birthday and decided she wanted to open her own health cafe, full of low-sugar, vegan treats. She hadn't always been vegan – when we were younger, vegetarians were the rare ones, and vegans were practically unheard of in our area – but she'd always avoided greasy kebabs and next-day fry-ups, and I'd had the privilege of being the taste tester for her various dishes over the years. It had come as no surprise when she'd told me she was opening her own bakery, but still, it was no small feat for someone her age.

'Everything okay?' Tom asked as I climbed in, his eyebrows raised.

I glared at him, but in my current state I wasn't sure it had the desired effect.

I called Tom the Instagram Vegan. He was tall and slim, with a shaved head and Buddhist symbols tattooed over his arms and chest. I knew this because on Instagram he rarely had a top on. He might have been slimline, but boy, he was ripped. His socials were full of pictures of him doing yoga in the woods and on hills, rocking his man-bun and making smoothies. I knew that he and Jess had slept together on occasion, and that they were both pretty keen on one another. But Tom was hiding a deep, dark secret. Every Wednesday, he did something that he would die to keep from anyone, but I knew – Steak and Beer Wednesday at The White Horse in Southampton.

I closed my eyes without answering and put my head back against the headrest, fighting nausea while Tom drove us back to Jessica's flat. Who had sent that message? Had Holly simply asked a boyfriend to reply to Jess without realising how much trouble that could cause? Or was it really something more sinister? Someone trying to get Jess to stop calling Holly for days, weeks… How long did they expect us to wait until we got suspicious?

Expect Jess *to wait, you mean,* a voice in my head chided. *She's the one who was really concerned about Holly. You probably wouldn't have tried again for days anyway.*

I felt like a naughty schoolkid being escorted home by her parents. I knew Jess hadn't approved of how much time I'd been spending at the bar recently, or some of the things I did afterwards – or the people I did them with.

But the fact was that I was a big girl, and she had no right to tell me how much to drink or who to sleep with. I worked every shift sober, my mask firmly in place. My daytime life was functioning just fine. I knew how much I could drink and what time to stop. I didn't have a problem.

It was understandable that Jess was being overprotective, given what I'd been through, and as annoying as it was, I was grateful to have someone who cared enough to lecture me. I suppose I hoped that's how Holly felt about me, grateful to have a pain-in-the-ass older sister who cared about her. Not that I'd shown her much of that recently. I had a sudden urge to apologise.

'Jesus Christ,' I groaned. 'I knew it was too soon for her to go off on her own. I should have stopped her.'

'Claire.' Jess leaned back between the seats and placed a hand on my knee. 'Holly is twenty-two years old. She might be your baby sister, but she's technically an adult. You couldn't have stopped her. We both know what she's like.'

'I could have tried harder.'

'And have her leave anyway, just mad at you?'

'She wasn't exactly over the moon at my reaction as it was.'

When Holly had told me she was going to spend the summer on Martha's Vineyard, my first reply had been a firm 'I don't think so.' She'd laughed and shown me the booking reservation. When most people said things like 'I'd love to go to Massachusetts,' they meant at some undetermined point in the future, and they knew that it would probably never happen. When my sister said it, she meant in three weeks – and she'd already found a job at a marina and an Airbnb to stay at. Holly was as bull-headed as I was when she set her mind to something, and this summer the thing she had set her mind on was Martha's Vineyard.

Tom pulled up outside Jessica's flat and let us out while he went to park the car.

'Should I add chauffeur and valet to his résumé?' I said.

Jess shook her head. 'You can be such a bitch sometimes. He didn't have to come and get you.'

'Neither of you had to come and get me,' I pointed out. 'I don't remember sending up the Bat-Signal.'

She stuck her middle finger up at me and buzzed us into the main door. Her flat was above a hairdresser, up a narrow winding staircase, then down what felt more like a tunnel than a hallway. When you got into the flat, though, despite it being small, you could see that Jess had really made it into a home. The entranceway was a pale grey with a huge mirror above a decorative shelf. The lounge was open plan in a light blue with navy and gold accents, leading to a bright white kitchen with splashes of colour courtesy of framed prints that said things like 'Home is where the fridge is' and 'Eating is my happy place'. Which was true for Jess: she loved food and, to her, family was whoever sat at your dining table. Unfortunately, her flat wasn't big enough for a dining table right now, but I had no doubt that Jess would eventually move into her dream kitchen – with some other rooms attached.

Tom let himself in and I wasn't too drunk to note this fact.

'I left it on the latch,' Jess said immediately, knowing what I would be thinking despite neither my face nor my lips moving. 'He doesn't have a key, so don't start with your conspiracy theory again.'

She was talking about the theory I had that her and Tom were secretly dating, and had been for years. In fact,

12

they would have to be secretly married with four secret kids by now too, given how long I'd been tied to this idea. I'd never come up with a good reason why they might be keeping this massive love affair secret from the rest of the world, but that was the thing about conspiracy theories: you got to ignore the bits that didn't fit.

'Who sent that text?' I asked, as Jess filled the kettle. The fresh air and bottle of water Tom had given me in the car had started to clear my head a little and added to the concern I was now feeling for my little sister, I was almost fully sober. Almost.

'Whoever it was doesn't know her very well,' Jess pointed out over the sound of the boiling water.

Whoever it was didn't know her well enough to know our mum had died eight months ago.

'What I don't get is that it said about missing your mum's call. Why say that when it's clearly a lie? They're taking a gamble there. Even if your mum was still here, she would know she hadn't called Holly this morning.'

'No, but I did,' I said, understanding where the texter had made their mistake. 'Holly would joke so often about how much I lectured her that she said it was like having Mum here anyway. She put me in her phone as 'Pain in the ass mum' as a joke.'

I hadn't been able to understand how she could see *mum* flash up on her phone – even as a joke – without it ripping her insides out. She said it was nice; that every time I rang her, she could pretend for a few seconds that it was going to be Mum. I still couldn't decide if I thought it was sweet, sadistic, or just really sad. Probably a bit of all three.

Since our mum had told us just over twelve months ago that she had been told she had lung cancer, Holly and I had become closer than ever. Holly now twenty-two and me just turned thirty, supporting each another through the toughest experience of our lives, taking turns to accompany Mum to chemo appointments, sleeping on chairs in hospitals after surgery. Clutching onto one another as we wept as quietly as we possibly could, so Mum didn't hear us crying. Adding songs to a joint playlist that reminded us of Mum. Doing one another's hair and then holding hands as the funeral car pulled up. And then, nine weeks ago, almost six months after our mother's death, Holly had announced she was going away.

'How long for?' I had demanded. 'A month? A year? Forever?'

Holly had shrugged. 'I don't know how long, Claire, I just have to do this. What happened to Mum… it could happen to anyone, at any time. I don't want to be left with regrets.'

Like Mum was, I had thought.

Samantha Matthews had been only fifty-seven when the cancer had taken her. She'd devoted so much of her life to making sure her daughters hadn't suffered from their dad's swift departure that she had never met anyone else – not anyone serious anyway. She'd always said she didn't want another man, but I knew that as Holly and I had grown up and moved out, she must have been lonely. I couldn't blame Holly for wanting to get out and explore the world, live her life: after all, that's what our mother had begged us to do, to really live each day as if it was our one day – the only day – promised to us. But there was that selfish, mean-spirited part of me that hadn't been able to be happy for Holly because what was I going to do without her?

'You don't really think something might have happened to her, do you?' I asked, tears threatening to fill my eyes.

No, I thought. I was not a crier. I'd cried enough tears after Mum: I wasn't going there again. I was afraid I would never stop.

'Probably not,' Jess said, her voice sounding more hopeful than certain. 'There will be a rational explanation for the message. Maybe she thought I knew that she called you Mum and she was carrying on the joke with me? Things don't always translate in text.'

'Maybe you're right,' I replied, wondering if I could allow myself to grasp onto that thought. That must be it. Holly would have probably been rolling her eyes when she sent it. *Tell 'Mum' I'm fine.* I was going to have to teach that girl to use inverted commas.

'Maybe she's lost her phone down the back of a sofa in a trendy bar or cafe,' Jess carried on. 'Or she's spent three days in bed with some cowboy and she'll call us in a couple of weeks telling us she got married in Vegas.'

'She doesn't ever ignore your calls. She's never even ignored my calls, even when she's annoyed at me.' I pulled out my phone and flicked through Holly's social media, my frown deepening more with each swipe. 'She's posted nothing on her socials for days. Since Friday, some pictures of a party at a big house and a bonfire on the beach.' As much as I wanted to grasp onto one of those possibilities, if Holly was ignoring Jess's calls on purpose it would be the very first time. The thought bugged me.

'She was trying to decide whether or not to go to a beach party when I spoke to her. She said some guy had told her about it, but she wasn't sure it was a good idea.

15

She made some joke about his intentions. Looks like she went. Maybe she's sleeping off a hangover.'

I looked at her sharply. 'Is this some kind of reverse psychology? You tried to convince me my sister was in mortal peril and now you're saying she's either married, phoneless or hungover. Which is it?'

'I don't know,' Jess replied, looking like she was going to cry. Great. Emotions were not my strong point.

I dialled Holly's number again and listened as it went straight to voicemail.

'Could she be at work?' Tom asked.

'Right now? Sure,' I said. 'Since Friday? No.' I turned to Jess. 'Are you sure you haven't spoken to her since then?'

Jess gave me a look that said she wasn't the one who had trouble keeping track of the days.

A bit unfair. I didn't have a drinking problem – and yes, I was well aware that that's what someone with a problem would say. It was just that my lifestyle lent itself to not always keeping up with the date. Or the day of the week. Basically, I knew it was the weekend because the bar was fuller, my tips were bigger, and doormen showed up at seven thirty p.m. I wasn't unhappy with my life, I liked working at the bar, and if I'd been staying on for a few drinks more often, or sometimes just staying over in the staffroom when I'd drunk too much to drive home and couldn't catch a lift, well, that was to be expected. I was grieving, if I hadn't mentioned.

'It was Friday,' she confirmed.

'Why don't you call her work?' Tom suggested.

'Because I don't want to completely embarrass her in front of her new workmates,' I replied.

Tom shrugged. 'I'll do it.' He pulled out his phone. 'What's it called?'

'Oak Bluffs Marina.' I pulled up the details of the marina my sister was working at for the summer. Despite being furious at her for running away so soon after Mum died, I still had all her contact details saved, in case there was an emergency. I knew my anger at Holly was temporary, and selfish. Eventually, I would eat humble pie and apologise, she knew that. She knew me better than anyone else and she knew how much pain I was in.

As I watched Tom type the numbers, my heart was pounding. Because this was it. This was either the moment they put me onto my sister, or the moment her silence turned into something more sinister.

'Hi, I'm looking for Holly Matthews? She put your name down as place of work... Yes, I'm from the car rental company, I can't seem to get through to her... Right, okay, um, okay.' He glanced at me, but I couldn't read his expression. 'Any idea where I might get hold of her?'

So she wasn't there. Jess and I stood rooted to the spot as he hung up the phone.

'She's not there,' Tom said, his face a mask of concern. 'She stopped showing up three days ago.'

Chapter Three

Claire

I sat down on the sofa, worried my legs wouldn't hold. My face must have shown my horror because both Jess and Tom started talking at once.

'She's probably taken a trip somewhere—'

'Met some new friends, being a bit irresponsible, but nothing to worry about—'

'If they were worried, they would have reported her missing.'

That one stopped my jumble of thoughts in their tracks.

'Why haven't her work reported her missing?' I demanded. 'What exactly did they say? Who did you speak to?'

Tom held up his hands. 'Calm down,' he said, reaching out to put his hands on my shoulders lightly. 'I spoke to a woman – she said her name was Stacy. I said I was looking for Holly and she said that Holly hadn't shown up to work for the last three days.'

'The exact amount of time she's been ignoring your calls,' I said to Jess.

As I waited for my heart to stop racing, I placed my head in my hands on my knees, pushing my hair back, and tried to think.

Breathe. That was what Jess always said. She'd been trying to get me to learn different types of breathing for years and I wished now I'd paid attention rather than making annoying remarks about how there was only one type of breathing that mattered: the in-out type.

'Here.' Jess passed me a mug of thick black coffee and I inhaled deeply. Oh look, I'm coffee breathing.

'Where is she?' I whispered. I wasn't the type to start sobbing. Since Mum had died, I kind of felt like I'd used up all my tears, fulfilled my quota of melodrama. Or maybe my cold black heart had learned not to show weakness.

Tom put his hand over mine, squeezed in support, then leaned across and tore off a page of branded paper from a pad on the coffee table in front of me He handed me a pen and pointed to the paper.

'What should I do?'

'First, you write down everything you know,' Tom instructed. 'Everything Holly has told you about where she is staying, any friends she might be with, her boss's name, her rental car type. Then you contact the police on Martha's Vineyard and give them all that information. They will go and find her, and they will call you back and tell you she's currently having mad passionate sex with a man who looks like Jason Momoa and you will text her and apologise for the interruption. Then, when she finally calls you, you will give the phone to me and I'll give her hell.'

I managed a small smile. 'Can I give her some hell too?'

'Just a little.' He held his finger and thumb up to demonstrate. Maybe I would let the fake vegan marry my best friend after all.

The list hardly took any time at all. For someone who was so protective over their little sister, I realised that I had asked very few questions, and listened even less to the answers. I managed to find the essentials in messages and emails though: where she was staying, the name of her boss. She mentioned in one message meeting another girl called Emmy for drinks so I wrote that down too.

When I dialled the number for the police station in Edgartown, a guy with a low, lazy voice answered. 'Martha's Vineyard PD. How can I help you?'

'Oh, hi,' I said, feeling stupid and self-conscious and still more than a little tipsy. 'I'm, um, I'm calling about my sister. Holly, her name is Holly. She's staying in Edgartown for the summer and I haven't had any contact with her in a few days, which is very unusual. I called her place of work and they said she hadn't been showing up either, when she's usually very responsible.'

'Age?'

The abrupt response threw me. 'Sorry, what?'

There was a sigh at the other end. 'What's your sister's age?'

'Oh, right, sorry. I thought you were asking for my... Never mind. She's twenty-two. Just. A few months ago. Well, five... five months ago.'

'Twenty-two?'

I knew from his tone of voice in that second that he wasn't going to take this seriously.

'Yes,' I sighed, 'but she's been in constant contact until three days ago, and her work said she just stopped showing up, which is so unlike her, she really wanted that job. And she sent a weird text message to my friend talking about her mum as if she's spoken to her, when our mum... We don't have our mum anymore.'

'Do you have an address for her?' the officer asked.

I reeled off the address Holly gave me. 'Are you going to do a missing person's report?'

'I'll send someone round to do a welfare check,' he promised. 'She's probably sleeping off the mother of all hangovers. There's an active social scene in the Vineyard over the summer season. Where did she work?'

'The marina,' I said. 'Not in Edgartown, actually, in Oak Bluffs.'

'Okay, sure, I think I know who you're talking about actually. It's a pretty small place and she stands out, right? Because she's English. I know her boss for sure. I'll check it out for you.'

'Thank you,' I said, relieved that someone was hopefully going to have eyes on my sister very soon.

Tom looked at me expectantly when I lay down the phone.

'The police are going to check on her,' I reported. 'He knew who she was. He sounded really nice.' I felt relieved and impatient at the same time.

'Right now?' Jess asked, mirroring my impatience.

'I have no idea. I guess so. How busy can a police force in paradise be?'

Jess disappeared into the other room and came back with a duvet, a pillow and a long T-shirt. 'You can stay here,' she said, not bothering to frame it as a question. 'Tom, help me pull the sofa out.'

'I'm not going to sleep until I've spoken to my sister,' I said.

'Well, that's a stupid decision, but fine,' Jess replied. 'If you want to sit up all night waiting for Deputy Dopey to call you back at least do it in comfort. If it was me, I'd be

21

getting some sleep in case I need to be a hundred per cent tomorrow for my sister, but you do you.'

'You don't have to be so snarky as well as being so bloody sanctimonious,' I grumbled, knowing she was obviously right.

I didn't think that I'd be able to sleep at all, but by eleven Tom had left with the promise that he'd open up Au Natural in the morning and Jess had forced a chamomile tea down my throat and my eyelids began to droop. I was aware of Jess asking Alexa to play relaxing sounds and I drifted off to the noise of waves crashing against the shore. My last thought before I fell asleep completely was that I hoped that, wherever she was, my little sister was okay, and that she could hear the same sound.

–

I was ripped from sleep by my mobile ringing. I glanced at the clock – Jesus it was gone eleven. I'd slept for nearly twelve hours straight.

'Holly?' I snatched the phone up and waited to hear my sister's voice. A dull ache spread across the inside of my head. The T-shirt Jess had loaned me was wrapped up around my armpits and I struggled to pull myself together.

'No, ma'am, this is Officer Waylans from the Martha's Vineyard Police Department,' an American voice announced. 'My colleague left me a note to do a welfare check on your sister this morning – he had an emergency call just after yours. Anyway, I've just got back from your sister's place, there's no sign of anything untoward.'

'Oh, thank God,' I sighed, relief flooding through me. Getting up from the sofa, I went over to get a glass of water and two Nurofen before Jess could get up and make me drink some vile ginger turmeric concoction to flush my toxins out. As far as I was aware, that was what my kidneys were for. 'Did she say why she wasn't answering her phone?' I readied myself for the embarrassment of hearing that my sister just didn't want to speak to us. I didn't care anymore, now that I knew she was safe.

'Well, I didn't actually see her,' he admitted, and my heart picked up speed once again. 'There's a car on the drive and I could see her suitcase through the window in the kitchen. She wouldn't have gone far without her car and suitcase, right? Everything looks normal, there's no sign of a struggle or a break-in. She's probably staying over with some guy.'

Dread swooped in to take the place of relief. I had to stop and reconsider what he was saying. He had been to Holly's house, seen her suitcase on her bed, no broken windows so he'd assumed she was fine? This guy was a real police officer, right?

'I swung by her place of work, too,' he continued, oblivious to my stunned silence. 'Carl said she was seeing one of the summer kids. He said she quit a couple-a days ago.'

'They told me she didn't show up – that's not the same as quitting,' I pointed out.

'Sounds like quitting to me.' He sounded bored and I could imagine him with his feet on his desk, polishing an apple on his uniform jacket.

'If someone doesn't turn up for work and no one's seen them for days, that's a disappearance,' I pressed.

'Your sister is a traveller, right?'

'Wrong.' My volume was rising with each stupid state-ment this guy made. 'My sister might have travelled to get there, but she had no plans to keep travelling once she

23

arrived. She had a job and a house lined up before she left the UK. She's not some teenage backpacker with a hippy van and a dreamcatcher in the window, changing her plans depending on the direction of the wind.'

'Listen,' he said, that one word indicating that his patience for the conversation was over. 'Give it a few days, I'm sure she'll be in touch. If you don't hear from her by the end of the week, I'll go on over there again, probably find her with some guy, exploring her *freedom*.' He emphasised the word freedom, the implication clear that it was me she needed freedom from.

'A few days?' I was floored. Anger flared. 'You want me to wait until she's been missing over a week before you even "go on over there again"? What kind of police officer are you?'

'Now, miss, there's no need to be insulting. We deal with these kinds of reports far more often than you do, and nine times out of ten it turns out that the missing person is just blowing off some steam.'

'And the other time?' I asked.

'Excuse me?'

'You said nine times out of ten,' I snapped. 'What about the other time? The tenth? What is it then?'

'Well, see that's just an expression, just a turn of phrase. Nothing like you're implying happens here, we're a real safe community. I'm sure your sister is fine.'

I was getting nowhere. Tears of frustration threatened to creep past my defences. 'Thanks for your help, *officer*.' I hissed the last word and hung up the phone before I could say anything worse.

When I looked up, utter shock still coursing through my veins, Jess was standing in the doorway. I felt a surge of guilt as I realised she'd missed work for me.

24

'You'll have to go and find her,' she said, as if Holly was down in the local pub and late for tea.

'And how am I supposed to do that?' I asked. 'She's three thousand miles away.'

'What else are you going to do? I can tell by the look on your face and you insulting the police officer that he hasn't found Holly?'

'No, he hasn't found Holly, he barely looked for her. I'm surprised he could be bothered to lift his wrist to knock the door.' I realised I was hungover and starting to get panicky about the fact that my sister was so far away and there was absolutely nothing I could do, no one I could turn to.

'So what's he going to do, nothing?' Jess walked into the kitchen to flick on the kettle, and I was relieved when she pulled out the instant coffee instead of her twirly spice rack.

'I have to call back if she hasn't got in touch by the end of the week. *A week,*' I repeated for effect. 'It's already been three days. She could be halfway across the country in the back of a van by the end of the week.'

'So you have to go,' Jess said, as if it was the most obvious thing in the world.

I downed the last of my water and refilled the glass. My mouth felt drier than the Sahara.

'You want some ginger tea?' Jess asked, seeing me drinking greedily.

'God no.' I shuddered at the thought. 'I'll take a vodka and orange if you have one. What?' I asked at her raised eyebrows. 'It's vitamin C, isn't it? Besides, I'm not the one who's sounding drunk. You think getting on a plane and flying to Massachusetts because my sister isn't answering her phone is the logical reaction?'

'It's not just that and you know it,' Jess said. 'You saw the text. And the police didn't speak to her. Plus, you know how excited she was about that job. She wouldn't have just quit without calling them to explain. And if there's nothing wrong and she's safe and sound, you get a few days on the beach with your sister. Win-win.'

I paused, considering what she was saying. I'd never done anything that spur of the moment in my life, but I'd also never felt as maternal and protective about anyone as I felt about Holly. Not to mention the excruciating guilt that it had taken my cousin kidnapping me from a bar for me to even realise there was anything out of the ordinary. If it wasn't for Jess, I'd be waking up with Chris this morning. Another shudder.

'When I find her, I'm telling her you sent me,' I said, not quite able to believe I was considering flying to Massachusetts.

Jess shrugged. 'I wouldn't expect any less. Go on.' She nudged my arm. 'You go home and pack a bag. I'll go into work and get Tom to sort you flights. He opened up for me this morning.'

Tom had worked everywhere you could think of, without ever having what I would call a real job until he went to work for Jess. For a guy of nearly thirty, that was impressive. He'd started coaching businesses, a virtual PA business, yoga businesses, organic health shots, a keto meal-planning business, holistic nutrition, marketing, social media management, and, most importantly for my current situation, a travel-planning business.

'You're amazing,' I told her, hoping she could hear how grateful I was. 'And so is Tom.'

I got a taxi back to the bar where I left my car last night and drove home. I wasn't over the limit, but I still didn't feel great – I usually handled my drink pretty well, but I was assuming the stress and panic hadn't helped with the pounding headache and feelings of existential dread. Luckily, the roads were quiet on my way home and I didn't have to contend with anyone pulling out on me or get stuck in any traffic.

My house was a three-bed end terrace that was left to me and my sister by Mum. Usually, Holly would be out at work when I dragged myself home in between shifts. Before she'd left to go to America, I had been going straight home from work, never stopping for a drink. I'd had someone to get back for. Despite having a job of her own to go to the next day, she'd always be curled up on the sofa under a blanket making sure I got home okay and ready to ask me about my night. Then she'd tell me about the customers she'd had come through the card shop she worked at, which regulars had been in, who had been buying apology cards and get well soon cards. It had felt like Holly knew practically everyone in Hampshire.

Ever since she'd gone, the house felt cold and empty, Mum's absence sitting heavier than it had in the eight months since she'd died.

Holly and I had both been renting when Mum had got ill, but we'd moved back home to take it in turns to care for her. Now I had no one to care for and I hated it here without them.

I pulled down my trusty old suitcase and chucked it onto my bed. Opening drawers, I counted in pairs of pants, socks, bras – I decided to take enough to cover four days. That was plenty of time for me to find Holly and spend a couple of days at the beach with her. Jess was right: if I was going to go all that way, I may as well get a few days' quality time with my sister. I grabbed my favourite T-shirt off the chair in the corner and gave it a sniff; it smelt fresh enough. As I chucked it in the case, I was reminded of watching Holly pack for her own trip.

She had practically everything she owned in a pile on her bed and was holding each item – most no bigger than a hanky – up for inspection. The agonising decision on whether to take each one took longer than it had just taken me to pack my entire case. The excitement she had felt at going had been so thick in the air that I had almost forgotten to be sick with worry. Almost.

Not now, though. Now I felt more and more nauseous with each passing minute.

I made sure I packed my phone charger and my laptop, and I threw a notebook and some pens into a rucksack, along with the copy of *Rose Madder* from my nightstand – not that I saw myself being able to concentrate long enough to read any of it.

My phone rang and I was disappointed to see that it wasn't Holly; it was Tom.

'Hey, how are you feeling?'

'I'm okay. Thanks again for coming to get me last night. Even though I know Jess made you.'

'I can't think why she felt like she needed backup,' Tom retorted. 'But you're welcome. I've booked your flights. I used my credit card—'

'Send me the details, I'll transfer the money when I get to the airport,' I said immediately. Thanks to my inheritance from my grandparents, half of Mum's inheritance and barely having a social life for the past three years, I had a decent amount of savings. The house was ex-council, paid off years ago and worth considerably more than Mum had bought it for, so I didn't have a mortgage.

'No rush,' Tom replied, but I knew he was nowhere near as good with money as I was and I made a mental note not to forget. 'I'll email you all the details now, with some info about a car rental place next to the airport. Do you want me to find you somewhere to stay?'

'No thanks, I'll stay with Holly.' I didn't allow myself to consider what I'd do if Holly was nowhere to be found. I'd sleep in the car on her drive, I guessed. I wanted to be close to where she was supposed to be. 'I don't know what I'd do without you,' I told him. 'Is Jess okay? She cares about Holly almost as much as me.'

And she's been a damn sight nicer to her since she left, too, that mean voice in my head reminded me. Jess had picked up the sisterly role that I'd been too much of a stupid, stubborn ass to take since Holly had gone away, and now she had been the one to tell me that there might be something wrong. I immediately felt ashamed of myself.

'I think she's more worried about Holly than she's letting on,' Tom said, lowering his voice.

Of course she was. Jess liked to pretend she was zen, but I'd seen her mainline three vegan muffins in a row when she was stressed in the past.

'Will you look after her for me?'

'She'll be fine,' Tom said. 'You look after yourself and that irresponsible sister of yours. Tell her we're all furious with her.'

'I'll do more than that when I find her. I'll wring her bloody neck.'

The email with my flight details was waiting for me when I hung up the phone. Tom had indeed worked his magic; I had a flight that evening.

I booked a taxi and rang work to tell them I wouldn't be in this week. If I'd needed any confirmation about how easily replaceable I was, then it came from the fact that my boss didn't even complain, he just told me he hoped Holly was okay and to keep him informed. Knowing how much he fancied one of the other shift workers, he was probably delighted at having an excuse to give her my shifts.

As I made myself some food and sorted out the house so that I wasn't coming home to the state I'd been leaving it in over the last few weeks, it half occurred to me that perhaps I didn't just need to get away to find Holly; maybe I needed some time away from here to sort myself out too. Jess was right – I couldn't just trudge through life, going from working at the bar to drinking at the bar to sleeping at the bar, showering and starting all over again. I also realised, as I bit into the grilled cheese and ham toastie I'd made myself, that I hadn't had a meal that couldn't be heated under the grill for six minutes for as long as I could remember. It was either grilled cheese and ham, potato waffles dipped in tomato ketchup or some form of cheese/beans/bacon on toast. I made a silent promise to myself that I'd eat a vegetable or two after I'd found my sister. Maybe even sign up for that meal delivery service I'd seen on TV, start to cook again.

God, listen to me, I'd be vowing to take up running and eating Jessica's vegan muffins next. I almost laughed – there was no danger of that.

Jess had texted me to remind me to call her as soon as I arrived, no matter what time it was in Hampshire, and apologised for the zillionth time about not being able to come.

I checked the flights again. I'd need to leave home at six p.m. to get to Heathrow for seven thirty. My eight-hour flight was due to leave at eleven p.m. According to Tom's email, I would arrive in Boston at around seven a.m. our time – just after three their time – and could get a flight to Martha's Vineyard arriving at six a.m. I checked that my passport was still in date and printed off everything Tom had sent me. I took a shower, washed and blow-dried my hair and was checking my passport for a final time when the taxi driver rang to say he was downstairs.

Taking a deep breath, I pulled my suitcase out of the house, dragged it to the boot of the car and ignored the driver's valiant and chivalrous attempt to help me haul it in. It was hard to believe that just under twenty-four hours ago I'd been trying to decide whether or not to sleep with my ex and in another eighteen hours' time I'd be touching down in Martha's Vineyard. *Please God, let my sister be okay when I get there.*

Chapter Four

Claire

The flight from London to Boston was just over eight hours and I felt horrifically sick for at least six and a half of those. I'd drunk my body weight in mineral water and orange juice and taken enough painkillers that I was sure if you shook me I would rattle, but as I touched down at Boston airport, I was almost feeling human again. If I hadn't needed to drive when I got to the Vineyard I'd have just turned to some hair of the dog, but I could already hear Jessica's voice telling me that you didn't solve your problems with the same mindset you had when you created them. See, I did listen to her sometimes.

I just had to get to Holly's place, demand she let me in and then enjoy myself. Maybe some yoga on the beach, swimming in the sea. I'd never been massively unfit, but I'd never done anything to help my fitness along, and at thirty I knew I needed to start doing something. Maybe I'd end up an Instagram vegan like Tom.

My stopover in Boston was two hours and the flight to Vineyard Haven Airport was another forty minutes. By the time I'd rented a car to take me to where Holly was staying, I would have been travelling for seventeen hours and was probably going to be in a near state of collapse. I figured I'd literally shout at her for fifteen minutes about how irresponsible she was and how much money she'd cost me, not to mention having to take time off work and just general inconvenience, and then I'd just crash on her sofa for the next twelve hours, until I was recharged enough to wake up and give her another lecture.

I closed my eyes and laid back my head. Please let that be the way it went. Please let me be able to yell at my little sister, then give her a hug and tell her never to worry me again like that. Please God.

–

Martha's Vineyard airport was adorable – smaller than some of the houses I'd seen for sale on the island when I'd been flicking through real estate pages on the journey. If you were travelling by air and this was your first glimpse at the island, you would know exactly what to expect from the airport alone. There was not an ounce of ugly concrete in sight; everything was timber framed and whitewashed – even the planes were adorable. It reminded me of the model village that used to pop up in the town centre once a year, with its perfect cottages and picket fences.

I felt terrified and hopeful all at once. Was this how Holly would have felt when she arrived here? Of course, she would have felt scared for different reasons – a new adventure, the unknown – but she couldn't have failed to feel a sense of being somewhere truly special. I was terrified because until now I'd been able to convince myself that Holly would be waiting to welcome me with open arms and much hilarity that I had travelled all this way because she'd ghosted us. The next hour would prove me very right or painfully wrong.

As I approached the desk at the car rental company, I wondered if Holly was served by the same person, if the same hands that handed me my keys were the ones that handed keys to my sister. These links made me feel closer to her and I realised just how much I had missed her since she had been gone. I wondered if I'd be able to convince her to come back with me... I wondered if I'd get the chance.

The car they gave me was old, but it was clean and started when I put the key in, so that was a bonus. Plus it was an automatic, and while I drove geared at home, an automatic made it easier to deal with the strangeness of driving in a completely different country on the wrong side of the road. I'd driven a few times in France, so it wasn't completely alien to me – the first time I'd attempted it I'd had to stop dead at every roundabout to make sure I went the right way around it, much to the consternation of the drivers behind me. It had a satnav too, so I punched in the address Holly had given me and was relieved to see it come up on the screen immediately.

My eyes were so tired, I was almost certain I shouldn't have been driving, but I was determined to draw a line under the fear that had gripped my stomach since Jess had showed me the message she'd received. *Tell Mum I'm fine.* An innocent enough phrase, if our mum had been still alive, but one that, under the circumstances, might prove that something untoward had happened to my sister, and that someone else had sent that message using her phone.

Chapter Five

FOUR WEEKS BEFORE

She'd only been on the Vineyard for eight days, but already it felt as though she'd been here a lifetime. It really was the picture of perfection. Holly had worried at first that there would be a real divide between the people who lived on the island year-round, and the tourists, but if there was, then it hadn't extended to her. Everyone she had come across had been so welcoming, genuinely warm and friendly. It was like she'd stepped onto the set of an All-American movie, surrounded by white wooden slatted homes with real-life, honest to God white-picket fences and American flags flying outside shops. Everything had a slightly surreal feel to it, a town engineered to represent model America. Even the air felt too clean, the smell of the salt from the ocean too obvious.

Martha's Vineyard was a dream you didn't ever want to wake up from. It almost felt too good to be true, the start of a movie where everyone is happy and content before the meteor hits and everything is thrown into turmoil. Holly knew it was crazy to feel anxious about everything being absolutely fine for the first time in a long time, but this kind of perfection felt like it could definitely come with a sharp edge.

Her job at the marina was fun, even if her boss Carl was entirely too touchy-feely, and his wife Stacy looked at her as though she'd quite like to punch Holly's lights out. They weren't around much – they liked to schmooze with the rich summer dwellers, a third category of islanders altogether. These weren't the people who came for a once-in-a-lifetime holiday, she'd discovered, or the locals who lived on the island come rain or shine, but an influx of filthy-rich country clubbers who owned summer homes here. They would turn up every year in June and depart at the end of August to go back to their high-powered jobs, rested and tanned from a summer playing tennis and boating.

It was here where the real divide seemed to exist, from what Holly could gather. Tourists knew they were tourists, they respected the hierarchy, they had saved all year round to spend their holiday money in the restaurants and cafes, and they bought their *Jaws*-themed novelty goods and they recognised that they were visitors to this magical place. Summer people – they were different altogether. They had spent every summer on the Vineyard since they were born, they were wealthy and entitled and treated the island like their own rich-kid playground. So Emmy had told her.

Holly had met Emmy just the day before, at a cute little coffee shop she'd found on Upper Main Street in Edgartown. Emmy had been cleaning tables, and she'd struck up a conversation with Holly when she'd seen the book Holly was reading – *Pig Island* by Mo Hayder.

'God I love that book!' the cute girl wiping down the tables exclaimed, leaning on the back of the empty chair facing her. 'Literally no one I know has read it. I feel like we should be friends.'

Holly put the book face down and open on the table.

'Hold on just a second,' she said with a smile. 'How do you know I'm not just hate-reading at this point?'

Emmy frowned. 'Hate reading? What on earth is hate reading?'

'Haven't you ever read a book that was so bad that you carried on reading until the end just so you could tell everyone how bad it was?'

Emmy's eyes widened. 'No! Why the flip would I do that?'

Holly had decided there and then that she was going to completely fall in love with this girl.

'I don't know,' she laughed. 'I've never done it either. But people do.'

'Yeah, crazy, weird people,' Emmy laughed. 'I'm Emmy. Can we *please* be friends?'

Holly couldn't remember the last time someone had asked to be her friend, with such openness and warmth. She found herself laughing too. 'Sure, as long as you're not a psychopath.'

'Me?' Emmy looked around the cafe and, not spotting her boss, pulled out the chair she had been leaning on and sat down. 'I'm not the one reading books I hate. Tell me more about you, English, tell me *more.*'

Chapter Six

Claire

Pulling up outside the address on the satnav, I couldn't actually believe that my sister had been living here. It felt like the most perfect place on earth. I didn't believe that anything bad could have happened to her here: it was paradise.

Holly's rental was a gorgeous grey-slatted, vintage wooden cottage. Around the front door was a cream moulded surround with a modern-looking number sixteen on slate plaque and the windows had freshly painted navy sash slats. The garden was well kept and – there was no other word for it – green. Everything here was green, until you reached the sky, which was a bright cornflower blue. There was even a white picket fence. A small white car with a rental sticker in the rear window sat on the driveway, just like Deputy Dopey said it was. At least he'd actually made it all the way over here, I guess.

Was Holly in there? What would she be doing at seven a.m. if she was? She wouldn't be at work, that much I knew. Bed then, maybe, or an early-morning run on the beach. She'd been trying to get me to go running with her for years.

Taking a deep breath, I got out of the car and walked up to the front door. Hoping this was the right place and I wasn't about to wake up some poor retiree on their summer vacation, I rang the doorbell and waited. Nothing.

I pressed my finger on the bell again, firmer this time and waited a few minutes longer before going over to the front window to peer through. The grass was damp from the early-morning dew and the moisture soaked through my canvas trainers and into my socks. I cupped my hands around my eyes and placed them on the cold glass. Inside the window, the blinds were slightly tilted but not fully and I could see where there was a comfy-looking sofa, a pine coffee table and a breakfast bar marking off the open-plan kitchen. As the police officer had said, there was a suitcase up against the breakfast bar, lying down and open, half packed and half unpacked. Had Holly been going somewhere? Had she been in the middle of packing? Or had she just been lazy and only half unpacked her suitcase as she used her clothes? Knowing Holly, the latter was just as likely as the former.

I banged on the window, but it was clear there was no one around. I could see the top of the back door from where I was standing, but not enough to see if there was a key in the lock. There was a six-foot fence closing off the back garden – or yard, as they would call it here – and when I tried the gate, it was locked. But no six-foot fence had defeated me in the past and I didn't intend for this one to. There were two empty, heavy-looking ceramic pots at the front of the house that might just get me high enough. The problem, I discovered, was that in order to stack one on top of the other I had to stack them rim to rim, which was hardly the sturdiest solution. Add that to the fact that it was broad daylight and this seemed like the kind of neighbourhood where people looked out for one another, and this came out looking like a pretty stupid plan.

'Let them call the police,' I muttered to myself. 'Saves me having to call them again.'

I put one foot on top of the plant pot and the whole thing wobbled precariously. If this worked, I would be astounded. Expecting it to fall the minute I put pressure on it, I held onto the handle of the gate and pulled myself fully onto the planter stack, shifting my weight as the top pot slid an inch to the side. Holy shit.

Now I was balanced on top of the planters, I grabbed the top of the fence to keep steady, shifted so I could stand on one leg, and swung the other leg up and over the top of the fence. It was a thick enough fence for me to lie along it, straddling either side, and look down to see just a six-foot drop. That was probably going to hurt. I'd learned to land from climbing trees as a kid, but I had older joints and more fear than I'd had back then. Still, I was here for Holly and prepared to throw my other leg over when someone shouted.

'Hey! What do you think you're doing?'

The voice belonged to a guy in his early sixties, dressed like he was about to spend a day on the golf course, which he probably was. He had a full head of slicked-back white hair and sea-blue eyes, tanned legs encased in white shorts and a polo shirt with an actual goddamn jumper wrapped around his shoulders. I reckoned I could take him.

'I'm breaking into this house,' I said, preparing to make the drop.

'I can see that. Why?'

I let out a sigh and looked back at him. 'Because my sister isn't answering my calls and I'm worried about her.'

'You're Holly's sister?'

For some reason, I was so surprised to hear him say my sister's name that I almost dropped off the fence. 'You know Holly?'

The guy smiled. 'Everyone here knows Holly. She's a real ray of sunshine, your sister.' He raised his eyebrows, almost as if he wanted to add that I was nothing like her. I don't suppose breaking and entering and blatant disregard for social norms counts as 'sunshine'.

'When was the last time you saw her?' The fence was painful between my legs after dangling there for so long. 'Hang on, can you just wait there while I get down?'

'Oh sure,' the guy said. 'You just finish your break-in, don't let me put you off.'

Wait, was that dry humour? And there was me thinking that that was purely a British trait.

I managed to wedge my left foot onto the gate's inside catch, which meant instead of dropping the entire six foot, I could lower myself for at least three of them. When I hit the ground, my ankle twisted sharply, but I was in. Ignoring the pain, I unbolted the gate from the inside and opened it to see the guy still waiting patiently for me.

'I live just down there,' he said, pointing down the street. 'And I see Holly most days, but I haven't seen her since before the weekend, I don't think. Do you need some help?'

Thinking about it, it might be a good idea to have him here, even if just to prove to the police that I wasn't trying to steal anything. I hadn't decided yet if I was actually going to break into the house.

'Thanks. My name is Claire,' I said.

'Gerry,' he replied.

The back door was locked and offered very little clue as to whether Holly was inside or not. I tried banging on the glass panes in the door, but there was no response.

'I think I'm really going to have to break in,' I told Gerry. 'I'll pay for any damage, I just need to know if she's in there hurt or something.'

'Of course you do,' he agreed immediately. 'But let me try the owners first. They live on the island, they might be able to open it for you.'

I didn't know if it was pure luck that it happened to be Gerry who had caught me breaking in, or if everyone had everyone else's phone number on the island, but whatever it was, I was grateful. The owners would surely know if Holly had any plans to go away, or if she'd decided to leave early.

Gerry was now talking to someone, which meant one of the landlords had answered their phone.

'They're on their way,' he said, hanging up. 'It will take them about half an hour, but Sheila said that if you think it's a life-threatening emergency, you should go ahead and break the window.'

I looked at the house once again and thought about the fact that Holly had been out of contact now for six days now, if you didn't count the possibly fake message to Jess. If something had happened to her inside there nearly a week ago, I couldn't imagine another half an hour would make a difference. Besides, despite how determined I had been to get in, another half an hour before I had to face any difficult truths was a welcome reprieve.

'I'll wait,' I said, and Gerry looked relieved.

'In that case, why don't you come and have a coffee at my house? Or do you Brits prefer tea?'

'Thank you for the offer, but I'd rather just wait here,' I said, planting myself on the doorstep. I'd come this far: I wasn't going anywhere until I'd made sure my sister wasn't in that house.

Chapter Seven

Holly

THREE WEEKS BEFORE

When she met Emmy, Holly's time on the island really began. Until then, her days had been divided between work and reading or drawing at the beach, or in cafes. It had been nice relaxing, taking stock of her life and where she wanted it to go next, thinking about her mum and trying her best to be grateful for all the love she had given Holly, all the lessons Holly had learned from her in life and the lessons she vowed to take from her death. But there was only so much of that a person could take before alone and pensive became lonely and maudlin.

Now, all of a sudden, she was on the inside of island life, being introduced to other locals and being pulled from one 'best spot on the island' to another by the charismatic and friendly Emmy. Her job at the marina had started to become an inconvenience – not that she would ever let her standard of work slip, and not once did she show up late or let Carl know just how hungover she might be feeling after an afternoon drinking pina colada at the beach club in Chappy. Holly was starting to feel as though this was the life she had always been cut out for, and she wanted to make a good impression at the marina in case she could find some way to stay on the island.

'Real estate here is a total bitch,' Emmy informed her, pulling her bright red bikini top into place over her tiny bosom. 'Most of the locals have had places here for generations – that's how we can afford it. You wanna buy a house now, you have to be Barack Obama. That's why I'm in my twenties and still living with Mommy and Daddy.'

Neither of them had a membership to the exclusive Chappaquiddick Beach Club full of rich summer islanders, but Emmy's ex-boyfriend worked behind the bar and could get them guest passes pretty much any time they wanted, she'd explained. Not that Emmy usually bothered, but she had wanted to give Holly a taste of the 'other side of island life'. It hadn't exactly been the relaxing spa day that the words 'beach club' conjured up. Young children splashed in and out of the sea, whilst harassed-looking nannies watched from the red, white, and blue umbrellaed tents, slathering on sun cream periodically and surreptitiously checking their phones. Holly had been expecting a massage and a topless waiter bringing them margaritas at the least, instead the waiters had their hands full with the demands of spoiled teenagers with trust funds.

'Uh-oh,' Emmy said, lowering her sunglasses to peer over them towards the sea. 'Look who it isn't.'

'Who isn't it?' Holly asked, glancing over in the direction Emmy was looking. Four boys in their early twenties were walking through the surf towards the pier opposite where they were sitting. None of them were unattractive, Holly noted, although only one of them was conventionally gorgeous. Holly noticed a few of the young nannies' heads turn. The whole atmosphere around them seemed to tense. 'Who are they?'

'Those boys there are the Slaytons,' Emmy replied, looking slightly wary and nervous with anticipation all at once. 'Well, two of them are, anyway. I don't know the other two. General interchangeable cling-ons.'

'What's a Slayton?' Holly asked, her nose screwed up. Probably some boating term she'd never heard of.

'Not a what, a who,' Emmy said. 'Bobby and Ryan Slayton. One of the richest families to own a place on the island. They've been coming every summer for as long as I can remember. Their mum Delilah's a real bitch. I remember one time she had a girl fired from Remmy's because she gave her the cheap whisky instead of the expensive one by accident. She said the girl did it on purpose to insult her by insinuating she couldn't afford the good stuff.'

'Jesus,' Holly whistled. 'That is a whole other level of "bitch".'

Emmy laughed. 'Well, they are related to the Kennedys, don'tcha know?'

'Honestly, dahhling, who isn't?' Holly said, fluttering her hand against her chest.

Emmy laughed again. 'Feels like that here, right? You should stay for the winter. It's like a different island. Seriously though, you're better off staying away from those boys. Bobby has looks to die for, but they are both trouble with all the capitals.'

Holly watched as the Slayton brothers and their friends messed around in the surf, kicking the water up at one another and laughing as they made their way to the pier. They didn't seem to look at a single other person, as though they were the only people on the beach, and yet somehow Holly got the impression that they knew that everyone was watching them.

Chapter Eight

Claire

Holly wasn't in the house. Sheila and her husband Hank had turned up after forty-five minutes that felt much longer and we had searched every room – there was no sign at all of my sister. Holly's handbag and phone weren't inside, but her phone charger and what looked to be all of her clothes were, she obviously hadn't gone anywhere in a hurry. Apart from the usual Holly mess – untidy rumpled bed, cold half-drunk cup of tea on the bedside table – there really wasn't anything to hang your hat on. It was a crushing blow not to find her, but at the same time a huge relief not to see her body at the bottom of the stairs or in the bathtub.

'She paid us up front for the whole summer,' Sheila explained. 'So we wouldn't have known there was anything wrong until she didn't contact us with her decision to renew or not in September.'

'Would it be okay if I leave her things here for now, please?'

'Of course,' Sheila said, reaching over and patting my hand. She was a lovely woman, with coiffed blonde hair that had been hairsprayed to within an inch of its life, far too much make-up, and perfume that could be smelled from the airport, if not from the plane but what seemed to be a heart of gold. 'The place is hers until September the first. Where are you staying?'

'I was hoping Holly would let me stay with her,' I admitted, feeling awkward all of a sudden. This was their house: what if they didn't allow tenants to have visitors? 'I was only planning on staying a couple of nights once I'd seen that she was okay,' I added quickly.

'Well, you must stay here until you find her,' Sheila said immediately.

I was struck by how kind, caring, but mostly trusting, the locals here were. I could be literally anyone, but Sheila had obviously sensed that I was being truthful and was desperate to find my sister. It felt like this couple repres- ented what Martha's Vineyard was all about: a community looking after one another.

'Do you really think something has happened to her?' She looked worried.

I'd already told her about the missed calls, and about her not turning up at work, the only thing I'd left out was the text message. To tell her about that would mean explaining about our mum, and I wasn't about to go into all that with a complete stranger unless I had to, even one as lovely as Sheila.

When Holly had first announced she was coming here, despite being absolutely furious, I'd looked into the island in as much detail as possible, reading stories about the islanders banding together to welcome asylum seekers and local families raising money to help another couple who had lost their home to an electrical fire two weeks after their home insurance expired. Sheila's concern for a girl she barely knew shone around her like a halo.

'I hope not,' I said honestly. 'But this is all very unlike her. Holly is young, but she's reliable, and considerate. She would know how much I would worry about her if she just stopped all communication.'

Not enough to notice that she was missing, apparently, my inner voice mocked.

That reminded me; I'd promised I would let Jess know what was going on. I shot off a text message updating her that Holly wasn't in the house and I'd call her as soon as I knew more. It was almost nine a.m. here now so Jess would have been clock watching for hours.

'I'll come with you to the police,' Sheila offered.

'That's very kind of you.' I was touched at the generosity of the woman who had only just met me. 'But I'll ask around a bit first, try to find someone who knows where she might be. I don't know how much help the police will be. I called them before I came here and an officer came to look through the window, then said she'd probably met a guy and was with him.'

Sheila scowled, then her face softened into some kind of understanding. 'I suppose they would,' she said quietly.

'Why? Why would they say that?'

She shook her head and I immediately got the feeling there was something she wasn't about to tell me. 'We get a lot of tourists. Over a hundred thousand people flood this island every year. I suppose it's easier to think that she moved on than to think the worst. But you must keep pushing them,' she said, suddenly grasping my hand. 'You must make sure they take you seriously. The police here are good people, most people here are good people, and Holly is a lovely girl. You must find her.'

'Oh I will,' I promised. 'I'm not giving up on her.'

It wasn't until after she'd gone, extracting a promise that I'd call her if I needed anything or if I found Holly, that I began to wonder what she meant by 'most people'.

Chapter Nine

Holly

THREE WEEKS BEFORE

It was the start of Holly's third week on the island when she met the Slayton brothers up close. She was into her last hour at work, cleaning one of the boats, when a text came through from Emmy.

> Drinks at Remmy's tonight? Some friends are meeting there at ten. Do you know where it is or should I pick you up?

Holly had seen the popular bar a few times and always wanted to visit, just not alone. She texted back immediately.

> Sounds great! Will meet you there xx

Grinning, she slipped her phone back into the pockets of the ridiculously short white shorts Carl had given her to wear. The T-shirt felt two sizes too small as well. Holly had noticed that Stacy's uniform fit perfectly – if anything, it was on the baggy side. She wondered how the harbour master's wife – not much older than she was – felt about the other girls looking like Hooters waitresses courtesy of her husband. That was probably one of the reasons she never said more than two words to Holly, and even they were usually curt instructions.

Holly started to plan what she would wear to the bar – something casual, not too try-hard, she'd learned. She didn't want to look like a preppy summer kid, she wanted to fit in with Emmy's laid-back island friends, the ones who smelt of the ocean and never seemed to wear shoes. The ones who knew how to handle a boat, not because they had had thousands of dollars of lessons but because their parents had been mooring the rich folks' boats since they were kids and had let them take a turn when no one else was looking. Emmy's friends had been so welcoming, Holly was starting to wonder if Martha's Vineyard wasn't just the most perfect place on earth.

'You missed a bit,' a deep male voice said from behind her.

She groaned at the age-old quip, expecting to see Carl standing far too close when she turned around. Instead, it was one of the boys Emmy had pointed out on the beach – the Slaytons.

'Oh,' she said, taking a step back.

The boy frowned. 'Sorry, I didn't mean to startle you,' he said, his American accent drawing the words out slowly.

'No, I'm sorry,' Holly said, 'I thought you were Carl.'

The boy smiled and, although he wasn't the one she'd thought of as conventionally attractive on the beach, there was something about him that drew you in. *It's the money*, she could almost hear her sister Claire saying. *You can smell money a mile away.*

For a second, it hit her how much she missed Claire, how she wished her sister could have been happier for her before she'd come away, rather than telling her she shouldn't be running off so soon after their mum's death. She knew how much Claire loved her, and that she only wanted to keep Holly close through fear of losing her so soon after losing Mum, but this trip would have been a whole lot easier if she'd had her sister's blessing.

'Now if I was Carl, I'd have leaned up close and showed you where you were missing a spot,' he said, and Holly laughed. At least she wasn't the only one who had noticed how up close and personal her boss could be.

'I can neither confirm nor deny,' she said, smiling back. Her face started to warm up. Had he come over to flirt with her? Or was he just being friendly as a prelude to asking her to wash his luxury yacht next?

'You don't have to. Carl's attention to his young female staff is legendary. I'm Ryan, by the way,' he held out his hand and Holly took it, feeling slightly silly. She couldn't remember the last time someone had offered her a hand to shake, but then again, nothing in this place was like anything else.

'Holly,' she said.

'Like Christmas,' Ryan replied, looking into her eyes, his entire attention focused on her. All of a sudden, she didn't know what to say, or where to look. Ryan didn't seem perturbed. 'Are you here for the summer?'

'Yeah, I'm working,' she said, then immediately felt like an idiot. 'Obviously,' she muttered, gesturing to the cloth in her hand.

'You've come a long way for a summer job.'

She started, wondering how he knew where she was from. Then she remembered: her accent. She was so used to the way everyone sounded on the island that she'd almost forgotten that she didn't sound like that.

'If you have to work, may as well work in paradise,' she shrugged. 'Not that you have that problem.'

As soon as the words were out of her mouth, her face flushed a deep red.

Ryan laughed. 'And how would you know I don't have a summer job?' he asked, clearly amused.

Holly sighed. 'I saw you on the beach,' she admitted. 'My friend told me who you were.'

'That would be Emmy, right?'

Holly raised her eyebrows.

His grin widened. 'Well, maybe I saw you on the beach too.'

It surprised her to know that he hadn't only seen her, but he'd remembered her. It made her feel slightly uneasy, reminded her that the island was such a small place. Nothing went unnoticed.

'So, is there something I can help you with?' Holly asked, spotting Carl emerging from the office. She wondered how long he'd been watching them, his face set in a grim line. He gave her the ick so badly, the way he stood so close. Once, she could have sworn, she heard him smelling her hair, but that could have been her imagination. Her paranoia did seem to fire up around her creepy boss.

'Nope,' Ryan said. 'I just came here to introduce myself to you.'

Once again, she was left stumbling for words. What were you supposed to say to that?

'That's very flattering,' she managed, looking across to where Carl was making his way towards them. 'But my boss doesn't really like me talking while I'm supposed to be working, and he's on his way over.'

Ryan turned to see Carl walking towards them.

'Carl, hi,' he held up a hand and Carl matched the gesture.

'Hey, Ryan, whatcha doing here, buddy? Anything I can help with?'

'No thanks,' Ryan said. 'I just came to introduce myself to Holly here, and to have a chat with her. You don't mind, do you? I hope she won't get in any trouble – it was my fault, I couldn't help myself.'

'No.' Carl shook his head vigorously. 'Oh no, no problem at all. How's your dad?'

'He's just great, thanks. I think he's going to put in another order for some of that marlin you got him last summer for a party we have planned. A real big order.'

'That would be great,' Carl was nodding, and Holly had to bite her lip to stop from laughing. He looked like one of those nodding dogs people put on their dashboards.

'Actually, I was wondering if Holly would be able to finish early today?' Ryan said, casually slinging an arm around her shoulders. The gesture was far too intimate from someone she had just met and she bristled, but she didn't push him away. She waited to see Carl's reaction.

'I, erm…' Carl looked flustered. Holly had expected him to say no straight away, but he sighed and shrugged. 'Sure. As long as you don't make a habit of it,' he added, almost as an afterthought.

He walked away and both of them burst out laughing.

'You could have asked for me to have a pay rise, while you were at it,' Holly said. She would usually be cringing at the blatant display of power and wealth Ryan had used to cut her boss down to size, but Carl was a creep and he deserved it. Besides, now she had more time to get ready for tonight.

'I know it was a shitty rich-boy thing to do,' Ryan admitted. 'But that guy really pisses me off. Anyway, you want a lift somewhere?'

Holly hesitated. Claire would absolutely lose her shit if she found out she had taken a ride with a guy she had met ten minutes before. Especially one who was so confident at getting his own way. The way he had used his family name to basically humiliate Carl right in front of her was a huge red flag. But he didn't *seem* like a serial killer and he had just got her off work, she didn't want to be rude…

'Hey, I get it,' Ryan held up his hands. 'I shouldn't have offered. It's different for guys, you know? We don't have to think about staying safe or not accepting lifts and stuff. And you double forget on the island…'

'No, it's fine,' Holly said, making up her mind. Ryan was one of the most well-known people on the island, it wasn't as if he was about to murder her and dump her in the sea. What harm could a lift home do?

Chapter Ten

Claire

Holly had been working in Oak Bluffs, a fifteen-minute drive from Edgartown across the famous *Jaws* bridge. I'd caught Holly watching *Jaws* countless times before her flight to Massachusetts – it had been one of our favourite films growing up and she couldn't believe she was actually going to be staying on Amity Island. 'Just stay out of the water,' I'd warned, and she'd smiled. Then I'd quickly remembered how angry I was that she was leaving and, like a petulant child, I'd added, 'It probably looks completely different now anyway.' It hurt now to recall the way her smile had crumpled.

And I'd been wrong. The coastline looked exactly how it had on the 80s film; beautiful clear blue water, soft sand dunes and tufts of beach grass. For a while, the sea disappeared almost completely and I was driving through a corridor of trees, past manicured grass and white picket fences, but it wasn't long before I was back on the famous coastline again, passing grey-and-white houses that had one of the best views the world had to offer.

I'd said goodbye to Sheila and Hank with the promise that I'd contact them as soon as I had news, thrown my stuff in Holly's house and set off for the marina straight away, but it was still nearly ten by the time I got there.

I parked up while my satnav said I still had five minutes' drive to the marina and walked the last stretch. I showed Holly's picture to everyone who passed me in the hope of finding someone who might say, 'Oh hell yeah, Holly? She's staying with me for a few days,' but no one I spoke to even recognised her.

When I arrived at the marina, I saw a cafe opposite. I went in, telling myself it was to show Holly's picture around rather than putting off speaking to her boss, even though I was expecting to be told *sorry but no* again. Instead, this time, a middle-aged woman with incredibly large eyebrows smiled and said, 'Oh yeah, Holly? She comes in sometimes for her lunch. She has seafood soup and a crusty roll. Haven't seen her in a while. She okay?'

In an instant, I felt a rush of closeness towards this place. My sister had sat in one of those seats, eaten from the bowls, buttered bread with one of the knives. I pictured her here just a few days earlier, probably reading a book or scrolling through Instagram. In my vision, she tucked her hair behind her ear continuously because it was so silky it kept falling out of her ponytail – I know, golden shoes problem, right? As she was eating her soup, she gazed out of the window, content to watch the world go by… God, I hoped so desperately that she was okay.

'When was the last time you saw her?' I asked, a bit too eagerly, I gathered, because the woman took a step back and her huge eyebrows narrowed. 'She's my sister,' I added, although I'd have assumed she'd be able to guess we were from the same place by my accent.

'I'm not totally sure, sweetie, but I'll go ask Marv if he knows,' she said, and left me standing on my own clutching the photograph of Holly like it was my lifeline.

A woman sitting at a table just to my left had been watching me intently since I'd asked about Holly, and I moved closer to her now. She looked to be late thirties and was slightly dishevelled, pretty but drawn. She had dark brown hair pulled back into a ponytail with wisps left loose, and tired brown eyes.

'Sorry to bother you, but have you seen this girl?' I asked her, thrusting my photo towards her face.

The woman looked at it and then at me. 'No,' she said, turning away. 'Sorry.'

I was about to say something else when the woman with the eyebrows came back out.

'Last Wednesday, Thursday,' she said, wriggling her hand side to side to indicate it could have been either. 'She was in here with Ryan Slayton.'

'Who's he?' I asked, relieved to finally have a name to hang onto. 'And where can I find him?'

'He's the son of one of the richest men on the island,' the woman said, lowering her voice. 'Practically a celebrity. They have the big house in Edgartown, the one with those awful marble pillars.' She looked around to see if anyone was listening, but the woman I just spoke to had gone and the place was empty.

'And this was Wednesday or Thursday?' I asked again, dread rolling around in my stomach.

She nodded.

'Thank you,' I said, not wanting to think about the implications of my sister being with some rich guy just before we lost contact with her. 'If I got one of these printed off would there be any chance I could get you to put it in your window please? If she was in here someone else might have seen her with this Ryan guy.'

The woman stepped back as though my photo might burn her.

'Sorry,' she said, her face apologetic. 'I can't. Not if...' she stopped.

'If...?' I said slowly, expecting her to elaborate, but instead she muttered, 'I hope you find her,' and practically ran to the back of the cafe.

Feeling slightly bewildered at the sudden change in the woman's demeanour, I left, pulling out my phone to google Ryan Slayton coupled with Martha's Vineyard. I clicked on images and the first thing to come up was a photograph of two boys, a man and a woman standing in front of a huge house, marble pillars and all. The woman from the cafe was right, they were obscene. The caption on the photograph read 'Annual Charity Fundraiser at the home of the Slayton Family on Martha's Vineyard'. My eyes scanned the article... incredibly wealthy family... cousin to the Kennedys... kind donations... Holly was talking to one of these people? Under the photo, the family were named in order, the father, Laurence Slayton, mother, Delilah Slayton, and the boys, Bobby and Ryan Slayton. They looked to be standing in age order, although you could hardly wedge a piece of cardboard between their ages by the looks of it. Bobby looked older than Ryan, and was the best looking, with his father's eyes and strong jawline. Ryan was plainer, but still not unattractive. They looked like a family who were used to getting their own way, and I didn't like that my sister had got herself involved with them.

Chapter Eleven

Holly

THREE WEEKS BEFORE

'So, this is Tara, Megan, Lucy and Minty. Her real name's Araminta, but her family are rolling in cash, so we call her Minty to piss her off.'

The girl Emmy had been talking about to her face held up a middle finger. 'They do as well,' she said. 'Bitches.' But it was said with a smile – and a moneyed accent.

Holly grinned. 'It's really nice to meet you,' she said, feeling slightly overwhelmed. Of course she'd wanted to make some friends – she didn't want to spend the entire summer reading on her own in cafes – but she didn't imagine having to meet this many people in one go. Lucky she wasn't as socially backwards as her sister. Claire would be moonwalking straight out of the bar faced with this many chirpy, smiley girlfriends.

'It's good to meet you too,' Megan, or maybe Tara, said. 'Emmy doesn't usually bring new friends into the group. You must have made quite an impression on her.' It was said without even the smallest hint of bitchiness.

Holly got it: it might have been a massive tourist attraction in the summer, but the rest of the year round it was still an island. When everyone else packed up and went home, these girls would still be together.

'She was reading *Pig Island*,' Emmy said.

There was a mixture of aaaahhhhs and groans.

'She's been trying to get us to read that book for years,' Minty explained.

'I did actually try it,' the ginger girl, who Holly had decided was definitely Megan, said. 'I hated it. Sorry, Holly.'

Holly laughed. 'And there was me just about to say I wrote it.'

The girls all laughed.

'Jesus, can you imagine, Emmy, if that were true? You'd never get rid of her,' Lucy said. 'Although you might not anyway with that gorgeous British accent.'

'You might not get rid of me,' Holly replied. 'This place is so beautiful. How does anyone ever leave it?'

'Not enough designer stores and Hollywood parties,' Minty said with an eye roll. 'We're good for a summer wellness retreat. Then it's back to the real world they go. You'd love it here early spring. All the benefits, none of the tourists.'

'No offence taken,' Holly quipped.

'You're not a tourist. You're a summer worker. Total difference.'

Holly raised her eyebrows and there was laughter again. She felt like she could really fit in here.

'Heads up, girls,' Tara said, nodding in the direction of the door. 'Look who just walked in.'

Somehow, Holly didn't need to look to know who it was going to be. It was like those boys were the only males on the island, the amount they were talked about. Okay, they were louder, and because there was always four or five of them they stood out more, but surely they weren't all the island had to offer in the way of male specimens?

No, she thought, her inner voice sardonic. *There's always Carl.*

Sure enough, it was the two Slaytons and two other boys.

'My, my, my that Bobby Slayton is fine,' Megan muttered.

'And arrogant, and narcissistic, and completely up himself,' Tara said.

'Didn't you sleep with him a few years ago?' Lucy asked, the hint of a smile on her lips.

'That's beside the point,' Tara grinned. 'But yes.'

Holly was just about to tell them about her lift home from Ryan earlier, and how he'd been sweet and charming when he was away from his brother, but before she had a chance, Megan let out a low whistle. 'They're coming over here.'

'Oh God,' Emmy groaned. 'What do they want?'

But Holly noticed her friend tuck her hair behind her ear nervously and check her reflection in the mirror on the wall behind them.

'Ladies.' It was Bobby who led the way over. His eyes fell on Tara first. He smiled slowly, the kind of smile that made you think he was undressing her mentally. 'Tara. How are you?'

Tara flushed bright red. 'I'm good, Bobby. Long time no see.'

'Well, I thought you were avoiding me,' he said, moving an inch or so closer.

Holly watched Tara find herself lost for words. Two minutes ago she had been running him into the ground, now she looked like she'd gladly have sex with him on the bar if he asked her. What was it about Bobby Slayton?

'Hey, Holly,' Ryan said, and Holly felt the group of girls all fix their eyes on them. 'I thought you were getting an early night tonight?'

Holly cringed. That was exactly what she'd told him when he'd dropped her off and asked her what she was doing later. She'd said she had an early shift at the marina and wanted to get plenty of rest.

'That was the plan,' she shrugged in what she hoped was an 'aw shucks' kind of way. 'But Emmy messaged me and said it was absolutely imperative that I came out for just one drink. She's not an easy person to say no to.'

'Unlike my little brother here, right?' Bobby said, slinging an arm around Ryan's shoulder. 'Who doesn't even know when he's being given the brush-off.' He ruffled Ryan's hair and Ryan looked furious. 'When a beautiful girl tells you she's having an early night, she's either telling you to get lost or that early night is in bed with a lucky man.'

The other boys laughed and Holly felt her face and chest redden, annoyed that Bobby could make his brother look and feel like shit in front of everyone.

'That's bullshit,' she said, her anger clear in her voice. 'I don't know how many women you've actually had a conversation with in your life, instead of just talking down to them, but you'll find that our whole lives don't revolve around whether we're sleeping with a man or not.'

Bobby held up his hands in mock surrender, but he had an infuriating smirk on his face. The other boys made 'oooooh' noises and broke down laughing.

Holly turned to Ryan. 'I really wasn't coming out tonight,' she lied. 'But I also wanted to meet the friends that Emmy had told me so much about. If the offer for a drink is still on, I'd like to take you up on it. Maybe Wednesday?'

Ryan's face was still burning red, but Holly didn't know if it was from his brother's ribbing of him or her offer of a date. He nodded. 'Sure, that would be great. Shall I pick you up at eight? Same place I dropped you off earlier, right?'

Holly nodded, noting the scowl that was on Bobby Slayton's attractive face. In a split second, it changed and Bobby broke into a grin, as if that was the best news he'd had all year.

'Well, if my little brother hasn't got himself a date with the pretty new girl,' he said, slapping a hand on Ryan's shoulder. 'Way to go, little bro. Now, if you ladies will excuse us, we have some drinking to do. Right, boys?'

The others whooped their consent and Ryan was dragged away, giving Holly a small smile as he left. She wasn't really sure what had made her ask him on a date in front of everyone, especially when she'd purposely refused him earlier on the grounds that him and his brothers were pure trouble, anyone could see that.

The tension hung in the air even after the boys had left. It was as though everyone was holding their breath, waiting for someone else to break the spell.

Holly turned to Emmy to see that she looked crest-fallen.

'Are you okay?' she asked, reaching out to touch her new friend's arm.

Emmy jerked away like she'd had an electric shock.

'Of course,' Emmy said. 'You just didn't tell me Ryan had given you a lift home.'

'Yeah, I was just about to say when they walked over,' Holly said. 'He showed up at the marina and made a bit of a tit of Carl. It was hilarious.'

'Yeah, I bet,' Emmy replied, her voice tight. 'Excuse me, I just need the loo.' She pushed through the girls, who all gave one another knowing looks.

'Why do I get the feeling I've massively fucked up?' Holly asked, looking to each of the girls in turn.

'No, no, it's not your fault,' Lucy said. 'It's just that... well, Emmy's a bit weird when Ryan is around, or when his name is mentioned. We think she has a crush on him, but she won't admit it.'

Holly's eyes widened and she slapped a hand to her face. 'No way! She made out like she wouldn't touch any of them with a bargepole!'

The girls all started talking at once, keen to reassure her.

'You obviously weren't to know.'

'She should just admit it.'

'No way you could have known if she won't even tell us.'

Holly didn't understand. 'But Emmy is gorgeous,' she said, confused. 'Like totally beautiful. If she's had a crush on Ryan for so long, why haven't they got together? It's not like he wouldn't fancy her, anyone would.'

'That's the thing we can't figure out,' Tara admitted. 'She just clams up and goes all silent when he's around, like a lovestruck teenager. I don't think he has any clue she likes him.'

Holly couldn't believe what a colossal mess of things she'd made. There was no way she wanted to upset Emmy over some guy. She'd have to fix this. She'd just tell Ryan she couldn't go out with him after all. Then everything could just go back to how it had been twenty-five minutes ago. Simple.

Chapter Twelve

Claire

I couldn't put off going to the marina any longer. It was, after all, what I was doing in Oak Bluffs, and they were most likely the people who knew the most about her. After travelling all night and barely sleeping on the plane what I really wanted to do was go back to Holly's and crash out for a few hours, but just being here and discovering that she was nowhere to be seen had given me a renewed sense of urgency to find out where my sister was. I knew that I was no use to her if I crashed my rental car through exhaustion, but I was also very aware the time since Jess had last heard from her – other than the fake text message – was increasing with every passing second.

I walked past the reception of the marina and towards a young girl I could see cleaning down a boat on the far side of the harbour. She was wearing a tight, light blue polo shirt and white shorts and she actually looked around Holly's age. She was shorter than Holly, and had dark brown hair. She was pretty, and looked open and friendly, and I wondered if she and Holly were friends.

She saw me walking towards her and held up a hand. 'Hi,' she called, 'can I help?'

'Maybe,' I said. 'I'm looking for my sister. Her name is Holly, she's been working here until recently.'

The girl smiled apologetically. 'Sorry, I don't know her. I only just started a couple of days ago, I think I actually replaced Holly. They said the girl before me quit unexpectedly and they were in a bit of a tough spot.'

'Who's they?'

'Carl and Stacy. Carl is the harbour master and Stacy is his wife. Carl's on one of the boats down there, if you want to speak to him?' She pointed towards where the larger boats were docked.

'Great, thanks.' I smiled and let her get back to her work. She hadn't seemed as though she was hiding some huge dark secret, although I'd never had to interrogate someone before. Perhaps I'd let her off too easily. Man, this was hard.

I wandered down the harbour, admiring the majestic boats that I passed alongside. I found Carl on the deck of one of the larger ones with a screwdriver in his hand. He was whistling as he tinkered with something out of my sightline. I watched him for a moment, taking in his wiry frame, his jet-black hair greying around the temples and slicked back with gel. He was wearing jeans and a polo shirt with the marina logo on. He looked to be in his late forties probably. When he turned to face me, I just knew I was going to dislike him – not just because he hadn't cared enough to find out why my sister had suddenly stopped turning up to work, choosing instead just to replace her like an old coffee filter, but because he had small, distrustful eyes and a shit-eating, butter-wouldn't-melt grin. His tan looked to be out of a bottle despite living in a place where a tan was practically a given. He looked me up and down in a way that made me think that he was probably a complete and utter prick, but I could see how he might have appealed to my sister who was younger, more impressionable. He was a relatively attractive older man with influence and probably a good salary. How had Holly felt when she first met him? Was she scared by him, or did she feel safe? Did he drive her back to her apartment after her shift one night? Was this the guy she had told Jess about, unsure of his intentions?

'Can I help you?' Carl asked, which seemed to be the mantra around here.

'I hope so,' I replied, and his eyes widened at my voice. 'Are you Carl?'

'You're English,' he stated.

Observant fella. I resisted the urge to tell him I could see why he was the boss and instead just nodded. Mum used to say something about vinegar and flies, but I was always too busy coming up with a sarcastic reply to listen properly.

'I'm Carl. I'm the harbour master. What can I do for you?'

'I'm Holly's sister,' I said, but I think he already knew that. And he wasn't only surprised to see me, but from the way his cheeks had flushed red and he was biting on his bottom lip I could see he was uncomfortable about it too.

'It's like I told Waylans when he came up here,' he said, his tone making it clear he resented having to answer to the police officer, 'I don't know where she is. She just stopped turning up. Didn't call, didn't explain. Left us in a right mess, middle of summer season.'

'Which day?' I asked.

He looked to one side as if he was trying to count the days off. I wished I could remember which side meant he was lying. Was it when you looked up to the left? Or was it up to the right? Either way, he was pretending to have to count the days. He knew exactly which day Holly had

69

failed to show up for work and I couldn't figure out why he was pretending not to know.

'I think it was Sunday,' he said eventually.

I raised my eyebrows to show him I had him worked out. 'And that didn't seem strange to you?'

'Like I said to the poh-lice,' he repeated, dragging out the word for emphasis. 'She won't be the first person we've had just not show up. People come here thinking it's an easy ride, then they realise that we do more than just book boats into the harbour. There's cleaning, maintenance. Some of the customers are real assholes. Then there's the fact that the beach always feels preferable to hard work. When she didn't show up, I didn't think anything of it except how I was going to have to find someone else now and that was a pain in the ass.'

'You found someone pretty quickly,' I said, glancing back at the young woman cleaning the boat.

His cheeks coloured. 'Just luck,' he shrugged.

'Did you try to call her?'

'I think Stacy might have.' He couldn't care less. I wanted to climb up there and push him off the boat and into the water.

'Did she mention any friends, anyone she might be with, any—'

'Look,' Carl cut my question off. 'I barely knew the girl. I was her boss, not her bestie. I'm not the one you need to be talking to.' I squared my shoulders, bristling at the way he had spoken to me.

'But—'

'You need to leave,' he said, this time forceful enough to let me know that the conversation was over and I would be stupid to try to go on.

I squeezed my lips shut to stop myself from hurling insults at him, turned on my heels and stormed towards the exit. As I was passing what I assumed was the office, I saw another flash of light blue polo, blonde hair. It couldn't be the first girl I saw – she was still out cleaning the boat, and besides, she was dark-haired. Whoever it was might be more helpful than Captain Asshole out there.

I pushed open the office door and the bell above my head rang. A woman who appeared to be in her mid-twenties glanced around the door opposite.

'Hi,' I called out, putting on my most winning smile. I was contemplating following up with a 'nice to meet y'all' in a loud Southern drawl; perhaps it was my clipped English accent that was causing people to be so unhelpful. But before I could give it some Southern charm, she disappeared, leaving me wondering if I'd even seen her at all.

I wasn't giving up that easily. I crossed through the office and peered into the room beyond. It looked like a staffroom, with a table, chairs, sink, microwave and kettle. The woman was standing in the corner in front of a fridge, as though she was hoping to blend into the brushed chrome. Her long blonde hair was pulled back into a plait and her face was free of make-up.

'You're not supposed to be in here,' she said defensively.

'I'm not, technically,' I pointed to the floor where my feet were still firmly in the office. 'My name is Claire.'

'I know who you are,' she said. 'You're Holly's sister.'

I felt a rush of warmth that Holly must have mentioned me to this woman, possibly even shown her my picture if she recognised me. I vaguely remembered Tom saying that Stacy was Carl's wife. 'Are you Stacy?' I asked.

She nodded. I could see the softly-softly approach wouldn't get me anywhere with this woman.

'Do you know why Holly stopped showing up to work?'

'How would I know? She never even told us she was quitting, let alone why.'

'I'm not asking what she told you, I'm asking what you know,' I said, gritting my teeth. I was getting annoyed with everyone being so unhelpful here, in such a contrast to Gerry and Sheila. What did they have to hide? Did something happen here that made Holly want to quit?

Stacy was pretty but she didn't seem to have any confidence whatsoever. She was constantly glancing down at her bitten nails and she spoke quietly as if she was scared of being overheard. Her own light blue T-shirt was long-sleeved and baggy, her bottoms were white cropped trousers, in stark contrast to the young girl I had met out front. I wondered if she always looked this nervous and downtrodden.

'Please,' I said. 'I'm really worried about her.'

'I don't think...' Stacy started. 'Well, nothing happened to her here. I don't think you need to worry. The island is very safe.'

'So everyone keeps telling me,' I muttered, glancing around at the photos on the wall and noticing that there were pictures of Carl with various celebrities. I saw Obama, Oprah, David Letterman. 'How long have you and Carl worked here?'

'Carl's worked here about fifteen years,' she replied. 'Me, not so long.'

She was a lot younger than him. She must have been about twenty-three, twenty-four. Barely older than my sister, but I couldn't picture the two of them as friends, they were so different. 'How long have you two been married?'

'Six years. What has that got to do with Holly?'

Six years. Carl would have been late thirties at the least, and Stacy would have been around eighteen. The thought made me shudder.

'Nothing, I'm just being friendly. Please, Stacy, is there anything you might be able to tell me? Did she get on okay with everyone here? With Carl?'

She wasn't stupid, she knew exactly what I was asking. 'Carl never touched your sister, if that's what you're implying,' Stacy snapped.

'It wasn't,' I said, even though we both knew it was. 'I'm just trying to find out where she might be. Do you really not know anything?'

She looked as though she was considering just saying no again, but either she was useless at lying or she thought I might go away quicker if she gave me something. 'Ryan Slayton,' she said, glancing out of the window. 'He'd been in here a couple of times chatting to your sister.'

'So what?' I asked, my tone challenging. 'What else?'

Stacy sighed. She looked as though she'd rather gouge her own eyes out than have seen anything that might help me find my sister. 'There was a party at the Slayton house, then a bonfire, at Left Fork. Last Friday night.'

'Holly went to that,' I said, remembering her Instagram. 'Did something happen to her there? Did this Ryan guy hurt her?'

'No,' Stacy said quickly. Too quickly. 'I don't know. I'm just telling you that she went to it. I think she went to it with Ryan, if you know what I mean. I think they went together.'

'You mean they were dating?'

Stacy scoffed. 'Do people still date? Or do they just hook up? It seems like this place is just a mating ground for kids every summer.'

I held my tongue from saying that my sister was almost the same age as she was, far from being a kid, but I didn't want to stop her talking.

'I'm pretty sure she was fine when she left,' Stacy said, then stopped as if she had said too much.

'How do you know?' I demanded. 'Were you there? At the bonfire? Did you see who she left with?'

Stacy shook her head, her lips firmly closed as if she was desperately trying to stop herself saying any more. I could see that I wasn't going to get anything else from her, she was practically in tears. Why? What else did she know? Who was she trying to protect?

I would leave her alone now, but if my sister didn't show up soon I would be back, and Stacy wouldn't get away with holding anything back from me then. I made for the harbour exit and walked back towards my rental car, but instead of driving straight back to Edgartown, I slowed down past the marina, almost to a stop. Carl was talking to the girl I'd met when I'd first arrived. I couldn't see the look on his face, he was too far away, but I could see the way his hand rested on her shoulder, how it dropped to her waist. I wondered if I was closer, what I would see on the girl's face. Would it be fear, or lust? Was Carl seen as a stud, or a sleaze?

I watched a second longer as the girl stepped abruptly back and folded her arms across her chest and I had my answer. And when I saw Stacy standing at the end of the harbour watching the pair of them, I knew that she was well aware of the type of man her husband was.

Chapter Thirteen

Holly

THREE WEEKS BEFORE

Holly's head was still pounding as she handed Emmy a steaming mug of coffee. She put her own on the small wicker table on the front porch and collapsed into the cushioned chair, closing her eyes. After their run-in with the Slaytons, and once Emmy had returned from the bathroom, the night had carried on as if there had never been an awkward interlude. Emmy's friends were funny, warm and welcoming, and although Holly still felt like an obvious outsider, she had allowed herself to think about what life might be like if she could move to the island permanently. They had discussed it at one point, as the evening had drawn on and the drinks had continued to flow. Minty had offered for Holly to stay in their family guest house once the season was over, until she could get permanent work. Lucy had mentioned that her father was in need of a PA, although she wasn't sure her mother would be keen on the idea of it being a gorgeous blonde English girl. They had all laughed at that, but Lucy had pulled a face to say she might just be serious. They had only seen the Slayton boys one more time, as they had been leaving the bar to walk home and Ryan and Bobby had been outside, looking like they might be having a row. Tara had said they were always like that, best of friends and worst of enemies. Holly thought she knew how that felt.

'You never told me that you liked Ryan Slayton?' Holly said now, trying to sound as casual as possible. Emmy's head snapped up from her mug of coffee. They had both stayed in Holly's rental house in Edgartown the night before, stumbling through the door in the early hours more than a little merry. Neither of them had woken until after eleven a.m., when Holly had made them mugs of coffee and carried them out to the front porch. Emmy was on the swing seat now dressed in one of Holly's T-shirts, the Vineyard summer sun already warming her skin. Her hair was in a crazy mess around her head and there were line marks on her tanned face from the deep slumber she had fallen into.

'I don't. Who said that?' Her voice was sharp and Holly held up a hand.

'Woah, calm down. I don't know why you're being all defensive about it. I bet he'd go out with you in a heartbeat.'

Emmy looked mutinous. 'I don't want to go out with him. Did Tara tell you I did? She doesn't know anything.'

'Okay, no worries.' Holly nodded slowly, then took a sip of her coffee. She didn't want to say anything that might upset Emmy further. She couldn't think for the life of her why her friend was being so secretive about a stupid crush. Wasn't that the sort of thing friends gossiped and laughed about, sharing every painful interaction? It wasn't as though Ryan was out of bounds, or smelled hideous, or had an extra head or something. They weren't teenagers, but Emmy was acting like one. Holly hadn't seen her this way before. 'Is there something you want to tell me?' Holly asked, trying to tread carefully. Perhaps there had been a one-night stand, or something that was making Emmy so defensive.

Emmy bit her lip. 'He's just... they're not like us, Hol,' she said eventually. 'They don't live in the same world as we do, where actions have consequences and...' She sighed. 'I just don't want you to get hurt. Just promise me you'll take it slow and...' She tailed off and Holly frowned.

'I really wish you'd just say what you want to say,' Holly grumbled.

'People don't just say what they want to say about the Slaytons,' Emmy remarked. 'That's kind of the point.'

Holly nodded as though she understood, and maybe she did. Rich boys were heartbreakers, they used girls then got bored and swapped them for shiny new toys. Emmy was just trying to watch out for her.

'Your friends are really nice,' she said after an awkward pause.

Emmy's face relaxed into a smile. 'They are, aren't they? We've all grown up here, so we've known each other our whole lives. We had another friend who went away to live in Boston, and I don't think Minty will be here much longer. She's been working away more and more, and it's clear she wants more than the Vineyard can give her. The rest of us just like the simple life.'

'I like it too,' Holly agreed.

'What are your friends like?' Emmy asked.

Holly sighed. 'My closest school friends are all engaged,' she said, and Emmy screwed up her nose.

'No way? At our age?'

'I know, right? I feel way too young to settle down. Especially after...' Holly stopped short. She hadn't

77

planned on telling anyone about her mum, but then she hadn't expected to meet anyone she liked as much as Emmy, whose face was now a picture of concern. 'My mum passed away,' she finished, a fresh rush of grief meeting the words. 'Nearly eight months ago.'

'Oh Hol, I'm so sorry,' Emmy said, her eyes looking like they might be filling with tears. 'That's awful.'

'It is,' Holly agreed. 'But it also made me realise that I was just coasting through life. Every day was the same, no new adventures, no experiences. So I made a decision that I'd live the rest of my life doing things I could tell Mum about. That by telling her something new and exciting every night before bed, it would be like she was still here, and that her death would have made my life richer, not emptier.'

'That's beautiful,' Emmy smiled. 'So that's why you came here?'

'Yep. Because of Mum. I might never have done this if she hadn't taught me how precious every moment is.'

'She'd be so pleased,' Emmy said. 'To think that you were trying to be happy.'

Holly sniffed. 'I wish my sister felt the same. She thinks I'm selfish to just up and go away so soon. She doesn't understand how I can feel anything but pain, just because she can't. It's like she thinks that being able to smile again or laugh would mean that we're not devastated about Mum anymore, or that we don't care that she's gone.'

'That's crazy,' Emmy said. 'You're grieving your mom by living your life in her memory. That's exactly what she would have wanted. Your sister probably feels bad that she can't bring herself to do the same yet. But no two people react the same to a situation. No one can judge how you behave or react because even people who have been in your situation have never been *you* in your situation. This specific circumstance, with all of the history and nuance you bring to it, has never happened to anyone else, ever.' Emmy let out a breath after this speech and Holly whistled a low whistle.

'Bloody hell, you sound like the Dalai Lama.'

Emmy laughed and Holly grinned, glad her joke had been well-received.

'Shut up,' Emmy said, in a faux-offended tone. 'You know what I mean though, right?'

'I know what you mean, and you're exactly right,' Holly said.

Because she *was* right. Holly just wasn't sure whether Emmy had been talking about her mum's death anymore, or something much closer to home, and she wondered what it was that Emmy had done to be judged for.

Chapter Fourteen

Holly

TWO WEEKS BEFORE

Wednesday night rolled around and Holly found that she was excited and nervous in equal measure. Although Ryan had seemed like a nice, normal guy, it was clear that the Slayton boys didn't inhabit a world that she was used to. No one here did. Martha's Vineyard wasn't just different from Hampshire because it was in America — it was as if it inhabited its own little universe with its own social rules. It felt like a permanent vacation. Perhaps it would feel differently off season, when the nights got shorter and the days started to become defined again. In all the time she had been here, Holly had discovered that weekdays and weekends didn't feel any different — people thought nothing of having a blowout on a Sunday or a Tuesday evening, the same as on a Friday.

She chose islander casual for her attire, trying once again to feel like she fit in. Denim shorts and a ruffle-fronted sleeveless cream blouse, not revealing anything other than her tanned arms and legs. She looked respectable and innocent, she decided, giving herself a once-over in the mirror, and a tan definitely looked good on her. She hoped she would be giving the right signals to Ryan – that she wasn't going to sleep her way through the summer boys on the Vineyard. She expected he would be used to girls throwing themselves at him given his money and family connections, so she guessed he would move on after tonight.

She had expected him to take her to a fancy expensive restaurant, so she was surprised when he pulled up outside her house – actually getting out of the car to ring the doorbell instead of honking his horn to let her know he was outside – with a picnic basket, and asked if he could take her on a picnic on Lighthouse Beach. She smiled and nodded, secretly impressed. The fancy restaurant would have been the simple choice, but a picnic showed a bit more effort.

So she had to laugh when they pulled up to the beach and Ryan led her around the lighthouse to where a table and chairs had been set up, complete with a candle, and fully laid.

'You did not do this,' she said, noticing that fairy lights had been strung up in a square around the table, stakes driven into the ground to suspend them from.

'Ummm, no,' he admitted with a wry smile. 'I had the staff do it. Which makes me sound like a complete asshole, doesn't it? But it was my idea, and I put that lantern up over there... see?'

Holly looked at where he was pointing, at the only giant lantern that had blown out. She laughed. 'It's definitely the thought that counts,' she said, taking the seat that he pulled out for her.

'Oh good,' Ryan said, opening the insulated picnic basket to reveal a stack of takeaway containers. 'I was hoping you'd say that.'

Holly burst out laughing and helped him empty the basket onto the table. Ryan handed her cutlery and they dug into the fake picnic as they watched the sun set over the sea.

Ryan was surprisingly funny, with a dry, self-deprecating sense of humour. He was both aware of and embarrassed by his family's ridiculous wealth, although Holly was glad that he didn't try to pretend that it was a huge drag being rich and well connected. They shared interests, dreams and wishes for the future and after a while Holly allowed herself to forget that they were from different worlds.

When the temperature dropped, Ryan produced a cashmere blanket from the side pocket of the magic basket and wrapped it around her shoulders. They sat together on the sand, looking up at the sky.

'Will you go back to Hampshire after the summer?' he asked her.

Holly shrugged. She dug her hands into the still warm sand beside her. 'I'm not sure anymore. That was the plan, yeah, but now that I'm here...'

'It's not the kind of place you want to leave, is it?' Ryan said.

'It's not, no. But I also just don't feel ready to go back to normality, either. It's like I've only just begun to see things from a different angle.'

'So keep travelling,' Ryan said, as if life was just that simple. And maybe for him it was, although she doubted it. He might have the money just to spend his life travelling, but that kind of family usually had high expectations, especially for the men, which included learning the family business. Ryan had suggested as much, clearly not wanting to seem ungrateful for his privileges but sounding like he would rather not follow in his father's footsteps.

'I might,' Holly said, 'if I can find a way to make some money while I travel. Maybe I could set up a van life blog or become a travel influencer.'

'You could get work that came with a house,' Ryan suggested. 'Like a live-in nanny. I bet I could find you work in New York as a childminder.'

'Are you asking me to emigrate with you already?' Holly teased, raising her eyebrows. Even in the fading light, she could see Ryan's face redden. She laughed. 'Don't worry, I won't be expecting a proposal on our second date.'

'So you'd like a second date?' Ryan asked, his voice so hopeful and nervous that Holly couldn't help finding him adorable.

'Sure,' she said, without needing to think. 'Why not?'

Chapter Fifteen

Claire

By the time I got back to Edgartown, it was midday and I was starving. I know that a lot of people find it hard to eat when they are stressed or worried, but that's not me. I find it pretty easy to eat at any given emotion. So despite how absolutely drained I was from travelling since six yesterday, I dropped my car off at Holly's place, checked she hadn't come back while I'd been at the marina, and then, finding the house still empty, set off on foot to look for food, hoping the fresh air would keep me awake.

The day had blossomed into full July sunshine now and I found myself wishing I'd packed a hat, or maybe some sun cream. As I wandered down Main Street, though, I realised that I'd be able to get everything I needed from Edgartown. The place was bustling with boutiques, smoothie bars, cafes and sunglasses shops. I imagined Holly's delight at the island chic there was on offer – I'd be willing to bet that she'd already spent a good chunk of her money on sunglasses and linen shorts alone. At the thought of this, something else occurred to me. If Holly really was involved with one of these rich Slayton kids... well, didn't that make it more likely that she'd taken off somewhere for a few days? If she'd fallen head over heels, it wouldn't be totally outlandish to think that maybe Ryan

Slayton had convinced her to jack in her job and let him pay for them to take a trip off the island. Maybe she didn't need clothes, just his daddy's credit card. In fact, the more I thought about it, the more likely it seemed that Holly was with some rich Kennedy relative and having the time of her life. I hadn't thought to ring her phone while I was in the house – although if she'd forgotten to take it the battery would be dead now, which is why it would be going straight to answerphone. It was all starting to add up. My sister had emigrated with US royalty. And like some kind of idiot, I'd followed her halfway across the world to check up on her.

I grabbed some supplies; food, drinks, sun cream and an adorably tacky trucker hat that said 'Honk if you want to go faster' and made my way back to Holly's place, the bags cutting into my fingers.

The longer I thought about it, the more convinced I became that Holly really had gone off with this guy, and the police officer had probably known it. He'd probably tried to keep Ryan Slayton's name out of it because that was what happened when you were rich and basically famous. It wouldn't have surprised me if the officer had called Ryan the minute he'd got off the phone to me, and Ryan had promised to see him right if he just told me all was fine. I wonder if Holly knew I was looking for her. It wouldn't make any sense for her not to get in touch – although perhaps she thought that after our last conversation I wouldn't care if she stopped calling me, or answering my calls. I highly doubted she thought that I'd buy a plane ticket and fly out to rescue her. What a bloody idiot I was.

Still, I thought as I let myself into Holly's front door, there were far worse places to spend a few days, and if

Holly could fly away from her responsibilities on a whim and end up in paradise, then why couldn't I? Okay, I'd feel ten times better if I could actually speak to Holly, but I needed to get some rest before I tried to drive anywhere again. My eyes were so heavy, I wondered how I was managing to keep them open. In fact, they started drooping shut as I was putting the shopping away. It felt like there was sand behind my eyelids and all I wanted to do was lay my head down on a soft pillow and close my eyes for a little while.

I locked the front door and took the key up to the spare room. As much as I desperately wanted to sleep in my sister's room, just to feel close to her, it felt too much like a trespass. Which was stupid, of course, Holly and I slept in the same bed all the time, especially since Mum had passed away. There's no way she would have minded. But it just didn't feel right.

The spare room was large and light, sparsely decorated but classy and welcoming all at once. Sheila had good taste, clearly. I took off my jewellery and put it on the bedside table, and without even getting undressed, I climbed into the bed, pulled the quilt up and over my shoulders and fell into an instant sleep.

–

I wasn't sure what it was that woke me, or how I became aware that there was someone in the house. I'd left the curtains slightly ajar in my exhausted state, but no light came in through them now, everywhere was pitch-black. I froze in the darkness, listening intently in the hope that whatever had woken me was a stray cat or the slamming of a car door. Then I heard another sound, a very distinctive

86

creak I'd heard earlier when I'd checked out the back garden.

I picked up my watch from the bedside table and the screen lit up, dazzling my eyes slightly. It was 10.47 p.m. And someone had just come in through the kitchen door.

I don't know how I knew that it wasn't Holly, but I did. There was something about the way the person moved lightly downstairs, as if they were trying not to be heard. If it was Holly and she knew I was here, she'd have bounded up the stairs to wake me up in true Goldilocks style. And if it was Holly and she didn't know I was upstairs – why would she be tiptoeing around?

No, this person was not supposed to be here. Perhaps Holly had taken in a lodger to help her pay the rental, or Sheila employed a midnight cleaner and this was par for the course. Either way, I had to make a decision before they came upstairs. Stay in the spare room and hope the intruder didn't come in, try to get out of the house, or confront the person downstairs.

Now, I could look after myself. I'd never been one to shy away from a fight, and much to my mother's consternation, I'd been known to start the odd one myself. However, I was also not a stupid person (unless you count flying three thousand miles based on a few calls sent to voicemail). For all I knew, this mystery person in my sister's rental property had a huge knife, or a gun, or a snake – because this was America – and I had no intention of facing down a madman with a snake. So, option number three was out of the question. Option number two also felt far more Lara Croft than I gave myself credit for, so the only real choice seemed to be staying put and hoping they didn't come into the spare room while I called the Vineyard police department. I listened for the sound of footsteps and scrolled through my phone to where I'd saved the number I'd called from the UK. Please Lord don't let it be Officer Waylans.

'Vineyard PD, which town do you require?'

'Edgartown, please,' my voice was barely above a whisper but sounded like a roar to my ears. I winced, hoping I hadn't been heard. The ringing of the transfer made me wince.

'Edgartown PD, can I help?'

'There's someone in my house, downstairs,' I whispered. 'An intruder. I can hear them.' I reeled off the address.

'I'm dispatching someone immediately, honey. There's a car not far away. Is there a lock on the door of the room you're in?'

'No. I don't think so, but I'm not sure, it's not my house. I'm down the side of the bed.' It sounded wimpy and I knew it, but the woman didn't seem to think so.

'Great, stay as low and hidden as possible, someone is minutes away. Can you still hear them?'

I took the phone from my ear and listened. I couldn't hear anything, then...

'I hear a car. Is that the police?'

'That'll be them, sweetheart. You stay there until you hear them calling you, okay?'

I heard the kitchen door slam shut and I stood up automatically to look out of the window. I could just make out a figure all in black running up the back path, the light of a torch bouncing along until it was suddenly flicked off.

'They must have heard the police, they've run out the back,' I told the dispatcher. 'Should I go down?'

'Do you know for sure there was only one intruder?'

I shook my head. 'No.'

'Then sit tight, sweetie.'

Moments later, shouts came from the front door. 'Police, you can come down, ma'am.'

'Thank you,' I whispered to the dispatcher. 'Thank you.'

'You're welcome, my love. The officers will look after you now. You're safe here.'

I'd heard that a lot, that the island was so safe, that I was safe here. But I'd lived in some difficult places in my life and I'd never once cowered behind a bed while an intruder stalked around downstairs. And my sister had never gone missing without a trace before. So exactly how safe was paradise? Or was it all just an illusion?

Chapter Sixteen

SIX DAYS BEFORE

The sun was scorching Holly's skin, but she was far too comfortable and too lethargic to reapply her sunscreen. She'd been listening to her favourite podcast as she lay on her scratchy towel on the soft sand, but the most up-to-date episode had come to an end and she couldn't even be bothered to sit up and find something else to listen to. Besides, she liked listening to the gentle roll of the waves and the squeals of children running in and out of the sea, the occasional calls from parents calling out to be careful, or not to go too far. It reminded her of summers at the beach with her mum and her sister, when everything seemed so permanent and unmoveable.

She was just thinking that she really had no choice but to get up and reapply, when a shadow fell over her. She opened her eyes and shielded them from the sun with her hands, ready to admonish the sun-blocker. Bobby Slayton stood over her.

Holly sat up, suddenly aware of the tiny bikini she had stripped down to, and reached for her cover-up, pulling it to her chest.

'I was just going to ask if you wanted some help with your sun cream,' he said, dropping down in the sand next to her and plucking the bottle of lotion from the mouth of her beach bag.

She scowled. 'I've been able to apply my own sun cream for a few years now,' she snapped. 'I'm a big girl.'

Bobby held up his hands. 'Just trying to be helpful. After all, you're practically part of the family now, right? Unless you don't trust yourself around your brother-in-law?'

He grinned, and Holly's heart thumped harder in her chest. She was glad now that she'd probably caught the sun, so that he couldn't see the rush of colour flood to her face. He really was incredibly good-looking. She'd met attractive boys before, but not boys who looked like Bobby. His floppy dark hair and his ice blue eyes made him look like a nineties film star, but it was the grin that really got you. And that look he could give girls, like they were the only ones in the entire world. Such a shame that he bore out the old cliché of the best-looking boys being the least trustworthy.

'Oh piss off,' she said.

Bobby laughed. 'Why is it that even insults sound sexy in an English accent?' he asked.

Before she could give him a witty answer, he flipped open the cap of the lotion and squirted it into his hand. He motioned for her to turn around and she did, allowing him to spread the cream over her shoulders and upper back. His fingers were warm and his skin soft – hands that had never known a minute of manual labour – and he purposely made it feel more like a sensual massage than the practicality of applying cream.

'How are things going with my little brother?' he asked, his voice low and close to her ear. His hands moved to her lower back, the cream cool and his fingers firm.

'Getting tired of screwing him just to teach me a lesson yet?'

Holly clenched her teeth. She'd been on a few dates with Ryan now and none of them had involved sex. She was starting to wonder if he wasn't just dating her because Bobby had manipulated them both into it. Either way, it was nothing to do with Bobby Slayton if they were having sex or not. Let him think they were.

'Do you know what?' Holly pulled away from him and turned around. 'You are just about the most arrogant, narcissistic, egotistical—' She stopped when she realised he was laughing again, and that she had given him the exact reaction he had wanted. 'What is it with you and Ryan?' she asked with a sigh. 'Why do you give him such a hard time?'

Bobby shrugged. 'I don't know. It's always been the same, we just clash. He hates me because he thinks I always get what I want, but he doesn't seem to appreciate the things I've done for *him*.'

'You Slayton boys sure are a therapist's wet dream,' Holly muttered.

Bobby chuckled. 'I suppose we are. Any guesses what my dreams have been about lately?' His eyes locked on hers and she felt her face flood with heat again. Goddam him and the effect he had on her. He smiled, clearly amused.

'Look, it's been a pleasure,' she said, her voice dripping with sarcasm as she moved to get up and away from this man who felt like danger in a way she'd never come across before. When she'd been with guys in the past, she'd always felt like the one in control, but Bobby Slayton made her feel all kinds of ways and none of them included cool, calm or collected.

Bobby got to his feet and held out his hand to help her up. When she was standing, he didn't loosen his grip on her hand, instead pulling her into his chest. Holly let out a gasp, thrown off guard. She took a step back, but he matched it with a step forwards, moving the grip of his strong fingers to her wrist.

'I know you only went out with my brother because I tried to make him look stupid,' he said, his voice low and his head dipping closer to hers. From anywhere else on the beach, it would just look as though they were a couple, about to share a kiss. Only Holly knew she was frozen in fear. 'And he knows it too. It would be kinder just to finish things with him, let him down gently.'

Holly looked up at him and set her jaw, trying not to show how scared he made her. 'And what if I don't want to?' she asked, hoping her voice didn't tremble and give her away. 'What if I actually like him?'

Bobby shook his head slowly. 'You know you're only going to break his heart eventually. It's safer if you stay away from him.'

'Oh, so this,' Holly waved a hand between them, 'this full-on Mills and Boon, panty-ripping, Channing Tatum act you've got going on is all out of *concern* for your brother?'

Bobby let out a low chuckle, his eyes dancing with amusement. 'Panty-ripping?'

'It's a thing,' Holly snapped, her fear edging out and irritation creeping back in. Even a Slayton wouldn't get away with hurting her on a crowded beach – would he?

Bobby laughed again. 'You think we aren't going to end up having sex, firecracker?' he asked. 'Does my brother make you feel like this?'

'You mean fucking irritated?'

93

'I think you know what I mean.' Bobby lifted her hand and placed it over her own chest, where she could feel her heart hammering as if it wanted to break free. 'I mean like this. Like the knowledge that if you walked away you would spend the rest of your life looking for this exact feeling again but never find it.'

Holly prised his hand from her wrist and rubbed it theatrically. Every instinct she had was telling her to get the hell away from Bobby and everyone in his family, including Ryan. And maybe she would, but she would never let Bobby Slayton know that it was because he terrified her and fascinated her in equal measure.

'How I spend the rest of my life is no concern of yours,' she said, reaching down to pick up her bag and towel. 'And you might be the one who always gets what he wants, but your brother is twice the man you are.'

Bobby's smile faltered, but he recovered quickly. Only the smallest flicker betrayed his fury. 'You have no idea who you're dealing with,' he said, his words slow and controlled. 'No idea at all.'

Chapter Seventeen

Claire

'Are you sure there was someone in the house?' Jess sounded horrified, and I didn't blame her. She was expecting to hear the news that I'd arrived to find Holly safe and well, and instead she was hearing that there was no trace of her cousin anywhere and her house had been broken into the first night I was there. I could imagine Tom standing in the background demanding I was put on speakerphone so he could keep up with the conversation.

'Definitely. It seems like too much of a coincidence not to be related to Holly being missing, but the police said it was probably just an opportunist thief.'

'In the safest place, like, ever? Seems a bit of a coincidence that Holly goes missing and now someone is sneaking around her house in the middle of the night... Hey, are you sure it wasn't Holly? Maybe she came back to pick up some stuff?'

'Without turning on any lights? Dressed in all black, swinging a torch around the place? Breaking the kitchen door open?'

'Okay, okay,' Jess said, probably with her hands in the air. 'What did the police say?'

'They were pretty good to be honest, came straight over to take a look, although they obviously thought I was just a hysterical female once they got here. Whoever it was was gone. There were no signs of a break-in, nothing looked out of place. They basically said that it was easy to imagine things when you're in a new place and alone. I told them about Holly. They said they were on emergency duty only as it was the middle of the night, and to head over to the PD today to make a missing person's report.'

'If there's no sign of a break-in, how did they get inside?' Jess asked.

'I don't know, but I know I wasn't imagining things. Someone was inside the house. And in a place like this I find it hard to believe it's a coincidence that it's my sister's place they got into.'

'A place like what?'

'It's beautiful,' I admitted. 'I can see why Holly loves it here so much. If it wasn't for the fact that she was missing, it would be the perfect getaway to deal with all the shit we've been through. I'm starting to think I really should have come with her, for my own sake as much as hers.'

'There's no rush to leave,' Jess reminded me. 'When you find Holly, you should definitely take some time there for yourself. Some rest and relaxation.'

'I will,' I promised. 'As soon as I find her, then I can relax.'

I rang off with the promise to update her the minute I got any news at all, and she promised to do some online searching into Carl. I could tell it was killing her having to wait at home by the phone, not able to be here and do something practical. Jess was definitely a doer.

I showered and dressed quickly and left the house, not for the first time wishing that I could be enjoying the beautiful sun here with my sister. Edgartown was busy today, people milling around the shops, cafes and restaurants. I wandered along, showing everyone I came across the picture of my sister. Plenty of people had recognised her, which didn't surprise me – Holly was slim and pretty, dressed well and had a friendly, open face that made you want to smile and speak to her. Everyone seemed to have something nice to say about her, it was just that none of them had seen her in days.

'You know what?' One of the waitresses at a small café pointed at the photo I was holding out to her. 'She was really good friends with Emmy, one of the waitresses here. And it's funny, because I haven't seen Emmy in a few days either. She's been off sick.'

My heart thudded in my chest. 'How long has she been off?'

I held myself back from grabbing the girl and shaking her. This was the first real piece of information I had about someone who might know something of where Holly was.

'My, um... I think the first day she called in was Sunday.'

'So she was in on Saturday?'

'No, uh uh,' the waitress shook her head. 'Emmy doesn't work Saturdays.'

'Did she say what was wrong with her?'

'I'm not sure, she spoke to Karen, not me. No one really tells me anything. But it must be bad because she's been off for five days now.'

Ever since the bonfire that Holly went to.

'But she's been calling in herself?' I asked.

The girl nodded. 'Yeah, I answered the phone one time, it was definitely Emmy.'

So Emmy wasn't missing. Did that mean Holly wasn't either? Perhaps she was holed up at Emmy's house and they were cutting work together. Perhaps I didn't know my sister as well as I thought, maybe she and Emmy were in a relationship and had been in bed together since the night of the bonfire. God, I hoped so.

'Where does she live?' I asked, my voice sounding a little too desperate. 'Emmy? Where can I find her?'

The waitress looked doubtful. 'I'm not sure I should give you her address, you know, like privacy or data protection or something?'

I nodded my head. 'I completely understand,' I said. 'And usually I would appreciate the position you're in and I'd leave, without any trouble at all. But you see my sister,' I waved the picture of Holly, 'is missing. And Emmy might know where she is. So it's really, really important to me that I speak to her.'

I saw her waver. 'I understand, really, I do.' She sighed. 'You didn't get this from me.' She pulled a pen out of her pocket and wrote something on her order pad. She ripped off the sheet and handed me Emmy's address. 'Please, don't tell her it was from me.'

'I won't,' I promised gratefully. 'Thank you so much.'

She nodded. 'I hope you find Holly. She's really lovely.'

'Thanks.'

I checked my phone and saw that the battery was almost completely run down. Not wanting to get stuck without a phone, I went back to Holly's place to charge it up – everything looked exactly how it had when I'd left, it didn't feel like whoever had been here last night had been back. Maybe they found what they were looking for. I just wished I knew what it was.

–

I'd bought a sandwich while I was out and I picked at bits of it now, sitting at Holly's kitchen counter waiting for my phone to charge so I could drive over to Emmy's house. If she knew where Holly was, I wouldn't even need to go to the police.

There was a hairbrush on the arm of the sofa, a pair of flip-flops kicked off at the back door. I recognised them as ones Holly had bought from Monsoon before she'd left, covered in brightly coloured jewels. It was so strange, being here without her but being surrounded by her things. Not for the first time, I wished I'd found somewhere else to stay, but I reasoned with myself that if anyone turned up looking for Holly, I wanted to be here to talk to them.

So far, a ton of people remembered seeing her, everyone had kind things to say about her, but no one had a clue where she might be now. It all went back to this bonfire. Had something happened at the party? Someone must know something.

I waited until my battery was at fifty per cent and unplugged it, not able to sit around any longer. I put the address the waitress gave me into Google Maps – Emmy lived in Oak Bluffs, back near the marina Holly was working at. I threw my handbag into the car and headed over.

I drove the long stretch of coast, gazing out across the sea. Had the bonfire been on this beach? Had something happened to my sister just feet away from where I was passing?

A battered old blue truck was driving towards me, flashing its lights. The driver honked the horn and I began to panic. Was I doing something wrong? I was on the right side of the road, I wasn't speeding...

It was only a second later when I realised he hadn't been chiding me; he'd been trying to warn me. A shiny red truck pulled out to overtake the blue one, speeding towards me on my side of the road. I got a glimpse of three, maybe four, shirtless, tanned guys in the truck bed whooping and laughing before I wrenched the wheel sideways and my car flew off the road onto long beach grass, spinning and sliding to a halt inches from a tall wooden sign announcing 'Welcome to Oak Bluffs'. My hands were gripping the wheel and my heart pounded, but I looked up in time to see one of the boys tipping a cowboy hat at me – in way of apology? Asshole had probably never been near a ranch in his life.

The sounds of the honking and hollering faded as the truck flew from sight. I put my head down on the wheel and tried to take in several deep breaths. I was fine, the car was fine. If only someone would tell my pounding heart that.

I gave myself a few minutes to calm down and was about to pull off when I saw the truck coming back towards me. Not the shiny red one full of idiots, but the bashed-up blue one whose driver had tried to warn me. I wound down the window and held up a hand.

'You okay?' he asked, his brows furrowed. He was perhaps a bit older than me, dark hair, tanned skin just starting to show the signs of age that made a man more attractive and a woman less marketable.

'I'm fine, thanks. Thanks for trying to warn me. I just thought I was speeding or something.'

His face relaxed into a smile. 'You're English?'

I nodded. 'I just arrived yesterday.'

'Do you want me to check your car over?'

'It's okay, I didn't hit anything, I think it's fine. But thank you.' I felt like an idiot, just thanking him on repeat. Good job us English were known for our manners. 'Do you know who they were? I should let the police know, right?'

The man scoffed. 'You can try, but I wouldn't bother. They get away with murder, idiot summer kids.'

I had a sinking feeling that I knew who the boys were. I tried to picture them standing outside the obscenely big house with the marble pillars, and then thought back to the guy in the cowboy hat. 'Let me guess... they were the Slaytons?'

He grinned and shook his head. 'Well, hell, those rich brats must have quite the reputation if a lady from England knows their names on her second day.'

'You could say that,' I muttered.

'If my advice means a dime, and I'm sure it doesn't...' He smiled and I realised it actually did. It wasn't just that he was cute, and friendly, but he'd driven back to check on me and there weren't many people who would do that these days. 'I'd stay clear of them if you can. Sure, they deserve to be reported to the police, but nothing is ever going to come of it, and it'll just put you on their radar, and you're best off the radar of people like that.'

'Okay, thanks.' Goddammit, why could I not stop saying thanks?

'No problem. If you need your car looking at, I'll be at Ripley's Auto.' He held up a hand and I was suddenly gutted that he hadn't asked me on a date like he would have done if this was a Hallmark movie.

'Thanks again.'

It wasn't until he'd driven off that I really thought about what he'd said about the Slayton boys. *You're best off the radar of people like that.* From what the waitress across from the marina had said, my sister had been with one of those boys just before she disappeared. Which meant she was very much on his radar.

Oh Holly, I thought, any thrill at my meeting with my handsome white knight disappearing fast. *What have you got yourself into?*

Chapter Eighteen

Claire

There didn't seem much point in turning around to report the accident; no one was hurt and I had a feeling that nothing would be done anyway. And anyway, now that I'd found someone who could potentially clear up the mystery of my sister's whereabouts, I was desperate to get to Emmy's house and find out what she knew.

I took a few deep breaths and steadied myself, then put the car into drive. I was only five minutes away from Emmy's house, but I had no idea if Emmy was living with her parents or on her own, or if I was going to be confronted with some irate boyfriend or husband. A showdown was the last thing I wanted, but what I did need was answers, and if I had to face down some asshole boyfriend to get them then that's what I was going to do.

I pulled up at the house, a beautiful light-grey slatted home with white wooden posts and white picket fences, a look I was coming to find was typical on the Vineyard. The houses here looked less grand than the huge ones I'd seen in Edgartown but still postcard perfect. There was a small car on the driveway, but everywhere looked quiet. So quiet that the slamming of my car door sounded like a gunshot against the stillness of the street.

I walked up to the door and pounded on the knocker. After a couple of minutes of no one answering, I knocked again. I stepped back off the porch in time to see the curtains in the room above drop back into place. So there was someone here.

'Hello?' I called up towards the window. 'I need to talk to Emmy. Is she here? Is that you? I'm Holly Matthew's sister. I need to know where she is.'

When there was still no answer, I went back to the car and grabbed a book out of my rucksack. I carried it over to the perfectly manicured grass and sat down, hoping Emmy didn't decide to just turn on the sprinklers. They had to have sprinklers to keep a lawn this beautiful in this heat.

And boy, was it hot. After about ten minutes, I was beginning to wish I'd made my stand on the porch instead of the grass, but I wanted to be seen from that top window. Sweat was rolling down my back and pooling in my butt crack, I was certain I looked a complete hot mess, but that wasn't going to stop me.

After twenty-five minutes and just as I was starting to worry I was going to be there all afternoon and end up with heatstroke, the front door opened. A woman much older than I had been expecting Emmy to be stood in the doorway holding a glass of what looked like iced tea. She descended the steps and crossed the grass.

'I'm Fran, Emmy's mom.' She held out the glass to me and I took it, drinking so greedily that it spilled down my chin and dripped onto my chest, but I didn't care. The ice-cold drink tasted amazing.

'Thank you,' I said when I caught my breath. 'I needed that.'

'Emmy won't come out of her room,' she said, almost apologetically. 'And believe me, I've tried to make her.'

'What do you mean?'

Fran shook her head. 'She's been in there for days. She won't talk to me, she just sits in silence or cries. I have no idea what's gone on. I've threatened to call the police, a doctor, her father.' She must have noticed the quizzical look on my face because she explained. 'Emmy's dad works on a fishing hauler. He's away for weeks on end. I can get a message to him in an emergency, and to be honest I think this might be one. Did you say you can't find Holly?'

'She isn't answering her phone,' I said. 'She hasn't turned up at work and she hasn't phoned in sick. I can't find a single person who might have seen her since Friday.'

'And you've come all the way from England?'

I shrugged. 'What else could I do? The police won't take me seriously, and I didn't have the first clue about who she might be with or where she might be. Then, when I got here, someone told me that she and Emmy are friends and she might be able to shed some light on where Holly is.'

Fran was chewing on her bottom lip. She looked worried, anxious, conflicted even.

'I don't believe that Emmy would know if something bad had happened to Holly and not say anything,' she said, but her voice was quiet and I wondered if she was feeling more hopeful than confident. 'She's really fond of Holly.'

'Have you met her?'

She smiled. 'Yes, she's a really wonderful girl.'

My stomach clenched. Here was another small link to my sister in this unfamiliar place. 'She is,' I whispered, 'and for the first time since arriving here, I thought I might start to cry.

Fran looked crestfallen. 'Come in,' she said, seeming to make a snap decision. 'If Emmy won't come down, then maybe I can at least try to help.'

–

The inside of Fran and Emmy's home was simply decorated, yet still beautiful. The walls and furniture were light greys and whites, but there were splashes of colour around, bright yellow cushions, a multicoloured painting, turquoise and blue breakfast bar stools. It gave the place a fun, creative feel. The cushions were screen printed, there were brightly coloured vinyl shapes on the walls. It almost looked like an artist's studio.

'You have a beautiful home,' I said as Fran gestured for me to take a seat at the breakfast bar.

'Thank you,' she replied. She pointed through the large double doors at the back of the kitchen to where there was a summerhouse. 'That's my studio outside. I'm a designer, I guess.'

'You guess?'

She looked embarrassed. 'I just do some local bits, touristy things to sell to the shops on the island – framed prints, cushions, that kind of thing. It makes me a living and I don't have to re-join the rat race.'

'Re-join?'

She nodded. 'I used to be a stockbroker. Until I came here for a holiday and married a fisherman.' I could almost see the love and pride emanating from her. Despite her humbleness about her design endeavours, I could tell she loved the life she'd built. I wondered if this was what Jess meant by sensing someone's aura. Maybe I'd stop being such a bitch to her about it. And maybe she was right about me needing to find my place in the world. Because I was starting to think it might not be behind a bar in Hampshire.

'Would you like another drink?'

'I'm okay, thanks,' I said, still slightly embarrassed about gulping down the iced tea.

We stared at one another for a moment, the awkward nature of the encounter hitting us both.

'What information do you have about Holly?' Fran asked, seeming to remember why I was here.

I pulled out my phone and notebook. 'I know that there was a bonfire on Friday night,' I said, showing her Holly's Instagram post. 'And I know that she hasn't been seen by anyone since. She hasn't answered her phone or been in touch with anyone and she hasn't been into any of the cafes or restaurants that I've been to. I think something happened to her at that party.'

Fran picked up her own phone and tapped the screen a few times. 'Here. This is Emmy's Instagram. She was uploading photographs that night.'

I took the phone from her outstretched hand. She had pulled up a picture of a beautiful girl, about the same age as Holly. She had thick, honey-coloured hair, long, lean, tanned limbs and a full mouth. I could see straight away that she was a younger, more beautiful version of Fran. I wrote down Emmy's Instagram name and I swiped through her photographs, some of the sea in the dusk, an inky black blot against the skyline, others of the bonfire with shadowy figures in the background.

My stomach lurched when I saw a picture of Holly. She was wearing an oversized red hoody with a tight black skirt underneath. Her blonde hair spilled over her shoulders in waves and her face was beautifully tanned with barely any make-up. She looked amazing, like she had grown up with the surf in her face and the sand on her feet. She was smiling and making a peace sign. Next to her was another girl with messy red hair and a smattering of freckles across her nose. She was wearing a bikini top and a long, flowing black skirt. On the other side of the redheaded girl was a young man dressed in a navy polo T-shirt and navy dress shorts. He looked out of place against the two girls who appeared to be part of the beach itself. He was clearly rich, his haircut and his tan and his clothes all screamed money. He had his hands in his shorts pocket and was turned at an angle, like he was modelling for a photo shoot.

'That's Araminta,' Fran said, and I scribbled down her name. 'Araminta Sandwell. And that's Cody Francis.'

The guy didn't look like he was particularly interested; it looked as though Emmy had just shouted 'say cheese' and everyone in range had posed.

The next few photographs were the same, cheesy poses or people putting their hands up to avoid the camera. I wrote down their names anyway, although my sister wasn't in any more of them. Until the last one. It was a picture of a guy, laughing and holding his hand up towards the camera as though to tell Emmy to get it out of his face. It wasn't him that interested me, though. In the background, the darkness lit up by Emmy's flash, you could see Holly, or at least a blonde girl in a tight black skirt and a blood-red hooded jumper. She looked shocked, as though she had been blindsided, by a girl with a ponytail, who seemed to be yelling at her. There was a man holding onto the girl's arm, as though he was trying to pull her away from Holly.

'What the...?' I murmured, picking up my phone and taking a picture of the post.

'That's Holly, isn't it?' Fran asked. 'Who's she arguing with?'

I knew exactly who it was, but before I could reply, a voice came from the stairs.

'It's Carl and Stacy,' Emmy said, emerging from the stairway. 'She was arguing with Stacy.'

Chapter Nineteen

Holly

THAT NIGHT

The Fourth of July celebrations on Martha's Vineyard were legendary, Holly had been assured. Somehow she had secured the next day off from the marina, and it was going to be a celebration to remember. First came the party at the Slayton mansion that it seemed the whole island was invited to, and then they would move on to the traditional Fourth of July bonfire at Left Fork Beach which would usually last until sunrise.

Emmy had completely taken Holly under her wing and they had been spending all of their free time together. Emmy had even taken Holly to Boston for the weekend to kit her out like a true islander; it had been amazing. Any rift that had threatened to open because of Holly's growing closeness to Ryan had all but been forgotten. Holly secretly thought that Lucy and the others must have exaggerated her feelings towards Ryan because Emmy had called Holly demanding all the details and they had fallen into the easy kind of gossip that Holly was used to. She was glad – as much as she'd been ready to make her excuses to Ryan and cancel their date to ensure her continuing friendship with Emmy, she'd found that he was really sweet, and she'd enjoyed his company. In the two weeks that had followed, Holly had seen him five more times, and each time she had felt her feelings for him growing. Avoiding Bobby hadn't been easy, though, and every time she saw him she was reminded of the day on the beach, feeling torn between lust and fear. But Holly knew that things with Ryan wouldn't be anything more than a summer fling and once he and his family went home to New York and back to whatever girlfriend he almost definitely had waiting there, she wouldn't see either of them again. Perhaps it was that which had made Emmy relax a little: the thought that Holly and Ryan would never be more than a drop in the ocean of one another's lives. Whereas Holly most likely would not be there the following year when Ryan came back – as much as she would love to be – Emmy definitely would.

But for now, tonight's celebrations were the top of everyone's thoughts. Holly was to get ready at Emmy's house and they were heading over to the Slaytons' mansion together.

–

'Is Derek going to be at this party?' Holly asked, wrapping her long blonde hair around Emmy's tongs.

Emmy's face reddened. Derek was a young police officer with the Vineyard Police Department and had recently let Emmy know of his interest in her. Holly got the feeling Emmy was more than a little interested in him too.

'He said he'd see me there,' she replied. 'I'm still feeling weird about the whole thing. We're friends. I've known him since I was a toddler; he was sixteen when I was eight. I've never seen him that way before.'

'Well, he's obviously seen you that way,' Holly grinned. 'And he's only thirty. That's mature, not gross old. He's got a good job...'

'Sounds like he'd have better luck with you,' Emmy smirked. Holly stuck up her middle finger. 'Oh I forgot, you're busy working on the millionaire.'

Holly froze, looking to see if there was any malice in Emmy's face, but she saw only teasing. 'Oh piss off.' She raised her eyebrow. 'I am thinking that tonight might be an interesting night for both of us.'

Holly pulled on her dress and studied herself in the mirror. She had ditched the island chic look for the evening and was wearing a tight, black mini-dress with long sleeves and a plunging sweetheart neckline. Her blonde hair had lightened even more in the sun and Emmy had shown her how to use sea salt spray to bring out the natural waves. She knew she looked good enough to be on Ryan's arm tonight, and she wasn't going to let herself think of what Bobby had said to her, or that when he looked at her he made her feel as though she was the only person on the island. Bobby Slayton was arrogant, and far too used to getting his own way. Well, he wasn't getting it with her.

They were just starting their fourth drink when the doorbell rang.

Emmy's mum called up the stairs, 'Holly! Someone just dropped off a package for you.'

Emmy raised her eyebrows at Holly, who shrugged, laughing. They ran down the stairs and Fran passed Holly the small square box, grinning.

'Come on, we want to see what's inside!'

Holly opened the box and gasped at the beautiful silver necklace that lay on a velvet cushion. Hanging off it was a large ruby pendant. It was stunning. She smiled at how thoughtful Ryan was and what her sister would say about such an obscenely expensive gift. Holly didn't care though – there was nothing wrong with enjoying being treated by someone you were dating.

'Holy shit!' Emmy exclaimed.

'Language,' Fran warned.

Emmy stuck her tongue out.

'Put it on,' Fran urged.

Holly turned around so that Emmy could fasten it behind her neck for her. She turned and looked in the hallway mirror.

'Holy shit,' Emmy breathed, and this time her mum didn't correct her.

–

The driveway leading up to the Slayton house was lined with lanterns floating in huge glass urns. They made the light sparkle and dance across the gravel and lawns, adding a magical feeling to the evening.

Holly glanced at Emmy, who looked completely unfazed. She'd seen all this before, of course, and as someone who lived here all year round was probably annoyed by the lavish displays of wealth the Slaytons were showing. Even more so when they got to the huge colonial-style house and the whole grounds were lit up with twinkling bulbs. Meteor lights were suspended from the trees and strings of white fairy lights swung between ornamental poles. A towering marquee bathed in golden light stood in the middle of the garden, clusters of giant lanterns in each corner. People gathered in groups, expensive-looking women and tennis club men, interspersed with twenty-somethings all wearing their mummy and daddy's money. Holly could make out a few local faces – Lucy was there, and Tara over by the marbled water fountain – but she couldn't see Ryan, or Bobby.

Emmy spotted her friends and grabbed Holly's hand, leading her over to where they stood. Her heels caught slightly in the manicured grass and Holly wondered if the Slaytons paid to have the lawn relaid each year after the annual bash.

She glanced around for the Slayton brothers once more, but they were nowhere to be seen. She tapped out a text to Ryan.

> I heard there's a big party at some rich asshole's house. Are you going to show up?

'Holly, great to see you again,' Lucy greeted her enthusiastically and Holly gave herself to the group. Drinks were brought to them by hired help and Holly accepted with a smile and a 'thank you'.

'Hey, Holly.'

Holly looked around to see Carl, striding across the lawn towards her. She set her face into a rigid smile. 'Hey. I didn't know you were going to be here.'

Carl moved closer than necessary and spent longer than was comfortable looking her up and down. 'You look great,' he said, eventually. Holly didn't let her fixed smile move.

'Thank you,' she said, her voice tight and her mind working overtime to try to think of an excuse to get away. She already had to put up with his creepiness enough at work – did she really have to put up with him leering over her here too? And where was his wife?

As if on cue, Holly saw Stacy looking around the grass in search of her errant husband.

'Oh, I think your wife is looking for you.' Holly tipped her wine glass towards Stacy, who hadn't spotted him yet. Carl didn't even turn to look, he just adjusted himself to block Holly's view of his wife.

'I don't doubt it,' he muttered. 'She's always looking for me. Look, Holly…' He stepped forwards and put a hand on her arm, rubbed it up and down against the fabric of her dress. Holly stiffened.

Jesus, working with Stacy was hard enough as it was, without him sleazing all over Holly in front of her. It was clear how much Stacy hated all of the girls Carl employed, even though it was her husband who was the one she should have been directing her ire towards. Seriously, if Holly had a pound for every time he moved into her personal space she wouldn't need the job at the marina at all. She knew he was the same with the other girls, and she also knew that the uniforms were his choice too – and the fact that the T-shirts all seemed to be a size too small. She was surprised Stacy stayed with him. She was young enough to find someone else, and tonight she looked really pretty. It made Holly want to take a blood oath never to settle for someone who didn't treat her like an absolute princess. Like Ryan had been, actually. She pictured herself spending summers here, in this huge mansion on the beach, maybe eventually with little Hollys and Ryans running around in the surf…

She realised Carl had been talking, but she didn't for the life of her know what he'd been saying.

'I'm sorry, what?' Holly said, just as she noticed Stacy coming close enough to them to hear her husband's words.

'I was just apologising for my wife's jealousy when you're around,' he said. Holly stepped towards her, and Carl, taking it as a step towards him, put his hands on her waist. She smelled the alcohol on his breath – he'd had plenty to drink already by the stench of him. He tried to pull her in towards him. 'It's just because you're so beautiful,' he said. He gripped her waist tightly and leaned in to kiss her.

Holly pitched backwards, out of his grasp, to see Stacy, frozen in shock just a metre away.

'Stacy,' she said, making to walk towards her.

Stacy pointed her empty champagne glass at Holly like a wand. 'Don't,' she hissed, her voice venomous. 'Don't. You. Come. Anywhere. Near. Me.' With each word, she thrust the glass forwards in punctuation.

Carl turned towards his wife, a half-exasperated, half-amused look on his face. Holly guessed that she wasn't the first woman Carl had made a fool of himself over – in fact, she probably wasn't even the first woman Carl had made a fool of himself over *tonight*.

Stacy glowered at the both of them in turn and stormed away as dignified as it was possible for a woman in heels on a grass lawn to do.

Before Carl could speak again, Holly shook her head.

'You had better go and make things right with your wife, Carl, because I want a job to come back to.'

Carl started to make noises about his wife not being the boss of him, and her job being perfectly safe, but Holly moved back over to Emmy and her friends, leaving him standing alone.

'What was all that about?' Emmy asked, looking amused. 'Stacy looked like she was going to skewer you with a champagne glass.'

Holly shuddered. 'Yeah, because her octopus-hands husband doesn't know what's good for him,' she replied. 'I swear to God if she makes things difficult at work because of that letch…'

'Letch?' Emmy laughed. 'I love your weird English words. Come on, I thought I saw Derek arrive a minute ago. I need to walk casually past him as though I haven't seen him.'

Holly grinned, but as she looked over to where Emmy was pointing, she noticed a face in the upstairs window of the house, staring straight at her. It was too far away to make out exactly who it was, but Holly was certain it was either one of the Slayton brothers, and whichever one it was they had seen the whole awful scene between her and Carl.

Chapter Twenty

Claire

Emmy looked awful; I could see why her mum was so worried about her. Her skin was pale and blotchy, not a hint of the healthy tan I'd seen on the photo from the bonfire. Dark semicircles were under her eyes and there was a spot on her chin that looked as though it had been scratched or picked at until it was inflamed and angry. Her beautiful thick hair was scraped off her face and didn't look as though it had been washed for days. Whatever had happened to her, it had had quite an impact.

'Emmy!' Fran jumped up and went to embrace her daughter. 'Can I get you anything to eat? Something to drink?'

'I could have some porridge,' she said, and her voice was raspy, like she hadn't spoken to anyone in a while. Fran shot into the kitchen like she'd been asked to make a life-saving elixir. Emmy gestured to the photograph. 'I didn't see that Carl and Stacy were in that when it was taken. Holly told me about what happened though. That was in the little car park, just off the beach where the bonfire was. Stacy was yelling at Holly because she thought she had been trying to steal Carl.'

'And was she?'

Emmy shook her head emphatically. 'No way. Carl is a creep. Holly wasn't even slightly interested in him. He'd tried it on with her earlier in the night, at the party at the Slaytons' place, but she told him to stop it. That didn't matter to Stacy though. Stacy is paranoid, sure, but she had reason to be with Carl.'

'Holly was at the Slaytons' house?'

Emmy nodded. 'I have so much to tell you.'

I didn't have time to ease her in gently to the conversation, or be delicate about it. 'Do you know where Holly is?' I asked, watching her cringe at my sister's name.

She shook her head. 'No,' she said, her eyes brimming with tears. 'I haven't seen her since that night. Since the bonfire. I don't know what's happened to her. I'm so sorry.'

I instantly felt sick to my stomach. Emmy had been my last chance, and I hadn't realised how much I was counting on Holly being holed up here sleeping off the mother of all hangovers, or just avoiding some one-night stand who wanted marriage and children. Seeing Emmy looking like this, I knew that something awful had happened to my sister.

'What happened?' Fran asked, something I realised I'd been unable to bring myself to say. 'Emmy, what happened at the bonfire? Is this why you've been locked away up there? What happened to Holly?'

Emmy looked between her mum and me, pain etched on her beautiful face. I could see my sister being friends with this girl – from the photos I'd seen, she looked bright and bubbly, fun and friendly. What could have happened that was so bad, and yet no one else on the island seemed to know about it?

'She disappeared,' Emmy whispered, her voice crackling with emotion. 'One minute she was there… then she was gone. We looked everywhere…'

'We?' I asked, trying not to react to what I'd just heard. I had to keep it together, losing it wouldn't help my sister. I needed to just keep my emotions together until I'd got enough information to take to the police.

'Me and Derek,' Emmy said. Her mum went back into the kitchen and reappeared with a steaming bowl of porridge and placed it in front of her daughter, but Emmy made no attempt to pick up the spoon. 'He came to pick us up. He's a police officer. He tried to get the others to believe me when I told them Holly was missing,' Emmy said. She gave her head a small shake. 'But Waylans said it wasn't unusual for tourists to come and go. I tried to say it wasn't like she packed up and moved on – she vanished from the middle of a packed beach party – but he's being a complete bull-headed asshole about it. It's like he didn't want to believe anything bad could happen here. Because we live in paradise. It's one of the safest towns ever, we're like the only place left in America where everyone still leaves their doors unlocked. Waylans isn't about to ruin an entire holiday season by starting a missing person search unless he's a hundred per cent convinced that he has to.'

'So what, he keeps the crime rate down by denying there's been a crime?' If I sounded furious it was because I was. My sister had been missing for a week, seen by no one, not turning up at work and all her possessions left behind, and this asshole was trying to protect his summer season like Mayor Larry fucking Vaughn.

'We have to do something,' Fran said, taking her daughter's hand.

I wanted to shake the stupid girl, ask her why she hadn't contacted me sooner, why she hadn't sat outside the police station until they listened to her, but she looked so forlorn, so wracked with guilt, that I couldn't bring myself to make her feel any worse. I couldn't turn back time by yelling at Emmy, and neither could I change the knowledge that I hadn't realised anything was wrong with my sister because of my own bull-headedness and inability to allow Holly her happiness. It had taken Jess practically putting me on a flight for me to come looking for my baby sister and I prayed with all my heart that I would get a chance to apologise to her in person.

'We are going to do something,' I promised. 'And I need you to tell me everything that happened that night. Starting with this argument with Stacy.'

Chapter Twenty-One

Holly

THAT NIGHT

Holly had been at the party for nearly forty minutes before she felt a tap on her shoulder. Holly turned and Ryan handed her a drink. She raised her eyebrows and pretended to look annoyed, despite how adorable he looked in his light blue polo T-shirt tucked into navy chino shorts. A real country clubber in the making. It was still hard to believe, though, that this house belonged to his family. That he called Robert Kennedy Jr 'Uncle Rob'. It was like stepping into a different world, one that she feared she really couldn't become part of. Especially looking around at the conservative women Ryan's mother called her friends. They were all buttoned up and preened – not a hint of cleavage on display anywhere. She knew that if things ever got serious she would be expected to change really quickly. She'd probably have to start pretending to believe in God and wearing tennis shoes. Holly shuddered. The boys back in England had been few and far between, and at twenty-two she'd been thinking more and more about the type of guy she would end up with. Was she prepared to change who she was for a chance at love?

Love. She felt stupid just thinking it. She'd known this guy a few weeks – barely at all. She hadn't even slept with him yet – although she liked that he'd never put any pressure on her. Even now, he kept a respectful distance – so unlike Carl, or Bobby.

'I was beginning to think you'd ditched your own party just to avoid me,' Holly said, still feigning annoyance. 'I've been here practically all night.'

'You've been here half an hour,' Ryan grinned. 'And I've been in the shower.'

He made no teasing remark about her joining him in there, like she knew his brother would have. They were so different. Ryan was sweet, and he seemed so dependable. Bobby was dangerous... and ridiculously attractive. She knew she could easily sleep with Bobby Slayton – probably mainly because he couldn't stand for his brother to have anything – but that would just be it. A one-night stand, a hook-up. And, as soon as he'd had her, he would move on to someone else, and she would be left feeling cheap and easy. She had to keep reminding herself of that fact: Bobby Slayton only wanted girls he couldn't have. As soon as she stopped being hard to get, she completely lost her appeal to a guy like that. What she needed was a guy like Ryan. Dependable, safe, nice.

'Okay, maybe not all night,' she dropped the act and smiled, taking a swig of the drink he'd handed to her. 'Besides, how can I stay mad at you after such a beautiful gift?' Her hand moved to her neck and touched the ruby necklace.

Ryan frowned. 'Gift?'

Holly's heart dropped. It was clear that Ryan knew nothing about the necklace. 'Oh God, I just assumed... It was probably from my sister,' she explained quickly. There

123

was no way Claire had sent her something so expensive halfway across the world. Anyway, it had been delivered to Emmy's house – it had to have been someone much closer.

Ryan nodded, but Holly could tell he wanted to question further. They both knew who had sent that necklace.

'Your house is beautiful,' Holly said, breaking the awkward silence.

He motioned to the patio doors which stood open, a huge kitchen lit up beyond. It was filled with food that was continuously being carried out by waiters, but Holly hadn't seen anyone cooking. 'Do you want a look around?'

Holly nodded. She'd been waiting for an excuse to go inside since she'd arrived, but the Slaytons had hired portable toilets that were fancier than her own bathroom back home. 'I'd love to. I've only ever seen houses this big on TV.'

Ryan grinned at her wide-eyed awe and led her into the grand kitchen.

Holly hovered her hand over the Aga, but it was stone cold.

'Where is all the food coming from?' she asked, confused.

'From the catering kitchen,' Ryan said, as though this was the most obvious thing on earth.

Of course, who used their actual massive gigantic kitchen when there was a bloody catering kitchen.

She put her empty glass down on top of the cold Aga. Beyond the kitchen door, she could see the hall opened out into a marble-floored entranceway, complete with sweeping spiral staircase. Ryan led her past that door and opened the one after it, that Holly assumed was a cupboard. Instead there was another staircase.

'We never use that front one,' he explained. 'Unless my parents want to make an entrance at some gathering or something. Come on.'

He took her hand and led her up the back staircase and onto a wide upstairs landing. The whole house was decorated in light grey, with black accents in the picture frames and black glass tables. A huge black vase was filled with white sprays of pampas grass and a giant black-and-white chandelier hung from the ceiling. The modern interior wasn't what Holly had been expecting from the grey-slatted traditional exterior, but it was breathtaking.

Ryan led her across the plush grey carpet. 'There are nine bedrooms, but only six of them have bathrooms,' he said, completely unaware of the irony in the word 'only'.

He was about to take Holly's hand to lead her towards one of the rooms when a woman's voice called up from below. Holly had never met Ryan's mother up close, but she was certain that was what she would sound like.

'Damn, I'd better go see what she wants or she'll just come up looking for me,' Ryan cursed. 'Why don't you wait here?'

Holly nodded, glad to be away from the party for a while. Since meeting Emmy, she'd rarely felt out of place on the island, but tonight she had no idea where her place was. She didn't belong with Ryan's crowd, that was certain, and yet she didn't feel like an islander either. She knew the encounter with Carl had shaken her, and she was glad she hadn't seen him since. Stacy had probably dragged him back home and was writing out her dismissal letter right now.

She was leaning over the balustrade when the arms snaked around her, one around her waist and one over her mouth. Before she could even try to scream, she felt herself being turned around, her nose inches from the tanned, smiling face of Bobby Slayton.

Bobby raised a finger to his lips and took his hand away from her mouth. Holly batted him on the shoulder, but her anger dissolved when she got a proper look at him. He was shirtless, with just a pair of denim jeans slung low on his hips. His chest was tanned and firm-looking; he was slim but muscular, and Holly felt her hand almost moving by itself to touch his torso. She caught herself at the last minute and lowered her hand.

'You scared me,' she whispered.

'That's one way to get your heart racing,' he murmured. He hadn't taken any steps back, and he hadn't removed his hand from her waist. He looked down at her dress, then back at her lips. 'God, you look beautiful. Nice necklace.'

Holly felt her face redden. She tried to remember all the reasons she'd told herself she should stay away from Bobby Slayton, but it was so much harder when she could smell the mint of his breath and the smoke and spice of his cologne. 'You know I'm dating Ryan,' she said, her voice low.

'And it's driving me mad with jealousy,' Bobby replied, moving his face even closer to hers. Their lips were almost touching now; from any angle a bystander looked, it would appear that they were kissing. Just one small head movement...

'Is that why you sent me the necklace?'

'I was just thinking about you and had to send you something beautiful. I think about you constantly,' he murmured, his breath warm against her lips. 'I hate that he can just hold your hand, kiss you, *touch you*, whenever he wants to.'

Holly's heart was beating so fast in her chest that she was certain he would be able to hear it. She wanted to say something cutting and feminist, something about no man being able to touch her whenever they wanted to. She wanted to play hard to get, but the truth was that as nice as it was to be with someone respectful and kind like Ryan, his sweet gentlemanly act didn't make her feel wanted. And here was Bobby telling her that she was all he could think about, that the thought of her drove him crazy. It was like a drug, like an aphrodisiac. She wanted to believe every word he was saying to her.

Their faces didn't move any closer, as if both of them knew that one kiss and it was all over, and the restraint they might have had would be gone. Instead, Holly lifted her hand and placed her fingers against the smooth bare skin of his chest, trailing a fingernail down to the faint outline of his stomach muscles. He let out a small groan that almost undid her. Bobby moved his hand slowly from her waist, sliding it up her back, his hand resting eventually on the back of her neck. His other hand slid up her side, lightly grazing the side of her breast. He gulped, then, when she didn't stop him, ran his thumb over the swell of her breast until it found her nipple. It hardened instantly at his touch, and Holly gave a small gasp, her back arching slightly against the balustrade. Bobby gently turned her around again, nuzzling his lips into her neck through her mane of blonde hair. He slid his hand down now, lifting the hem of her dress at the back, and running his fingers up in-between her legs, so close to where she wanted them to be. Holly knew she should tell him to stop, that this was as wrong as a kiss – worse, of course – but it was like a spell had been cast over them both, and to speak would ruin everything.

'Yeah, fine Mom, I'll tell him now.'

Ryan's voice snapped her back to the present, and Holly's eyes flew open. She could see Ryan below her in the reception area now, and at the sound of his voice the weight behind her disappeared as fast as it had snuck up on her. Holly almost could have believed that she had imagined it all, if her legs hadn't still been shaking.

Ryan appeared at the top of the staircase and smiled at her. She hoped he didn't get too close, that he wouldn't smell his brother on her skin. But, of course, he wouldn't get too close – not without written permission.

'Sorry,' he said, and his voice sounded too loud into the silence, after the murmured words of his brother close to her ear. 'Mom wants Bobby to come down. This is her chance to show her family off and he's not playing ball.' Ryan handed her a glass of wine, then crossed the hall to one of the doors and banged against it with a closed fist. 'Bob,' he called. 'Bobby, get out here now.'

Holly waited, her heart still hammering, as Bobby opened the door to his room. He was wearing a black shirt with his jeans now, half of the buttons undone. His hair was glistening as if he'd just jumped out of the shower, and he looked at Ryan without the least bit of concern. She took a sip of her drink.

'What's the problem?' he asked, looking from Ryan to Holly. 'Wow, Holly, you look beautiful.'

Holly's cheeks burned and Ryan just looked irritated.

'Mom wants to know when you're going to grace us with your presence.'

'Well, if I'd known this kind of beauty was out there waiting, I'd have been ready long ago.'

Ryan scowled.

Holly found her voice. 'Give it a rest, Bobby,' she said, raising her eyebrows at him. 'Any more cheese and I'll end up lactose intolerant.'

Ryan laughed and it was Bobby's turn to glare at his younger brother.

He held up his hands. 'Whatever you say, sweetheart,' he retorted. 'I'll watch out for you later.'

Seeing the look on Ryan's face, Holly slid her hand into his and tugged him towards the stairs. 'Ignore him,' she said, trying not to glance back at Bobby. 'He only does it because he knows it winds you up so much.'

Ryan shook his head as they made their way down the staircase. 'Just avoid him at all costs,' Ryan warned. 'Nothing good will come of you being around my brother.'

Chapter Twenty-Two

Claire

'Every year after the Slaytons' party, there's a bonfire at South Beach,' Emmy continued. She'd told me all about what had happened with Stacy and Carl at the Slaytons' house, and how Holly had gone for a tour of the house with Ryan. 'Although we call it Left Fork. I couldn't find Holly, so I texted her saying I'd meet her there. I don't know how, but she ended up getting a lift with Carl. It wasn't exactly far, but it's not well lit and Holly had heels on. I don't think either of them knew that Stacy was going to be at the bonfire – she was supposed to have gone home, but when she saw Holly and Carl arrive together, she hit the roof.'

'What did she do?' I asked.

'She was just screaming,' Holly said. Total nutjob. I guess looking at that photo, Carl must have pulled her away and that's when Holly found me.'

'Do you think Stacy could have come back again? Is she capable of hurting Holly?'

Emmy looked at her mum and then back at me.

'I don't know,' she said, her voice quiet. 'I don't want to say anyone I know is capable of hurting someone, not really hurting them, but… how do we know?'

'Fair,' I admitted. My mind was working overtime on what Emmy had said. A fight between Stacy and Holly... Stacy accusing my sister of trying to steal her husband... neither Carl nor Stacy reporting my sister missing when she didn't turn up for work. Did it mean anything, or was it just a coincidence? 'What happened after that?'

'We partied,' Emmy said. 'We had a drink, and a dance, then Derek came to pick me up.'

'And where was Holly?'

'She wasn't ready to leave. She told me to go and she'd get a lift back with someone.'

'What, and you just left her there alone?'

Emmy bit on her lip, but Fran interjected before her daughter could say anything.

'With all due respect, Claire,' she said. 'Holly travelled to the island on her own. If she wants to stay at a party, what's Emmy supposed to do, drag her away kicking and screaming? Martha's Vineyard is a safe place. Holly was there with the boy she had been seeing. Emmy thought she was fine.'

'I wish I hadn't left her now,' Emmy whispered. 'Of course I do.'

'Your mum is right,' I said, shame washing over me. Emmy clearly felt awful about Holly being missing, she looked an absolute mess, and she'd tried to get the police to listen to her. She didn't need me making her feel worse. 'So she was with Ryan when you left her?'

'Not exactly,' Emmy said.

I frowned.

'Well, Ryan was grabbing them both a drink, which was when I said I was going to meet Derek. She said she wanted to stay a bit longer and she'd see me the next day. She was alone when I left her. Completely alone.'

Chapter Twenty-Three

Holly

THAT NIGHT

They found Emmy again in the garden, just heading towards the driveway.

'Holly, there you are! Where have you... Oooooh.' She looked between Holly and Ryan and nodded. 'Never mind. Are you okay?'

Holly had no idea why her friend was looking at her so strangely, but then she clocked the vodka bottle in her hand.

'Emmy! Did you take that from the house?'

Emmy's eyes widened and she looked at Ryan. 'Ummmm...'

Ryan laughed. 'You think my parents care about a bottle of vodka, Em? I'll bring a few crates of beer and some more spirits to the bonfire. Is that where you're going now?'

Emmy nodded and gestured to where the other girls and a group of guys were waiting at the end of the Slaytons' drive. 'Yeah, you can't beat watching the legendary Slayton fireworks from the beach. You coming, Hol?'

Holly looked at Ryan, who gestured for her to go ahead.

'I've got to stay here a bit longer,' he said. 'Mom'll go nuts if I leave now. But you go ahead and I'll meet you there.'

'Great,' Holly leaned over to kiss his cheek, and caught a scowl cross Emmy's face. This was driving her crazy now. What was her friend's problem? She hadn't planned to confront Emmy about her issue with Ryan – after all, he'd be gone in a few weeks and Holly still had no idea where she was going to go after the summer had ended. Back to the UK? Try to stay on the island? Or move on and experience somewhere else? The not knowing didn't panic her, far from it – it excited her. Thanks to her mother's will, she had enough money to survive if she couldn't pick up another job straight away. Accommodation was trickier, but she'd been thinking about investing some of her inheritance in a little van, travel for a while sleeping in the van and then sell it before she left the country. She felt like the world was literally at her feet. And if Ryan asked her to go to New York with him, well, why not?

Bobby, that was why not. Holly knew she was playing with fire with the Slayton brothers, falling for the sweet one while being unable to resist the temptation of his more dangerous brother. She'd caught a glimpse of Bobby joining the party and her heart had begun to pump faster, her face flooding with colour at the memory of the way he had touched her, the heat of his breath against her lips... No, staying involved with these boys was a bad idea indeed. She would wait for them go home after the summer, then she would make her next move. She couldn't think clearly while romance was clouding her judgement. Not to mention the thought that sooner or later she was going to have to confront Emmy over her feelings about Ryan.

'Wait,' Ryan said as she turned to leave. 'Emmy, can you wait a sec?'

Emmy huffed impatiently. 'I'll go down to the truck and get them to hold on for two minutes. Two minutes,' she warned, holding up three fingers, then noticing and giggling.

Holly laughed. The buzz of the alcohol made everything seem hilarious.

Emmy headed in the direction of the road where a big blue truck was waiting. She wasn't stumbling exactly, but she wasn't steady either.

Holly turned to Ryan. 'What is it?'

'It drops cold out on the beach later on,' he said, looking at her dress. 'I'm going to grab you a sweater. Wait here.'

Holly grinned, unable to keep the smile off her face. Until Ryan disappeared and she saw a familiar figure walking towards her. She smoothed down the front of her dress and tried to put an indifferent look on her face. She knew she had failed when Bobby said, 'No need to look so scared, beautiful. I'm not going to try to seduce you here, in front of everyone.'

Holly bristled. He was so arrogant! Okay, he was attractive, and used to getting his own way, but she hated that he thought that he would be able to seduce her anywhere he liked if he so chose. The insinuation was that the only reason they weren't getting it on in the middle of the lawn was because he was choosing not to seduce her. What she hated more was the fact that he was probably right. 'Why not?' she asked. 'That's what you want, isn't it?

134

To be caught with the girl your brother has been seeing? You think I'm stupid, Bobby? You think I don't know that the only reason you're doing this is to get one over on Ryan?'

Bobby smiled then, and any hope she'd had that he would deny what she was saying evaporated. 'Okay, I'll admit that my brother and I have always wanted what the other one had,' Bobby shrugged, holding up his hands. 'But I have spent every day since I saw you kicking myself that my brother saw you first. It's not just about him this time… I promise.'

Holly tried to fight the rush of intense longing that rose inside her. How could her stupid emotions betray her so easily, when her brain knew exactly what she should be doing, exactly what she should be saying? This was all going to end badly, that much she knew. It was like there was an undercurrent of fear in every interaction she had with Bobby, the fear that she was getting herself involved in something that shouldn't involve her. That with every interaction the trajectory of her life shifted ever so slightly off the path such that by the end of the summer, the course of her life might be irreversibly and permanently altered.

'It doesn't matter what you say,' Holly told him. 'You and I are not a thing. There is no you and I. I like Ryan, and he doesn't deserve you doing this to him.'

Bobby laughed, a deep throaty laugh. 'You think you know my brother? You don't know a single thing about him. He is not the Prince Charming he pretends to be when he's with you. It's all an act, and you are falling for it. At least I don't pretend to be something I ain't.'

Holly faltered. She knew she shouldn't believe anything that came out of Bobby Slayton's mouth. Every word, every action, was carefully planned to illicit his desired outcome. And she wasn't falling for it.

'Piss off, Bobby,' she said.

Bobby laughed again. 'I love it when you talk dirty in that sexy English accent,' he said.

Holly stuck up her middle finger, relieved to see Ryan striding back across the lawn.

'Jesus, Bobby,' he said, handing Holly a hooded sweater. 'I leave her side for five minutes and you're here trying to weasel your way in.'

Bobby held his hands up once again. 'I was just keeping her warm for you, little brother.'

'Fuck you, Bobby,' Holly snapped. 'Thank you, for the jumper.' Her phone buzzed and she looked down at it. 'Shit! Emmy. She says they wouldn't wait any longer.' She looked over to where the truck had been parked. She'd been so distracted by Bobby that she hadn't seen it leave.

'I'll take you,' Ryan said instantly.

Holly frowned. 'I thought you said you couldn't leave?'

'Shit,' he cursed. 'I promised I'd do the fireworks. Bobby, could you—'

'Sure,' Bobby said. 'I'll get my keys.'

Ryan scowled. 'I was going to say could you help Dad with the fireworks so I can take Holly?'

'It's fine, I'll wait,' Holly said, unable to keep the disappointment from her voice. 'I'll watch the fireworks from here.'

'You don't trust me with your girlfriend, Ryan?' There was a hint of a challenge in Bobby's voice, something dark that Holly didn't entirely understand. Or maybe it was just the drink.

Ryan glared at him for a second before looking at Holly. 'Are you okay to get a lift with Bobby? I'll be there straight after the fireworks.'

Bobby raised his eyebrows at her, and she knew that she didn't trust herself to be alone in a car with Bobby Slayton in the slightest. She looked across the grass at the rest of the party, scanning the crowd for someone she might stay with while Ryan went off with his dad. She cringed as she realised there was only one person left who she knew.

'I'll get Carl to take me,' Holly said, trying not to laugh at the surprise on Bobby's face. Ryan went to object, but she silenced him with a long, lingering kiss. When she stepped back, his face was flushed and he looked at her with eyes dark with lust. 'I'll see you at the beach later, okay? Don't be too long.'

She walked away without looking at Bobby, but she enjoyed imagining the look of disbelief on his face. Bobby Slayton was about to learn that she wasn't the easy catch he had her down as.

Chapter Twenty-Four

Claire

Emmy had been exhausted when I left. Holly's disappearance had clearly had a huge effect on her, and for the first time since I'd arrived, I started to really dread what might have happened to my sister. I couldn't put off going to the police station any longer, even though I felt as though it was going to be a waste of time.

Edgartown Police Station looked, from the outside, like a pretty little house with a white picket fence. Like whoever had made the island had neglected to realise they might need a police department and they'd had to commandeer one of the homes for use. I half expected to see a sofa, rug and a log fire when I walked in. Instead, the inside looked sleek and professional – and freshly painted white.

The woman behind the counter smiled and looked up as I approached. She had hair that could only be described as… large, backcombed curls sprayed into place like the fire risks of the eighties. She was wearing light pink glasses that matched her lipstick. Her smile was all teeth but inviting and friendly, not predator versus prey.

'Hi, I spoke to someone on the phone on Tuesday about my sister, Holly Matthews,' I said. 'She's been missing a week now.'

The woman frowned, looked immediately concerned and I felt a rush of relief. 'You've already reported this?' She screwed her mouth into a tight line. 'Then why don't I know about a missing woman? Let me look. Sorry, what did you say her name was?'

'Holly Matthews,' I repeated, and watched her tap on her computer. The frown didn't leave her face.

'She's not listed as a missing person,' she said, looking up at me. 'Did the officer you spoke to file a report?'

'I doubt it,' I said, my worst fears concerned. He hadn't taken my call seriously at all.

'Well, did you get his name? Oh wait,' she bit her lip. 'I've got a welfare check here, done by Officer Waylans. It says that there was no sign of a break-in at the house and no signs of distress.'

'I'm staying at her place,' I said, 'and someone broke in last night. No one can tell me where Holly is. She quit her job out of the blue and—'

'Oh sweetie, you're going way too fast for me. Let me get you a coffee and I can get this all down properly.'

She disappeared into the back and I leaned against the counter, letting out a huge sigh. Finally, someone was taking me seriously. My hopes, though, were short-lived. When the woman came back out clutching a mug of steaming coffee, she was followed by a short, stocky man in police uniform and his face looked less than open and friendly.

'This is Officer Waylans,' she said quickly. 'He is the officer you spoke to on the phone.'

She looked almost apologetic. He wasn't going to take my sister's disappearance seriously, he'd made that much clear.

'Thanks Brenda,' he said pointedly, dismissing her back to her desk. 'You've come a long way.' He raised his eyebrows at me.

'My sister is missing and the police weren't taking me seriously – what did you expect?'

He glanced at Brenda, who pretended not to be listening, then scowled back at me making me regret my flippant remark. I needed him to help me: being my usual asshole self wasn't going to encourage that but this guy's flippant attitude was pushing my bitch button.

'Why don't you bring your coffee into an interview room and I'll take a statement,' he said. Then louder, for Brenda's benefit I thought, he added, 'Officially.'

'Thank you,' I said, more to Brenda than to Waylans.

She smiled and nodded encouragingly.

Waylans led me into one of the interview rooms, which was nothing like the bare, cell-like interview rooms you see on television. There was actually framed art on the wall. I was tempted to commit a crime to get locked up here, I was willing to bet the cells were like luxury hotels. Waylans gestured to a chair and I sat down.

'So, your sister is still ignoring your phone calls?'

'It's a bit more than that.' I tried to keep the impatience out of my voice. 'She isn't at home, no one has seen her since last Friday. She hasn't been to work, to her usual cafes…'

He leaned back in his chair. 'We're a tourist island. People wash in and out. She probably met a boy and is holed up in his place in the throes of passion. You know what these young girls are like.'

I took a sip of my coffee, trying me best to ensure my response was measured and calm. By now, they were practically my middle names. 'I don't know how many twenty-two-year-old women you know, officer, but my sister is not the type of person to spend a week in bed with some guy she just met.' I refrained from saying that that would be much more my style since my mum had died. But Holly absolutely never made stupid decisions like that. Even if she'd fallen head over heels in love, she would have at the very least called in sick at work, and she definitely would have answered Jess's calls. 'She's missing. What do I have to do to convince you? Are people just allowed to disappear around here and you don't do anything about it?'

'People don't disappear here, it isn't that kind of place. We can't be expected to keep track of every traveller who comes on and off the island. We're a police service, not a babysitting service. Perhaps if you had proof of a crime...'

'Someone broke into her house last night.'

'Which we are investigating.'

'She left behind all her stuff!'

'She left behind *some* of her stuff. Her handbag, purse, phone, all gone. Maybe she left in a hurry, maybe she just didn't want to take them. She had everything she needed to leave town.'

'Except her car.'

'You don't need a car to get off this island, Ms Matthews.'

I made a mental note to call the island's taxi companies, find out if anyone had taken my sister to the ferry port the morning after the bonfire. Come to think of it – did either the ferry terminal or the airport have CCTV? I mentioned both to Officer Waylans, who sighed and wrote some notes on a scrap of paper. What could he possibly have to do that meant he didn't have time to look for my sister? We weren't in New York for crying out loud. He made a show of filling in some details about my sister on the missing person's report, but I absolutely knew it was going nowhere. He didn't believe she was missing and he wasn't going to make any effort to find her. If I wanted my sister found, I was going to have to do it myself.

–

'Wait, stop!' a voice called after me as I was leaving the station.

I spun around to see a police officer following me out of the building, not Waylans, a guy I'd never seen before. He was tall and slim with floppy blond hair – he looked like he should be wearing board shorts and clutching a surfboard rather than wearing a cop uniform.

I stopped and waited for him to catch up with me; he seemed to take about five strides to cross the car park.

'Hey, I'm Officer Howes,' he said. 'I know Holly. Emmy Hindle has been trying to report her missing for days, but that jackass in there threatened my job if I start shouting about missing travellers at the height of summer season.'

'He's an idiot if he thinks she's run off with some cabana boy,' I said.

'Yeah, well, he's got his reasons.'

'What reasons?' My face must have looked mutinous because he stepped back and held his hands up.

'None good enough not to look for your sister. I came out because I want to help you.'

'Sorry,' I said. Not really sorry at all. If I was feeling stabby, it was because his fellow officer had treated me like a stupid little girl. I had every right to be shirty. 'Thank you.'

'Here's my number,' he said, holding out a small rectangular card. 'Call me if you find anything or if you need anything.'

'Okay,' I said, suspicion creeping into my voice. Please tell me this guy wasn't using my sister's disappearance to hit on me. That might just be the last straw.

'I'm not hitting on you,' he said immediately, as if he could read my mind.

'I didn't think you were,' I lied. He smiled. 'Oh, by the way,' I added, 'some assholes ran me off the road doing a highly illegal overtake about an hour and a half ago. Shiny red truck. No shirts. Small dicks.'

He smiled even bigger at this, then frowned. 'Yeah, I know who you mean. Do you know who they are?'

'Apparently everyone here knows who they are,' I said. 'Major island celebrities. I'm guessing they could have killed me and Daddy would pay for the charges to disappear.'

'Probably,' Officer Howes admitted. 'Not by my choice, but yeah, I reckon those boys could get away with murder.'

As I climbed back into my car, I couldn't shake the feeling that Officer Howes had seen the Slayton boys get away with their fair share of trouble in the past. What that had to do with Holly, I was yet to discover.

Chapter Twenty-Five

Holly

THAT NIGHT

Carl had readily agreed to drive Holly to the beach, and it wasn't until she was in his car that she considered that she might have made a big mistake. Despite the air still being warm, she pulled Ryan's hoodie on, covering as much exposed skin as possible, and tugged the hem of her dress down as far as it would go.

'Isn't Stacy coming?' she asked, looking around for his wife.

Carl screwed up his face. 'She got a taxi back after she saw us talking,' he said. He looked completely unabashed, as if he hadn't tried to throw himself at her in front of his wife. That was fine by Holly – if he was going to pretend it had never happened, she was happy to do that too. They were still going to have to work together, after all. 'She gets weird about the girls at work sometimes. It's because I was married when we met, I think… She used to work for me.'

The information did not surprise Holly whatsoever. She wanted to tell Carl that he was treating his wife like shit, and if he wasn't careful, he was going to lose her altogether, but now didn't seem the time to poke the bear.

He'd sobered up enough since their encounter to drive her to the beach, but she wasn't about to piss him off.

She imagined what her sister would say if she saw Holly getting into a car with a guy who had been drinking and had hit on her already once that night and she shuddered. What was wrong with her? Ever since she'd arrived on Martha's Vineyard she'd been acting like some kind of stupid teenager, getting into ridiculous love triangles and putting herself in dangerous situations. She would never have acted this way in England... she would never have acted this way before her mum died.

Is that what this was? Her way of hitting some sort of self-destruct button? She had been so smug about the way she had dealt with her mum's passing, following her dreams in the name of her mum's memory. But was this her dream? Feeling slightly nauseous in the passenger seat of her lecherous boss's car, hoping he kept his hands to himself and managed to stay on the road?

You have got to rethink your decision-making process, she told herself. *Stop seeing Ryan, stop fooling around with Bobby, and never, ever get into a car alone with Carl again.*

The coastline was a solid black expanse by now, only distinguishable from the night sky by the reflection of the moon on the surface.

Carl pulled up in a small car park and turned to her. 'Look, after what happened earlier, I know I don't have any right to say anything to you about who you date, and I know I'm just your boss and we're not friends or anything, but I just think you should know—'

But before he could tell her what she should know, there was a thump on the window at the side of Holly's head. She swung around to see Stacy hammering on the glass.

'How fucking dare you!' she was shouting. 'Get the fuck out of my husband's car!'

Holly shoved the door open, causing Stacy to stumble backwards. She caught herself and launched back towards Holly, screaming in her face, words like 'whore' and 'hussy'. Holly started trying to defend herself, but it was useless, Stacy was hearing none of it.

Carl was out of the car now, and he grabbed his wife's arm, practically dragging her away from Holly. She didn't wait to see what Carl said to Stacy, or what happened next; Holly kicked off her heels and strode in the direction of the huge fire she could see on the beach as fast as she could in the darkness and on the pebbled surface. When her feet hit sand, she relaxed a little, seeing that neither Stacy nor Carl were following her.

Looking around, she was relieved to spot Emmy standing a little way away from the fire, taking photos of anyone who stood still long enough.

Emmy threw her arms up at the sight of her, spilling the wine she was drinking. 'There you are!' she shouted over the crackling of the fire and the music, not even noticing the wine dripping down her arm. 'I'm soooo sorry that dickhead wouldn't wait. I tried to get out of the truck to wait for you myself, but he just took off like a fucking kidnapping. How did you get here, did Ryan bring you?'

'No, Carl,' Holly said, and even in the light of the fire, she saw Emmy's eyebrows raise.

'Holy shit, don't tell Stacy,' Emmy warned. 'She was here just five minutes ago raving about you – you are not her favourite person. I would be looking for another job if I were you.'

'Stacy saw us pull up,' Holly admitted. 'She went batshit crazy.'

Emmy gasped. 'Jesus, you're lucky you don't have a black eye. You know I heard…' she looked around as though expecting Stacy to jump out at them any second. 'I heard that once she shoved some girl's head into the side of one of the boats for flirting with Carl. Nearly fractured her skull.'

Holly laughed. 'Liar!'

Emmy grinned and shrugged. 'Yeah, probably bullshit. But I wouldn't put it past her. She has that murderous psychopath look about her, don't you think?'

Holly's smile faltered a little as she pictured the crazed look in Stacy's eyes as she launched herself at the window. She wasn't sure she would put anything past a woman that desperate. Anything at all.

'So did you enjoy your tour of the Slaytons' mansion?' Emmy asked, a little too casually.

Holly raised her eyebrows. 'It's a beautiful house.'

Emmy nodded and Holly gave her a playful smack on the arm.

'Just spit it out, Emmy. Come on, what are you dying to say?'

'What?' She held up her hands in mock innocence. 'Okay, fine, let's find somewhere to sit.'

They grabbed a rug from the pile near the bonfire and laid it out on the sand. Emmy sat herself down and patted for Holly to join her.

Emmy took a deep breath. 'Look, I've gone back and forth about whether to talk to you about this,' she said. 'It's about Ryan.'

Holly sighed. 'You told me you weren't interested in him,' she said, her voice weary. 'I don't get it, we're not stupid teenagers. If you wanted to go out with him, why wouldn't you just ask him? Or have you tried it on with him and he's knocked you back? I can't personally see why any guy wouldn't jump at the chance to go out with you, but then I've only known you a few weeks, and clearly you're a bit of a nutcase.' She smiled to show she was teasing.

'I'm not a nutcase and I don't have a stupid crush on Ryan Slayton,' Emmy scowled. She glanced at the party-goers lit up in the glow of the flames and, satisfied that none of them were looking their way, she carried on. 'It's you I like.'

Holly frowned in confusion, then her eyes widened in shock. 'Oh... oh, God, Emmy, I'm so sorry, but I'm straight. I thought you knew that?'

Emmy let out a delighted laugh and Holly was even more confused than before. 'I don't fancy you, you fucking idiot.' She shook her head as though she couldn't believe how dense Holly was being. 'But I do like you. A lot, as a friend. I never wanted you to go out with Ryan because... because of Natalie.'

'Who's Natalie?' Holly asked. She felt more confused than ever, although she couldn't be sure that wasn't the alcohol. She'd never even heard of a Natalie. Was that Ryan's girlfriend back home? If so, why hadn't Emmy told her sooner?

'Sit down,' Emmy motioned to the rug but Holly shook her head. The alcohol in her system made her head hurt when she moved it too fast, and the adrenaline now coursing through her veins didn't help.

'No. Tell me what the hell is going on, Emmy. Who is Natalie? If Ryan has a girlfriend back home I want to know now. I don't need to be swept up in his shallow promises and look like a fool.'

'Natalie isn't his girlfriend,' Emmy said. 'It's worse than that. Natalie died, here, on the island, five years ago. And I'm pretty sure Ryan had something to do with it.'

Chapter Twenty-Six

Claire

I was still fast asleep at ten a.m. on Saturday morning when Tom's number flashed up on my phone. Ever since I'd started working at the bar, my sleep patterns had been screwed up, and the travelling and the previous night's break-in drama obviously hadn't helped.

'Tom, what's up?' I asked, panic hitting me. 'Is Jess okay?'

'Jess is fine,' Tom replied, and I realised how nice it was to hear his voice. A small slice of normality in all of this madness. 'She said to say hi and to tell you that she would call you after work. I'm just ringing because we were just randomly searching stuff about Martha's Vineyard and we came across this article and we weren't sure if it was relevant or not. Jess said not, but I thought maybe, and so Jess said—'

'Tom,' I interrupted. 'I love you, but I could fly home and print the article off myself in the time it takes you to tell a story. Try bullet points.'

'Oh.' I could imagine the adorable kicked-puppy look on his face and I rolled my eyes. 'Yeah, sure, bullet points. Okay. Fifteen-year-old girl missing on the island five years ago. Was found in the marina. The police ruled it a suicide, but eventually the ruling was changed to an accidental drowning after a petition from the girl's sister. It doesn't say why they decided to change it though.'

I processed the information as quickly as I could. A girl accidentally drowned in the marina five years ago. 'Doesn't really sound relevant,' I said.

'No, we didn't think so. Neither did the media. Until we got to one blog post, and a Reddit thread. The sister, it seems, didn't just disagree with it being suicide; she was convinced that her sister was murdered, but the police refused to reopen the case. Tons of people agree with her. Some guys were with her that night, rich "do you know who I am" types.'

My breath caught in my throat. A possible murder and police refusing to look into it – now that sounded a lot more relevant to me given how quickly Waylans had been to dismiss the idea of my sister even being missing.

'Can you send it to me?' I asked, flicking my phone onto loudspeaker and waiting for the notification.

'No problem…'

Seconds later, the link dropped into my WhatsApp messages. When I clicked on it, a blog post started to load, complete with pictures of the dead girl, and the dead girl's sister. The one who refused to believe her sister's death was an accident. The woman who had been watching me in the cafe on Thursday.

'I'll have a read of these, thanks, Tom,' I said, glad of another path to follow. And one that involved me not having to accost people on the streets.

'No worries,' he replied. 'Anything else you need, Claire?'

'No, you've been efficient, as always. Must be all the red meat,' I said.

Tom hissed down the phone, 'Keep your bloody voice down.'

I managed a chuckle. 'Thank you for everything. And for looking after Jess. I'll keep you posted.'

'Make sure you do. We're just looking forward to some good news here.'

'Yeah, me too,' I said, hanging up the phone.

I made myself a cup of coffee and scrolled through the Reddit thread on my phone. From what I could make out, there were a group of people, all anonymous of course, who believed that the original police investigation determined suicide too quickly, and that the wounds on Natalie's body were more consistent with a knife than with a boat propellor like the autopsy claimed. Added to the fact that Natalie went missing after a party – that particular fact grabbed my interest – and that there shouldn't have been any boats running in the marina that late at night for their propellors to do the kind of damage that was done... it was clear to see why people had ques- tions. The biggest question, of course, was why such a short investigation was carried out before ruling the death an accident.

Another article read 'Memorial service for Natalie', showing pictures of people holding candles, their cheeks tear-soaked. This was an official newspaper article and made no mention of the claims made by Natalie's sister that the investigation wasn't thorough enough. Aside from the first initial days of the search, there was barely any coverage at all, but then I supposed an accidental death was a tragedy for friends and family but hardly newsworthy. What was interesting, though, was that the woman who had been watching me in the café was in at least three of the photographs of the memorial. One of the captions read 'Gina Burton lights a candle for her sister'.

Despite the reluctance of the local businesses to put up photos of Holly – at least three places I'd asked had said they couldn't – I'd decided to have some printed anyway. I googled printing places on the island and came across a business that made huge signs for gardens, to celebrate birthdays or baby showers, right here in Edgartown. I pictured a huge sign saying 'FIND HOLLY' spread across it and dialled the number instantly.

Fiona, the woman on the other end of the phone, sounded shocked and upset to hear that there was a girl missing on the island, and worse – no one was talking about it. She agreed to help in an instant, promising only to charge for the materials she used. It was amazing to think that everyone I'd come across was so friendly and concerned, and yet I still wasn't any closer to finding out where Holly might be. I cast my mind back to Carl and Stacy, and Officer Waylans – okay, *almost* everyone was willing to help.

Fiona promised to deliver the signage as soon as possible, and agreed to print me some fliers as well. She suggested a few places that might be able to help, and asked if I'd checked CCTV around the area Holly had last been seen. I'd only been here forty-eight hours and I hadn't known until yesterday afternoon where the bonfire had even been – I needed to take stock and get my information straight. Not for the first time it struck me how much better Jess would have been at this. In the time it had taken me to decide I needed a map and some coloured pens she probably would have found Holly and set up her own missing persons investigation bureau on the island.

She'd call it 'Island Investigations' or something equally as cute.

But Jess wasn't here, and I was the only person looking for my sister on this whole damn island. So I was going to have to pull my finger out and get organised.

Chapter Twenty-Seven

Claire

I was coming out of the tourist information with my trusty new map when I saw the woman again. Only this time I knew who she was. She was Gina Burton, the sister of Natalie Burton, the girl who had died accidentally in the marina five years ago. She stared at me more openly now, and she had positioned herself so she could see exactly what I was doing. Had she followed me here after seeing me in Oak Bluffs the other day?

I spun around and strode towards her and watched her eyes widen in surprise.

'You've been following me,' I challenged.

Her face reddened and she looked as though she might deny it but instead she nodded. 'Yes,' she admitted. 'I'm sorry.' Her face was pale and drawn, her eyes sunken dark circles.

'No, I'm sorry,' I said. Clearly this woman was harmless and grieving, and I knew how that felt. Grief didn't make you crazy, but it made you feel that way. Like no one on earth could ever be experiencing the exact pain that you were. Like that hole inside you could only ever be filled with despair and madness. Since Mum had died, I had been consumed by it on an almost daily basis. 'I know what happened to your sister, I'm really sorry.'

She paused, as if that was the last thing she expected me to say. 'I suppose they told you I'm crazy, and to stay away from me,' she said.

'No one has said anything about you. But then again no one's exactly been forthcoming with any information about anything.'

'That's because you're asking too many questions. I know why you're here – they won't like you asking questions.'

Okay, now she really did sound crazy. All right, so no one had exactly showered me with information, but the locals had been as nice as nice could be to me. There had been no covert warnings or horses' heads on my pillow.

'Who's they?' I asked, trying not to sound overly sceptical. I didn't want to upset her, but my patience was wearing thin. Every moment I wasted entertaining this grieving sister was a moment my own was still missing.

She opened her arms in response to my question and gestured wildly around her. 'Everyone!' She must have caught my look because she scowled. 'I know, you think I sound crazy too, but if I'm crazy it's because the people here made me crazy. Denying facts, twisting evidence. You know they tried to say my sister's death was suicide? *Suicide.* She'd been knifed twelve times in the stomach. Then they said it was an accident – that they weren't knife marks but propeller blades, that she'd slipped into the marina and been cut up by a boat. They ruled that there was no foul play within twenty-four hours of finding her. No investigation, barely any evidence gathered...' She was talking so quickly that I thought she was going to pass out. What the hell was she going on about? Stabbing, murder? The article had said tragic suicide – was she saying that wasn't true?

I put my hands on her shoulders tightly, and told her to calm down. She was making a scene outside the coffee shop, no doubt people inside were watching.

'I'm sorry,' she said, sounding defeated. 'This is why I didn't approach you sooner. Because I know how crazy I sound. Like a grief-stricken big sister desperate to see conspiracy theories because her sister killed herself and she feels guilty. I've heard it before.'

It was exactly what I'd been thinking, and it was the obvious conclusion to come to – but something about her was so real, so raw and convincing that I couldn't help but want to hear what she had to say.

'I don't think that,' I lied. 'But you're right, it does sound pretty unbelievable.'

'Even with your own sister missing?'

The words hit me like a gut punch. 'Are you trying to say the two things are related? Your sister's accident and my sister being missing?'

'My sister's murder,' she hissed. She sighed. 'I had hoped we could help each other. Given the similarities.'

I could feel my face flush and my heart begin to race. 'The similarities?'

'You don't know?' She looked like a poker player, about to play her trump card. 'The last people my sister was seen with were Bobby and Ryan Slayton and their friends. And your sister had sex with one of them the night she went missing.'

Four aces.

'You can't know for a fact she had sex with Ryan that night,' I said, once I'd recovered from the surprise of her words. 'You didn't even know Holly – why would she tell you that?'

Gina shrugged. 'I saw them getting onto the Slaytons' boat at the marina the night of the bonfire.'

'Wait,' I said. 'You were at the bonfire?'

'Obviously not,' Gina scoffed. 'I'm not exactly top of everyone's invite list, if you hadn't noticed. I was at the marina though. I saw Bobby's truck pull up and I saw a girl getting onto the boat. I had no idea that the girl I'd seen was missing until I saw the picture on Thursday. It was definitely her though, I'm sure of it.'

'Wait, Bobby's truck? Are you saying she went there with Bobby, not Ryan?'

Gina shook her head. 'I'm pretty sure it was Ryan. Maybe he borrowed Bobby's truck?'

'What was she was wearing?' I asked, hoping desperately that she was wrong. I didn't know why, because a lead was better than no lead, but for some reason the thought of my sister being alone with either of the Slaytons on the last night she was seen by anyone filled me with dread.

'It was dark, but I think her dress was black, or at least a really dark colour. When they arrived, she had a bright red hooded jumper on, but she, um...' Gina looked down at the floor, her face awkward. 'She took that off. That's how I could tell it was a dress, not a skirt.'

'And you just watched them have sex?' My tone must have given away my disgust because Gina's face coloured even darker red.

'No! Well, I didn't exactly mean to. At first I didn't know what they were going to do. I saw her take her jumper off, and they started kissing... to be honest, I was considering going over there to warn her that he was bad news – that he was a rapist and a killer.'

'Wait, now he's a rapist too?' my stomach clenched at the thought of Holly being around this guy. Had she known what he'd been accused of?

Gina scowled. 'Why do you think my sister ended up dead? Everyone on the island knows that Ryan had sex with her that night. She was fifteen and too drunk to consent, so yes – he's a rapist. And when he realised the trouble he was in he killed her.'

'Then why didn't you warn my sister?' I asked, even though I knew the answer. It was easy for me to will past Gina to go and save my sister, drag her from the arms of Ryan Slayton and get her into a taxi home, but in reality Holly would have likely thought her crazy and told her to get lost.

'I mean, it wouldn't be the first time I'd done that,' Gina said, her voice low. 'Last time I warned a girl to stay away from Ryan, he threatened to have me arrested if I went near him again.'

'So you've been stalking him,' I said, matter of factly. 'And you didn't want to be seen.'

'Okay fine, and I'm sure you think I'm a crazy obsessed stalker like everyone else does, but I just can't bear the thought that someone else could go through what my sister went through and that another family—' She broke off because she was sobbing then – heavy, wracking sobs. The poor woman. I might have been the only person on the island at that moment who knew exactly how she felt.

'Look,' I said, putting a hand on her arm. 'Come with me, back to Holly's place. We can talk more then, without prying eyes. You can tell me everything. I think I know someone who can help us.'

She looked up at me, hope in her dark eyes. She looked like a person who had given up all hope and I had just handed her the tiniest bit back. 'You think so? Maybe they won't be able to ignore two of us,' she said, wiping her tears from her eyes. She looked at me as though I was some kind of hero, swooping in to save the day like Jessica Fletcher in *Murder She Wrote*. 'Thank you so much,' she said. 'You wouldn't believe how long I've waited for someone to help me.'

Chapter Twenty-Eight

Claire

I got back to Holly's place and still felt that familiar pang of disappointment that she hadn't turned up while I was out. I let us both in and gestured to Gina to sit down on the couch, apologising for the mess.

'I didn't want to, um… I haven't been able to…'

Gina nodded despite my inability to finish my sentence. 'You don't want to tidy up her stuff,' she said. 'I understand.'

That annoyed me, the way she was already treating me as if I was like her. As if our stories were the same. We weren't the same, she and I. Her sister was gone and I felt terrible about it, of course I did, but there was no proof at all that something terrible had happened to Holly and I refused to believe just yet that that could be the case.

I didn't let my irritation show. Emmy had been nice enough, and she seemed to have known my sister well, but Gina was determined and steadfast and I needed her as much as she felt she needed me. We had talked a bit on the walk back and even after all these years she had refused to give up on trying to get justice for Natalie. People on the island were tired of seeing her, she said, she reminded them of their ability to sweep murder and injustice under the carpet for the sake of their happy, perfect community.

She was convinced that plenty more people in Edgartown believed there was more to her sister's death than an accident, but no one wanted to admit it. It would be better for everyone, she told me, if she were to go away, to disappear. Everyone except Natalie.

'You know I have to tell the police what you just told me, about seeing Ryan with Holly the night she disappeared,' I said.

Gina shook her head sadly. 'They won't believe you. Surely you can see that? There were dozens of witnesses who saw my sister get into the Slaytons' truck that night. It didn't make any difference then and it won't now, especially if their only witness is crazy Gina with the Slayton obsession. They have their fingers in every law enforcement pie around here, and further. They're related to the Kennedys, for goodness' sake.'

'If the Slayton family are murderers and the rest of the island are happy to cover up their crimes, why wouldn't they just have got rid of you?' I asked her.

She smiled. 'Firstly, I don't think the whole island is involved in some cover-up conspiracy,' she said. 'Despite what people say about me, I'm not crazy. I just think that Officer Waylans was quick to label Nat's death as a suicide because he didn't believe that someone would have murdered her. She'd been drinking, she'd come to the marina with the Slaytons and she'd ended up dead. No one wanted to believe it was a murder, so they were happy to believe when he said she'd brought it on herself. It obviously helped that he is friends with Laurence Slayton. According to the police, the Slayton boys and their friends were all more than happy to help with the investigation.'

'Waylans,' I muttered. And that must have been what Holly's landlady Sheila was referring to when she'd said that the police department wouldn't want to believe that anything had happened to my sister. Because if it turned out that something bad had happened to her, people might start asking questions about a young girl's 'accidental' death five years ago. And it might just come out that Officer Waylans hadn't looked into Natalie's death quite as thoroughly as he should have. 'If you don't mind me asking,' I said, trying to keep my voice as non-accusatory as possible. 'What makes you so sure that Natalie's death was murder? I mean, I understand that it's an awful tragedy, but people do have accidents all the time. Especially young girls who aren't used to drinking.'

Gina nodded. 'Of course. It's not that I don't realise that Natalie had had too much to drink – from what people at the party say, she could barely stand, she was that out of it. And that was her own stupid fault – although I really wish someone there would have just called me to come and get her. And as much as I want to blame someone for her death, if it really was an accident, well, that would be a bit of a relief, to know she hadn't suffered at the hands of someone she trusted. But there are so many things that just don't quite add up. I mean, if – as the Slaytons say – they dropped Natalie at our house, why didn't she just come inside?'

I was about to interrupt to say that we all do stupid, illogical things when we're intoxicated, but she held up her hand.

'I know,' she said. 'It's not enough. She absolutely could have been too scared to come inside and face the music from our parents, maybe she wanted to get some fresh air in the hope of sobering up. Except people at the party reported her as being so drunk she could barely stand. They had to carry her to Bobby's truck and put her inside.

163

But a ten-minute drive later she can go for a walk from my place to the marina? It's half a mile. Then she would have had to get in – the gate was locked and no one reported it being open the next morning. So how did she get inside?'

I nodded, starting to understand why the Slaytons' story hadn't made sense to Gina.

'So they allegedly leave the party just to drop Natalie at her front gate in some altruistic act of chivalry,' she continued. 'But none of them bother to check she actually came inside? Even though she could barely stand? Let's accept that that's true. Natalie walks, no, stumbles – half a mile to the marina, in the dark. No one can say whether she did that in bare feet or in heels – she had no shoes on when she was found. So either she made that walk in these shoes...' She holds up her mobile phone with a zoomed-in, grainy shot of a pair of feet in at least six-inch stilettos. 'Or barefoot. And yet she didn't have a single cut or scratch on her feet. I get that she was in the water, so most of the dirt and sand would be washed away, but her feet were completely unscathed.'

I had to admit, that sounded unlikely. It would be almost impossible for this young girl, intoxicated as she reportedly was, to walk half a mile in those shoes, and yet how would she have walked that far in bare feet but shown no signs of her expedition?

'I'm starting to see why you didn't think things added up,' I remarked.

Gina's eyebrows raised. 'And you've only heard half of the story,' she reminded me. 'So why do you think the PD are being so pig-headed about denying it could have been anything other than an accident?'

'Tell me the rest,' I said, getting up and going to the kitchen. I took a couple of glasses out of the cupboard and opened the fridge. 'Would you like some orange juice?'

'Oh yes, please,' Gina said.

It was still strange to me to be using Holly's things, the glasses she would have used and the fridge she would have stood at trying to decide what to have for dinner. It was almost like she was standing next to me sometimes, a Holly from a parallel dimension where whatever happened the night of that bonfire never happened at all.

I passed Gina the orange juice and she accepted with a smile. She took a small sip, and then a deep breath.

'So even if we're believing that Nat walked all the way to the marina in high heels, or she walked barefoot without hurting her feet, then we have to believe that for some unknown reason she went to the marina where the Slaytons' boat was moored, instead of just going down to the beach, or one of the other million beauty spots she loved on the island. She'd never even been interested in the marina.'

'Okay,' I said, not pointing out once more that drunk people aren't always logical. I had a feeling there was more.

'And let's say we believe all of that, then she eventually is now so drunk that she falls over and hits her head repeatedly, according to the autopsy, on the edge of the dock. Then, after knocking herself out and dying in the water *without drowning*, she remains in the marina until a boat comes along and she gets cut up by a propellor without any sailor noticing a dead body stuck in their blades. Then she gets trapped under the dock until she is found a day later.' Gina finished her story and looked at me expectantly. It seemed clear that the media hadn't covered exactly what had happened the night of Natalie's death, and I didn't understand how more of an investigation hadn't been done.

'What I don't understand,' I said at last, 'is how anyone can hear the whole story and still be convinced that your sister's death was one hundred per cent accidental.'

Gina looked at me as though I had just asked for her hand in marriage. 'You have no idea how long I've been waiting to hear someone say that to me,' she said, her eyes brimming with tears.

Chapter Twenty-Nine

Claire

It wasn't that Gina didn't have any supporters, she told me after she'd finished Natalie's story. We took our orange juice outside into the back garden, where there was a beautiful grey decking area, some patio chairs and a table with a firepit in the middle, and what was possibly a hot tub covered over in the corner. I hadn't noticed that before. We chose to settle onto the oversized, brightly coloured outdoor beanbags on the perfectly manicured lawn. We could have been two friends catching up on old times, or making plans for weddings or baby showers. To the outside world, the last thing we would have looked like were two women discussing the disappearance and potential murder of their little sisters.

'There are some voracious true crime fans out there,' Gina continued, smoothing bits of her hair back into her ponytail. She took a sip of her orange juice and looked out towards the sea in the distance. 'It can be a bit of a double-edged sword. Sure, it's nice to have people tell you that your suspicions are justified, and at first it can feel like you've found your tribe. Then you get people coming forward with theories, treating my sister's death like some Netflix show to binge-watch and try to figure out the surprise ending. You wouldn't believe how many times I've seen people say horrible things about Nat, about me, about our parents.'

I frowned. 'What do they say?'

'They say that Natalie shouldn't have been allowed to get that drunk – which is true, but that doesn't mean you need it pointed out by some holier-than-thou keyboard warrior. We all wish more than anything that we hadn't let her go to that party, or that I'd arranged to go and get her. She was out with friends all the time, she'd never really been interested in getting wasted. I don't know what made her drink too much that night. The most popular theory is that one of the Slayton boys did it and everyone is covering up for them. People love a conspiracy theory and because of the Kennedy connection it got some traction for a while. But I've also seen...' She cleared her throat and her discomfort was clear. 'People try to outdo themselves, by coming up with a theory no one else has thought of. I've seen people say that Natalie did come home after the party and my dad did it, maybe because he was mad at her that she'd got drunk and disgraced him, or to cover up the fact that he was abusing her...' Her voice cracked at this last bit. 'Which just couldn't be crazier. My dad loved us both, and he was so proud of us. He would never have laid a finger on either of us, whatever we did. Other people said that it was probably me because I was jealous of Nat – people are never quite exact on the reason why, maybe just because she was younger and prettier than me, maybe I was in love with one of the Slayton boys. One person...' She half laughed and half sobbed, the emotion just too much for her. She swallowed hard and I leaned forwards to squeeze her knee in what I hoped was a reassuring way, not a creepy one. She didn't seem to notice either way. Her grief was a pair of blinkers, she could see nothing but the pain. 'One person said that maybe I was jealous because my dad was abusing her and not me, so I killed her for having sex with my father.' She closed her eyes to block out the pain those words caused.

'Oh Jesus,' I whispered.

'My mom and dad couldn't take it. It was worse than when everyone said her death was accidental. I asked was it worse than never getting justice for Natalie? My father said if I'd ever been asked if I'd had sex with my fifteen-year-old daughter I wouldn't need to ask.'

'It must have been horrible,' I breathed, thinking of what a cruel place the internet could be, how people never felt the need to hold back from behind their computer screens, the theatre of the damned.

Gina nodded. 'I stopped reading them,' she said. 'And so I was back where I started, alone and with people who either believed me and wondered if I'd done it, or people who didn't believe me.'

'What happened to your parents?' I almost didn't want to ask.

Gina closed her eyes gently, as if that memory hurt more than any of them. 'My father died two years after Natalie,' she said. 'His heart just gave up. My mother moved off the island to live with her sister in Oregon. She couldn't bear it here anymore. She begged me to go with her but said if I had to stay I could keep the house. She...' The tears began to flow now, and once the dam was open they didn't stop.

I grabbed a box of tissues from the bathroom and handed them to her. Gina pulled them out of the box by the fistful and pushed them into her eyes. When her sobbing eventually subsided, she looked over at me and she just seemed exhausted and defeated once more by her living nightmare.

'She committed suicide a year after Dad died. I was the only person who could have kept her alive and I wasn't there. All because of a promise I made to Natalie the day her body was found. I promised that I wouldn't leave this island until I'd seen the people who did this to her behind bars. So I'm stuck here. Same as you.'

Chapter Thirty

Holly

THAT NIGHT

It took a few seconds for Emmy's words to register, and even when they did, Holly didn't understand what she could possibly mean. *Natalie died, here, on the island, five years ago. And I'm pretty sure Ryan had something to do with it.*

'How?' she asked, shock numbing her arms and feet. She shivered, unsure why she was suddenly so cold when there was a gigantic fire just feet away. 'How could Ryan be involved? He's never mentioned—'

Emmy scoffed. 'Well, it's not exactly first-date kind of chit-chat, is it? Or second, or third for that matter.' She wrapped her cardigan around herself and looked a mixture of terrified and upset.

'Stop trying to pretend everything is a joke and tell me what's going on,' Holly demanded.

'Let's go back to mine,' Emmy pleaded, looking again at the group. 'Ryan and the others will be back in a minute and if he finds out I've told you...'

'Told me what?' Holly practically shouted. She looked sharply around to see if anyone had heard her over the crackling fire, the music and the chatter, but no one was

171

looking their way. 'You haven't told me anything and I'm not moving until you do.'

Emmy sighed. 'Fine, okay, but as soon as I tell you, I want you to come home with me. Things feel weird here tonight, it doesn't feel safe. Derek will come and fetch us.'

'Start talking,' Holly instructed.

Emmy bit her lip and nodded.

'Natalie lived here for a while,' she said. 'She wasn't born and brought up here, but her parents lived here year-round so she wasn't a summer kid and she wasn't a tourist. She hadn't been here long enough to be a proper local, but she was getting there, her and her sister were really nice, and they fitted in great. She was just a kid. Gina, her sister, was a few years older. Anyway, when the summer came around, five years ago, Natalie went missing.'

Holly bit her lip as her last drink threatened to come back up again. She didn't know whether it was the amount of alcohol she had consumed or the horrible feeling she was getting about where this story was going. She didn't trust herself to speak.

'We spent two days looking for her,' Emmy said. 'Her parents and her sister were frantic; she was only fifteen years old. Then her body turned up in the marina at Oak Bluffs.'

That last detail was too much. Holly turned and expelled warm, acidic vomit onto the sand behind her. She started to heave again. Emmy rubbed her back and put an arm around her shoulders.

'I knew I shouldn't have told you now,' Emmy said. 'Are you okay? Can we go home now? Let me call Derek.'

'No,' Holly said, wiping her mouth on her sleeve. Her head still felt as though it was spinning, but her stomach felt a little easier after her purge. 'I want to hear the rest. How did she die?'

Emmy sighed. She sat back on her knees and held Holly's arms at length. 'Everyone said it was an accident. Well, a few said it was suicide, but most people thought it was just a tragic accident. And it probably was...'

'But?' Holly said. Obviously Emmy thought differently, or she wouldn't be telling her this story, not now, not like this.

Emmy looked away for what felt like the longest time, then looked back at her new friend. 'But Gina, Natalie's sister, was convinced that Natalie was murdered. And I believe her. I saw Natalie the night she went missing, getting into a car with the Slaytons. She looked really drunk – way too drunk to be going anywhere with a boy older than her. It was a Saturday night and we'd all been drinking, but she was younger than us and it didn't feel right. Bobby was holding her up, and he slid her into the car next to Ryan, basically dumped her into the passenger seat. Bobby got into the car with another couple of guys and they drove off after them. I was too far away to stop them, so I called Gina. She came out straight away, but no one knew where they had gone. Gina called the police, tried to get them to go and look for her little sister, but as soon as she said the Slayton name it was like she was talking to a brick wall. The police said they'd go out and have a look, but we're not sure if they did or not, at least not that night. When Natalie was still missing the next morning, Gina had to tell her parents and they kicked up one hell of a fuss. The police went round to the Slayton house and found all the boys asleep in the front room, sprawled over sofas and on the floor. They said they'd just given Natalie a lift home, she must have wandered off after they left.'

'And how do you know she didn't?' Holly said, the feeling of dread so heavy in her stomach she was glad there was nothing left to heave up.

'I told Ryan that I'd seen her getting into his car, and that she was too drunk to have just wandered off alone,' Emmy said, her eyes as dark as the inky black sky. 'We were friends back then, I guess; I mean we hung out in the same places over the summer, with a lot of the same people. He got really upset – I'd never seen him like that before – and he said that she'd been a silly little girl who had only been with him to make his brother jealous, and if anything bad had happened to her at the marina, then it was her own fault.'

Holly cringed. 'That's a shitty thing to say. But I don't see how it makes you suspect Ryan of hurting her. It makes him look like an asshole, sure, but—'

'Don't you get it?' Emmy asked. 'That conversation was before Natalie's body was found. Before any of us had any idea she'd even gone to the marina.'

Chapter Thirty-One

Claire

I peered over the top of the book I was pretending to read, watching the steady stream of passengers join the queue for the ferry to Chappaquiddick Island. Most people who visited Edgartown wanted to see the famous island where Senator Ted Kennedy drove his car off the bridge over fifty years ago, but that wasn't why I was interested in the place. Gina had told me how the Slaytons visited their beach club on Chappy most days in the summer, and I'd hung around the Edgartown ferry most of the afternoon to try to catch them either going out or coming back. I wasn't a member of the beach club, and although Gina had said she could get me in without any trouble, I hadn't wanted it to look as if I'd deliberately sought the brothers out. Instead I had taken up residence in the Seafood Shanty with a book and a regular supply of iced lemonade. The seafood looked amazing, and I'd been assured that it was the best I'd find on the whole Vineyard, but I knew that the minute I ordered a lobster roll the boys would show up and I'd have missed my chance. Holly was going to owe me some good seafood when I found her.

I was ready to give up when I saw two familiar figures stepping off the ferry with a third one I didn't recognise. Gina had shown me Facebook and Instagram accounts for the Slayton brothers and their friends – she'd been following them under fake accounts for a long time, by the looks of it. I felt like I already knew them, and had to remind myself that they would have no idea who I was.

I downed the rest of my lemonade, threw down a generous tip for the waitress and shot out onto Dock Street to make it look as if I'd been there the whole time, handing out the fliers Fiona had dropped off for me.

As they walked towards me, I couldn't help thinking that the older brother, Bobby, really was one of the most attractive men I'd ever seen in real life. Even if I didn't know he was related to Bobby Kennedy, I could have probably guessed, such was the confidence in his walk: his whole demeanour was one of importance. He had dark hair, longish, and he ran his hand through it often. He had clear blue eyes with long lashes – although I couldn't see them from where I was, I had seen them on many photographs. His face was tanned and his lips were full.

His brother, in comparison, was like shining a torch next to a floodlight. Sure, a torch would produce enough light for you to see, but it could never shine quite as brightly. Ryan had short, sandy brown hair, and the same shaped eyes as his brother, except his were brown. He was attractive, kind of quiet-looking.

As they got closer to me, I pretended to have spotted them for the first time. 'Oh, hi,' I said, holding up a picture of Holly. 'I'm looking for my sister, do you know her?'

Bobby looked at the photo and nodded. Ryan's face paled slightly, I thought, but it might just have been my imagination.

'Yeah, of course,' Bobby said. 'You're Holly's sister? You've come a long way.'

I let out a sigh of what I hoped sounded like relief, but my heart was pounding. 'Oh thank God I've found someone. Do you live here? How did you know Holly? She hasn't been answering my calls since she went to a party on Friday.'

Ryan looked as though he was about to speak, but Bobby held up a hand and Ryan closed his mouth. Bobby looked at me with a hint of suspicion. He wasn't stupid.

'We have a summer place in Edgartown, but our boats are moored at Oak Bluffs. A gorgeous girl like Holly starts working at the marina, she's going to turn heads. She seemed like a really nice girl. You say she's missing?'

I looked at him, waiting for him to say more. He obviously wasn't aware that I already knew of their relationship with my sister. Something told me to hold this detail back though, call it a gut instinct.

Bobby was good at the waiting game and didn't say anything more to fill the awkward silence.

Eventually I said, 'No one's seen or heard from her since last Friday. It was your Fourth of July party she was at, wasn't it?'

Bobby grinned. 'You should have said that you already know who we are, Claire. As a matter of fact, she had left our party and gone to the bonfire at Left Fork, like most people under forty do.'

I raised one eyebrow – a trick Holly had always wished she could do – and dropped the act. 'I was under the impression that everyone knows who you are, Bobby. You're used to that, aren't you? Do you know where my sister might have gone after your party?'

He shrugged. 'We haven't seen her since then.'

I gestured to Ryan and the other guy whose name I didn't know. 'Are you speaking for everyone?'

'Why ah guess ah am, little missy,' Bobby said, putting on a loud southern cowboy drawl. 'Are you the sheriff in theyse parts now? Do ah need to get mahseylf a loyyer?'

The other guy started to laugh, but Ryan just looked slightly uncomfortable at his brother's showboating.

'I'm just really desperate to find my sister,' I said, my fake smile threatening to morph into a much more familiar scowl. 'I just want to know that she's okay. If you know anything that might help, I'd be really grateful.'

Bobby shrugged again. 'Just trying to have a little fun. Holly was nice, like I said. A bit naïve for twenty-two, mind you. Especially to be showing up at the beach party with Carl when his wife was right here, looking like the two of them had been… well, you know.'

Emmy had told me that Carl had given Holly a lift to the party, and that Stacy hadn't been pleased, but had she really slept with him? Surely not. He was just trying to throw me in a different direction.

'So you're saying Holly was having sex with her boss?' I asked.

Ryan jumped in before his brother could stop him. 'No, she wouldn't have done that. Stacy just got the wrong end of the stick.'

'How would you know?' Bobby demanded. 'You were still up at the house helping with the fireworks when they left.'

Ryan looked mutinous. 'I just know that she wouldn't have slept with him, okay?'

I wished I could get Ryan on his own, see what he had to say when his organ grinder wasn't around, but there didn't seem much chance of that.

'How do you know?' I asked.

It was Ryan's turn to shrug. 'I just knew her a bit, that's all. We went on a few dates. She was great.'

My blood ran cold as I realised he was talking about my sister in the past tense.

'She is,' I agreed, goosebumps raising on my arms.

'Look, we saw Holly at the party,' Bobby interjected, glaring at his brother. Had he noticed Ryan's mistake? Did it mean anything? 'She got a bit too drunk. I mean, we were all drunk, but she was making a bit of a fool of herself, throwing herself at the guys, dancing around them all sexy. The guys mainly just found it funny, but the girls were getting annoyed and no one wanted a fight. I had a word with her, told her to go home and sleep it off.'

I didn't believe a word of it, but I acted as if I was lapping up every word he said. 'Didn't you make sure she got home okay?' I asked.

Bobby held up his hands. 'Look, I'm a gentleman, but I'm not an idiot. I walk her home and she makes a pass at me, what's to stop her waking up and saying I came on too strong? When you grow up like we have, you learn not to be alone with drunken women.'

'*Like you have?*'

'Yes, like we have,' he repeated. 'With money. Some women just want to get with us because we're rich and our uncle is famous, but others...' He lowered his voice as if he was letting me in on a secret. 'There are others who do it on purpose so that they can get themselves a payday. We have to be extra careful.'

'Must be awful,' I muttered. I stepped closer and looked him square in the eyes. 'And it wouldn't be the first time you've been accused of hurting a woman, would it?'

Surprisingly, Ryan was the first to react to my words. 'What's that supposed to mean?' he practically yelled, stepping closer to me, and I got a hint of the angry, angry man inside.

Bobby grabbed at him and pulled him back, giving him a look that didn't need words. 'We didn't do anything to Gina's sister,' he said, his voice like ice now. 'But that didn't stop Gina trying to ruin our lives. She didn't want to accept that her sister couldn't handle her drink and fell into the marina. But you can see why I didn't want to get involved with Holly after that. People here suffered because of Gina's accusations. The media made us out to be monsters. On the night of the beach party, your sister was drunk and making a fool of herself. There are a dozen people who could have followed her off that beach.'

'You won't pin this on any of us,' Ryan hissed.

'Cool it, man,' Bobby said, slapping him lightly on the shoulder. 'Claire is upset about her sister. She didn't mean to accuse us of anything, did you, Claire?'

'Of course not,' I said, my voice tight. I was still reeling from the way he had turned so quickly from mild-mannered younger brother to Rottweiler.

'There you go.' Bobby smiled. 'If we could help you, we would. When Holly quit the marina, we all just assumed she was embarrassed about her behaviour and had moved on, or gone home.'

I nodded, just wanting to get away from them now. I could feel that something in the air had turned ugly and I knew better than to push it. Still, I had to ask. 'So the last time you saw her she was on her own, leaving the beach party? What time was it?'

'Around eleven,' Bobby said, making to move away in a signal that the conversation was over. 'Sorry I can't be more specific, but we were all pretty wasted. I offered to call her a taxi, but Stacy went after her.'

'Stacy?' I repeated, thrown by this sudden detail.

'Yeah, Stacy from the marina... Carl's wife.'

Chapter Thirty-Two

Holly

THAT NIGHT

Holly sat there, frozen, trying to take in what Emmy had just said about Ryan knowing where Natalie's body would be found the next day. God, she wished she hadn't had so much to drink. Already the story Emmy had told her had started to jumble in her mind, warping and rewriting itself. Did she say that Ryan had driven off with her in his car? That Bobby had put her in there because she was so drunk she couldn't stand? And two days later she was found floating in the marina. That just sounded really bad for Ryan. Unless they were just trying to get her home safely. After all, if they dropped her off at home, they couldn't exactly be responsible for what happened after they left, could they? If Natalie had decided to go for a walk to sober up, for example, or if she had met someone else after Ryan and his brother had gone home. What Emmy was saying, it didn't have to mean anything.

'Say something,' Emmy said, and her eyes were pleading.

'Why didn't you tell the police?' Holly asked, and even in her inebriated state she knew from the look on

Emmy's face that her friend had been hoping she would say something else, maybe reassurance that she couldn't have known anything would happen to Natalie, or that Emmy was so much younger then, and had been drinking, that what had happened wasn't her fault.

'I did,' Emmy said. She was looking at a spot over Holly's shoulder, far into the distance, and Holly wondered what she was remembering. 'I did tell them and I was told that Ryan Slayton had already admitted giving Natalie a lift home. He claimed he saw her walk up her path but didn't see her go inside, he just presumed she had. Naturally, he said he regretted it afterwards, when he found out she'd gone missing. He'd been beating himself up about it all day. Officer Waylans sounded like he felt sorrier for Ryan Slayton than for Natalie – he said that such a promising future shouldn't be tarnished over a drunken girl having an accident. And that was that. Natalie's death was ruled an accident and every time I see Ryan or Bobby Slayton, I picture her getting into his car and me not doing a single thing to stop her.'

Tears were rolling down Emmy's cheeks now and this time Holly did what she should have done in the first place and pulled Emmy to her feet, enveloping her into a hug, reassuring her that she wasn't to blame, she wasn't to know what was going to happen. She held Emmy tight as she sobbed into Holly's shoulder, draining herself of the emotion she had been holding in all these years. Holly knew why Emmy had never told anyone else, the guilt and shame of thinking that she could have done more, that the young girl's life might have been saved if only she had spoken out. When the reality was that even if Emmy had spoken out, she would probably have been ignored, nothing would have changed. That was the reality of boys like the Slaytons against girls like Emmy. She would have been called hysterical, prudish, jealous even. Five years of guilt, and probably a lifetime to come, wondering 'what if'.

'Hope I'm not interrupting anything?'

Holly felt Emmy's body go rigid in her arms. They broke apart to see the grinning face of Ryan Slayton standing in front of them. He was holding up a six-pack of beer in one hand and a bottle of wine in another.

'I got you some more wine,' he said to Holly, then, noticing Emmy's tear-streaked face in the light of the fire he frowned. 'You okay, Emmy?'

'She's fine,' Holly said, before Emmy could say anything. She felt Emmy's hand slip into her own and squeeze ever so slightly, a gentle warning not to say anything about what she had just been told. 'Just boy stuff.'

'Well, any guy that upsets you is a fool,' Ryan said, dropping the drink at his feet and reaching over to cuff her playfully on the arm. 'You're an absolute beauty. Want me to sort him out?'

Emmy shook her head, but said nothing. The three of them stood there in awkward silence before Holly cleared her throat and picked up the bottle of wine from the sand.

'Thanks for this, Ry,' she said. 'But I can't drink out of the bottle. Would you see if there's any more of those plastic cups? I think I saw a pile by the red truck over there.'

Ryan smiled and leaned forwards to kiss her on the head. It was the first time he had been so brazen – usually he had waited for her to make any sort of physical contact. It was why Emmy's story felt so unbelievable now, looking Ryan in the eye. Sure, she had hardly known him any time, but he'd always been so shy and respectful with her.

Now, Bobby, she could see him getting a young girl drunk and taking advantage, but not Ryan.

'I'll be right back,' he said, and turned to get her a cup without argument.

'What the hell am I supposed to do with this information?' Holly said, putting her hands over her eyes. She took them away and looked at Emmy. 'You said yourself that you have no idea that they did anything but give her a lift home. And I just can't see Ryan doing anything to hurt a woman, let alone a young girl, a kid for God's sake. But if I'm wrong about him...'

'I had to tell you,' Emmy said, her voice pleading with Holly to understand. 'You were talking about going back with him – what if the two of you stayed together, got married? Had kids?' She sounded like the idea repulsed her, and Holly knew that Emmy really believed Ryan and his brother had had something to do with what happened to Natalie that night. She grabbed Emmy's arm, making her decision. She needed time to process this, she needed to sober up, to calm down and to talk it over with Emmy properly.

'Can you call Derek? Get him to come and get us out of here?'

Emmy nodded and pulled out her phone.

Holly looked to where Ryan had been caught up talking to a large guy with short blond hair. Emmy was talking on the phone now, and she held five fingers up to Holly: five minutes. The car park was on the other side of the bonfire, but they could go around and get to it without walking directly past Ryan. The other way was through a sparse patch of bushes to their right, but it was pitch black in that direction, with no light from the fire breaking through. It would be just her luck to break her leg and not be able to work the rest of the season.

'Come on,' Emmy said, hanging up the phone and grabbing Holly's arm.

Ryan had his back to them, and there were enough people on the beach to slip in-between the groups and get lost in the darkness. They weaved in and out of groups, trying to stay out of Ryan's sightline across the roaring fire.

Suddenly, Holly stopped short, her stomach dropping with panic. 'Shit,' she said, grabbing Emmy's arm. 'My bag! I left it on the sand, where we were sitting.'

Emmy's eyes widened. 'Leave it.'

'I can't just leave it,' Holly said, close to tears of frustration. 'It's got my purse, my phone... I'll have to go back.'

'I'll come,' Emmy said, but Holly shook her head.

'You go and meet Derek. Tell him to have the car running and pull up as close to the beach as he can, I'll be two minutes behind you.'

Emmy hesitated, not looking altogether pleased with the arrangement.

Holly pushed her arm lightly. 'Go,' she urged. 'Make sure he doesn't think you've changed your mind, or get called away or something. I'll be right behind you.'

Emmy nodded and carried on walking hurriedly towards the car park, while Holly made her way back to where they had been sitting moments before. The spot was near impossible to find again in the dark, and Holly cursed herself for urging Emmy to go on without her; she should have made her ring her phone over and over so that she could find it on the inky black sand.

She stopped, looking over to where Ryan had been talking to the blonde guy. Ryan was gone.

Holly swore under her breath, looking side to side at the people gathered around the bonfire. So many faces were in darkness or half illuminated by firelight – she could barely make out if she knew anyone. Where was he?

She was scanning the sand desperately when the hand grabbed her from behind, clamping around her mouth.

'Lost something?' a voice hissed, and Holly was dragged backwards into the long grass.

Chapter Thirty-Three

Claire

My first stop the next morning was the marina. I was going in search of Stacy and I was going to find out if she had seen Holly after their argument. The day was warm but not as sweltering as it had been and there was a cool breeze coming in off the sea. The marina was busier today than it had been on Thursday and I saw Carl talking to a group of people, his back to me and his voice carrying confidently. I found Stacy sitting behind the desk in the reception area.

She saw me and her face dropped. 'I don't know what you're doing back here,' she said, putting her pen down on the desk. 'I've already told you everything I know about your sister.'

'That's not true though, is it?' I said, my voice as level and as cool as I could keep it. I'd never had to hold my temper as much as I had these last couple of days. I honestly felt as though if you sliced into a vein, you could use my blood to fill a hot-water bottle. I was looking at Stacy differently this time, and I noticed a scratch on her neck, near her chin. Was that new or had I missed it before? Had that been caused by her errant husband or by a fight with my sister? Holly had never been a physical fighter, but I did think that she would try to defend herself if someone was hurting her. Unless of course they had caught her off guard. Or unless there were two of them. Stacy's eyes looked puffy too, as though she hadn't been sleeping well. Was she wandering the halls trying to wash imaginary blood off her hands?

'Are you calling me a liar?' she asked, a flash of anger crossing her face.

'Well, I suppose I am, yeah,' I replied. I stood at the edge of her desk, towering over her and wondering if I was confronting the woman who had hurt my sister. Had Stacy flown into a jealous rage that night and done something to Holly? Or had she scared my sister so badly that she had no choice but to run away? 'Why didn't you tell me you had a fight with my sister the night she disappeared?'

Stacy's eyebrows raised and her eyes grew wider. It was as though it was just dawning on her that I suspected her of something.

'Oh no, no, no, no,' she said, shaking her head. 'You are not pulling that bullshit on me. I shouted at her, yes, because she was a home-wrecking, husband-stealing whore. But I never touched her and you are not going to try to say I did. She walked away from me onto the beach and I never saw her again. If you want to know who hurt her, you'd better find out who else's husband she was trying to steal.'

My blood raised another degree in temperature. I leaned forwards, placing both hands on the desk. 'My sister wouldn't have touched your husband with a barge-pole.'

'I saw them together! At the party, and then in the car park. I'd already been watching her at work, the way she hung off him, the way she flirted with him to get the easier jobs, the overtime. Then she'd seen me watching them at the party and tried to pretend she was telling him to get off her. Carl might be weak-willed, but if your sister hadn't been leading him on...'

I could tell she'd been through these lines dozens of times since that night, trying over and over to convince herself that her husband wasn't to blame somehow. Suddenly all I could feel for her was pity, and disgust. I didn't honestly believe she could have hurt my sister, but she'd lied to me the first time I'd been here and I wasn't letting her off that easily.

'Bobby Slayton said he saw you leave the party to go after my sister.'

She laughed. 'Bobby Slayton? That's where you're getting your information? Oh Lord, you really don't know anything, do you? Bobby Slayton would say just about anything to protect himself and his family – he's proved that numerous times.'

'So you're saying you don't know where Holly is? Or what's happened to her?'

She looked at me, her face inches from my own, and she seemed unsure. 'The police say she cleared off of her own accord. They said she was travelling.'

'And you just believed them?' I shook my head. 'Weren't you worried when she didn't turn up for work?'

'Why would I be?' Stacy snapped. 'After what happened at the bonfire, there was no way she could carry on working here. If she'd have turned up, I'd have had Carl fire her anyway. I just thought she'd saved us the trouble. We weren't expecting her to show up and she didn't. No surprise there.'

'And where did Carl go after you left the party?'

Stacy's face fell and that was when I realised I'd hit on it. The real reason Stacy had looked nervous to see me, and unsure in her protestations that Holly was fine. She was worried her husband had done something to hurt my sister. 'He came home with me,' she said, but there was a change in her whole demeanour.

'And he stayed there all night?' I asked, watching her jaw set.

'Yes. All night.'

'You'd been drinking,' I said. 'How would you know if he'd slipped out when you were asleep? Maybe he went back to the beach to meet my sister. Maybe something happened between them. Can you be sure he wouldn't hurt her? How did you get that scratch, Stacy?'

She pushed back her chair and moved from behind the desk to pick her mobile up from on the bookshelf. 'You need to leave now,' she said, 'before I call the police. They don't take kindly to people stirring up trouble.' She held up the phone for me to see that she was serious.

'And is that what Holly did?' I asked. 'Stir up trouble? Did she do something that made Carl have to hurt her?'

Stacy scowled. 'Shut your mouth. We don't have that kind of thing happen here, and no one will believe Carl had anything to do with your sister leaving. It's been five years since we had trouble like your sister show up. And look what happened then.'

'Are you talking about Natalie Burton? Did Carl hurt her too? Are you afraid of him? Because I can help you. Do you know what happened to my sister? It's just the two of us here, Stacy, I can't prove anything you tell me. And even if I could, I have a feeling I know who the police will believe. So why don't you just tell me where she is and I can help you get away from him?'

Stacy looked as though she was going to say something, then she stopped. Her face softened and she began to speak. 'I knew Natalie Burton. She was my friend. *Gina* was my friend. What happened to Natalie was nothing to do with Carl, and everyone around here knows it. We all know what those boys did to Natalie, and whether they killed her or if she did commit suicide… well, they are to blame either way. Now Natalie is gone and Gina has spent five years going out of her mind trying to prove they are to blame. If I knew where your sister was, I'd tell you. But if she did go with those Slayton boys again that night…' She paused. 'You'd be better off leaving things alone and going home. Don't end up like Gina. Don't let them ruin your life too.'

Chapter Thirty-Four

Claire

'You lied about Stacy following my sister away from the bonfire,' I called to the figure lounging on the swinging chair. The chair was on the biggest porch of the biggest house – no, mansion – that I had ever seen up close in real life, but I wasn't about to let that intimidate me.

Bobby opened his eyes and looked at me in surprise, although I wasn't sure why. It wasn't as if there were armed guards at the gates; there weren't even any gates. For a trillion-dollar house, it was remarkably unprotected. Maybe that's why Bobby looked so surprised, maybe on Martha's Vineyard strangers didn't just accost you while you were having a snooze on your million-dollar swingy chair.

'Claire, it's nice to see you again,' he said, sitting up. 'I take it you've spoken to Stacy?'

'Yes, and she said you were lying.'

Bobby shrugged. 'I suppose she would, wouldn't she?' He waved a hand as if the conversation was considered over. I could not believe this asshole. 'Listen,' he said, as if he had been the one to seek *me* out. 'I wanted to apologise for Ryan's outburst yesterday. He's my little brother and I love him, but he's always had a spontaneous temper.'

I raised my eyebrows but didn't say the obvious.

'And if I seemed flippant or uncaring about your sister...' His voice trailed off and he actually looked sad. He looked me in the eyes. 'I had to put a bit of an act on in front of Ryan. You heard him say that he and Holly had been on a few dates... well, he was pretty keen on her.'

'And so were you,' I finished.

He looked surprised. 'Is it that obvious?'

I shrugged. 'I know sibling rivalry when I see it.' I didn't mention what Gina had said about seeing Holly getting onto their boat on the night of the bonfire. 'Were the two of you sleeping together?'

Bobby shook his head and motioned for me to take a seat.

I hesitated. Part of me was telling me to stay standing, that this family was dangerous and I should leave right now. But even Bobby Slayton wouldn't get away with murdering me on his porch in broad daylight. Probably. I obliged, sinking into the expensive chair opposite his.

'It hadn't gone that far,' he said. 'I can't say it wouldn't have, but she was pretty certain that Ryan had seen us together at the house. We had kissed and he came up the stairs; he didn't say anything, but he was acting really strange afterwards.'

I sighed. I didn't know if I could believe a single word that came out of his mouth. He seemed more genuine this time, though. It didn't feel like he was putting on a show and when he talked about Holly his face really did soften. And if Ryan had seen them together – would he be mad enough to hurt Holly?

'If you both cared about my sister so much, then why didn't you report her missing?' I asked.

He grimaced, his attractive face scrunching up. 'Ryan said she'd sent him a message telling him that she'd gone to stay in Boston for a few weeks.'

'And you believed him?' I asked, well aware of the incredulous tone to my voice.

'Why wouldn't I?' Bobby asked. 'I didn't really know your sister, none of us did. But what we did know is that she'd most probably lost her job at the marina thanks to Stacy being convinced that she was sleeping with Carl—'

'Which she wasn't,' I cut in.

Bobby shook his head. 'No, she thought he was a creep. I let Ryan wonder about that to take his attention off what was growing between the two of us. But when Holly took off, we just thought it was to lick her wounds after Stacy firing her. I called her to see if I could go and join her in Boston for a few days, but I never got an answer. Then you showed up.'

I stopped to consider what he was saying. There were three options. Option number one: Ryan was telling the truth about the message from Holly and she had told him she was going to Boston. Option number two: he was telling the truth but didn't know that the message was really from whoever had texted Jess on Holly's phone. Option number three: Ryan was lying about getting the message to account for the fact that Holly wasn't around anymore. Which would imply that he had something to do with why Holly wasn't around anymore.

'My sister hasn't gone to Boston. You know that, right?'

A dark look crossed Bobby's face. He looked as though he was about to say something but thought better of it. Instead he nodded. 'I believe that you don't think Holly would stop answering your calls,' he said. 'But I'm not lying when I say that Ryan and I barely know her. And people are different on the island. I know I am.'

'What do you mean?' I asked.

He shrugged. 'It's like a paradise playground. Sure, for the people who live here year round it might just be home, but for us summer kids it's an escape… it's freedom.'

'Except you're not kids anymore,' I reminded him. 'You're what, twenty-two?'

'Twenty-three,' he corrected. 'But here I may as well be eighteen. That's what I'm trying to say. Back home, I'm constantly being groomed to work in Dad's business. Like, literally everyone hates me. They've all worked their asses off to get to where they are and I'm leapfrogging them up the corporate ladder because of who daddy is.'

'Your golden shoes are sounding awfully tight,' I retorted. 'But I fail to see how you sobbing on my shoulder about your life of privilege has anything to do with me finding Holly.'

He grinned as if I hadn't just insulted him. He had the most disarming smile of anyone I'd ever met. I could see easily why Holly would be tempted away from the younger, less charismatic brother by that smile alone. 'I'm just saying that anyone can be anything on this island. Even a nice girl like Holly.'

I shook my head and frustrated tears pricked at the corner of my eyes. 'She didn't just meet someone at that Fourth of July bonfire and run off to Boston with them the next day,' I insisted, through gritted teeth. 'She was with your brother that night, and I think she left with him and went to your boat. Maybe she let it go too far, maybe she said no at the last minute. Or maybe she was too drunk, like you said, and there was an accident. What happened? Are you covering for him again?'

Bobby's face underwent a transformation, from charming and handsome to a dangerous scowl. 'Again?' he asked, his voice even but low.

I should have stopped there. If either of the Slaytons had hurt my sister, then possibly aggravating one of them at his own home, shielded from the road by about an acre and a line of trees, would be extremely stupid. But I had never been accused of being sensible before, and I didn't disappoint now. 'Which one of you killed Natalie Burton? Or was it both of you? See, I don't think so. I think Ryan is the one with the temper, and I think you're the one who covers up his mess.'

Bobby stood up and took a step towards me. I flinched but didn't step back. I didn't think he was going to hit me – but why? I was questioning if he was capable of murder to protect his brother and yet I was fairly confident he wasn't about to hurt me.

He clenched his jaw and leaned in close to me. I set my own jaw and stared him in the eye. 'You should watch who you let fill your head with ideas,' he snarled. 'Gina Burton has been harassing my family for five years because her sister was obsessed with us. You want to end up like her, no life, no future? Be my guest. But don't expect me to stand here and listen to you throwing accusations in my face. I like Holly and I never would have hurt her. I hope she's okay, honestly I do. But Ryan is my brother and at the end of the day I'll protect him, the same way you would do for her. However I have to.'

He carried on walking past me, down the steps of the decking and across the grass. I wanted to shout something to him, but what? An apology? I wasn't sorry for asking the same question everyone else wanted to know. And I was also very aware that he hadn't denied that Ryan had hurt either Gina or my sister.

Chapter Thirty-Five

Claire

I didn't expect to see Bobby again so soon, let alone later that afternoon. He'd just walked out of an ice-cream shop, and despite the fact that I'd just been about to get an ice cream myself as a way to cool off after being told Officer Waylans 'wasn't available right now', it irritated me to see him doing something so casual and mundane. My sister was still missing and he and his brother who apparently 'really cared about her' were acting like they really couldn't have cared less. After our run-in this morning, however, I had no intention of getting into another threatening match with him and tried to duck out of sight behind a truck. He clearly wasn't done with me though, and as he walked towards my cleverly concealed hiding place, I bristled, ready to stand my ground.

'Claire, hey,' he said, looking thoroughly uncomfortable. 'I wanted to apologise for how I spoke to you this morning.'

He looked different somehow, tired and a bit, what, defeated? I didn't know him well enough to judge properly, but he didn't look as polished and arrogant as he had previously.

'Why?'

He looked surprised. 'Excuse me?'

'Why did you want to apologise?'

He held up his hands. 'No ulterior motive. I just don't usually speak to women that way. I'm sure you have a different impression of me, but I don't.'

'Okay,' I said, not completely satisfied that this wasn't some ploy to get something he wanted, or just to get me to back off from asking questions. 'Thanks.'

'Is there... um...' He shoved a hand through his hair. 'Is there any news on Holly?'

I don't know why, but something about hearing him say her name pushed my anger button. It's a large one and protrudes more than other people's on a normal day. 'How could there be when no one's looking for her but me?' I snapped. I gave him my best glare. 'You know you could get Officer Waylans to look into my sister's disappearance, right? If you really wanted to find out if she's okay. But you haven't, and you won't. Because you don't care, so don't pretend to.'

Bobby's face looked almost pained and I was pretty sure that I knew in that moment that he thought Holly was hurt, or worse. And I could only guess that he thought Ryan was to blame. That's why he wouldn't ask Waylans to open a missing person's report on her. He was scared of what they would uncover. I was surprised by what he said next.

'We were going to be together,' he announced.

'What?' I noticed a couple look our way and lowered my voice. I'd forgotten the kind of attention the Slayton family got around here.

'That night, at the bonfire. We kissed. She said she'd made a mistake, she wanted to be with me, not Ryan. She asked me to go back to hers and I... I said no.'

'You said no?'

200

He sighed, and I could see in his face that there was something, pain, regret? But for what, I had no idea. 'She'd had too much to drink to make decisions like that. She'd only been seeing Ryan a couple of weeks, but still, I didn't want her to sleep with me when she was drunk and then regret it. She said Emmy was waiting for her in the car park and she was going straight home. She was supposed to call me the next day and we were going to talk. I said I'd take her on a boat trip, we could spend some time together. She could make her decision in the right... in the right state of mind. She walked away and I never saw her again. I know I don't have any proof of this, and it all sounds pretty convenient...'

It did, and yet he seemed sincere. Then again, Ted Bundy had looked pretty sincere also, so I wasn't stupid enough to rule Bobby out completely.

'Why didn't you tell me this earlier?'

He shrugged. 'I almost did. I told you that we liked each other, and that I thought it would go further.'

'But if you'd told me that Holly was going to dump Ryan for you, that puts Ryan under suspicion.'

Bobby nodded. 'I guess I hoped that if I put it off long enough she'd come back and that would be that. I don't want to think about what might have happened to her.'

'Do you know she was seen at the boat with Ryan? Your boat?'

Bobby looked down at his feet. 'I heard stuff. Nothing concrete.'

'Why would she be there, if she had planned to run away with you? What made her change her mind and go with Ryan?'

'Did anyone see her with Ryan?' he challenged. 'Because I heard she'd been seen on the boat, but I can't find anyone who saw her there with Ryan.'

I thought about it and realised he was right – Gina never claimed to have seen Ryan on the boat, just Bobby's truck and Holly getting on board with someone.

'Was it you?' I challenged back.

'No.'

'Then who else would it be?'

He let out a breath. 'Why would she go with Ryan after we'd just... it doesn't make sense. Unless she was playing us both.'

'Holly would not do that,' I said firmly. 'She might be a bit naïve, but she's not cruel. If she said she was going home, then that's where she was going.'

'Me and Ryan...' He looked as though he was getting close to saying what he didn't want to say. 'We have this thing going on, we always want what the other has. He wouldn't have been happy that she wanted me.' He hung his head. 'Seems really fucking stupid when I say that out loud.'

I thought about me and Holly, and the relationship we'd had over the years. 'It actually doesn't,' I admitted. 'A sibling relationship is one of the weirdest there is, if you ask me.'

He looked at me strangely for that. 'You obviously have a close relationship with Holly though, to come all this way to find her?'

I nodded. 'Sure, we're close. That doesn't mean that we always get along. After Mum died...' I let the words trail off, this wasn't the time or the place.

Bobby nodded. 'Holly told me that she felt like she'd let you down coming here. Like she was running from her grief instead of facing it, like you were.'

The words were like a sucker punch. 'She told you that?'

Bobby nodded and I let out a dry laugh.

'I never faced anything head on in my life, and Holly could never let me down. I hated Holly coming here because I needed her with me. I was being selfish, but instead of facing up to that I told her she was selfish. It was probably the last thing I told her.' The thought brings tears to my eyes and I look down so Bobby can't see them.

'Which is why you came all this way to find her.' Bobby nodded. 'I understand. Me and Ryan fight like anything, we steal each other's stuff and everything is a competition, but I love him and I'd do... I've done... everything I can to protect him. You understand?'

I had a feeling he was talking about Natalie but if I pressed the issue he'd clam up. I nodded. Bobby had covered for his brother once and he would do it again if he needed to.

'Have you been to Left Fork yet? Where the bonfire was?' Bobby asked, breaking the silence.

I shook my head. 'I haven't had a chance.' It was partly true. I hadn't wanted to go on my own.

'Why don't I take you? The bonfire will probably be lit again – nothing like the Fourth of July party, but there's usually a few people around in the evenings.'

I considered his offer. I did want to see the beach where Holly had last been seen – not that I thought that there would be any evidence to find there after all this time – but the idea of going with one of the people who I suspected of knowing more than they were telling me didn't seem very sensible. Especially given what he'd just told me. *I've done everything I can to protect Ryan...* Had that been a threat?

'I can meet you there if you don't want to get in my truck,' he said, and I almost smiled at how he had read my thoughts.

'I don't want to get in your truck, if I'm honest,' I admitted. 'No offence meant, I'm just a naturally suspicious person.'

'No offence taken. I'll meet you there, say seven? It's just a short walk from where Holly was staying. It'll still be light, so you won't get trapped with me in the dark.' He winked and I couldn't help noticing how attractive he really was. But, unlike my sister, I knew how dangerous that could be.

—

I didn't dress up to go to the beach – for a start I hadn't brought any party clothes with me and secondly I didn't want to give Bobby the Bighead any ideas that I was trying to come onto him. I was too old and too tired for his shit. I was ready for him.

What I wasn't ready for was for him to actually be quite pleasant.

He met me at Left Fork, where the dirt parking lot met the sandy beach. There were no street lights, but the evening was still plenty light enough for me to see my way to the huge bonfire roaring on the sand. I looked around the parking lot, thinking about how that must have been where Emmy went to meet Derek, and where Carl had pulled up and Stacy had started screaming at Holly. Then Holly would have made her way onto the sand – just like I was doing now.

'The bonfire is always in the same place,' Bobby told me, 'and we usually put all our drinks down there.' He pointed at a stack of bottles spilling out of coolers next to some grassy dunes. The dunes rose up slightly and the grass got longer, bushier. Past the fire, children still played on the white sand, kicking balls with their parents. There were signs declaring 'no alcohol on the beach'.

'How many people were here that night?' I asked Bobby, as he moved closer to the coolers and grabbed two beers. He held up the two different brands and I pointed to one. He turned and picked up a bottle opener that had been partially buried in the sand.

'About fifty,' he said, handing me the beer. It was cold and refreshing and I guzzled at it greedily. 'A mix of summer kids and locals. It's a tradition: we host the party, then some walk, others drive down here and we carry on drinking and partying.'

Bobby walked me around the party, introducing me to people, explaining how I was looking for Holly and helping to give out fliers. It seemed like I was with a totally different person than the guy that had mocked and teased me so flippantly. A few people said they knew Holly and expressed concern that she hadn't been seen in so long. I felt for the first time like I actually might be getting through to people. With the signs for the front garden due to be delivered and installed tomorrow, word might actually spread.

And what if I had been wrong about Bobby? With his connections perhaps I could get the police to take Holly's disappearance seriously. As Bobby handed me another beer and started talking about ways we could get the local media involved in the search, I felt more hopeful than I had in days.

Chapter Thirty-Six

Claire

I woke up to the angry shriek of a seagull, gritty sand beneath my legs and the smell of salt and decay. Pain shot through the back of my neck as I dared to open my eyes and pull myself into a sitting position. Everything hurt. Every inch of my body objected to movement and the brightness pierced my eyes, making me hold up an arm to shield them from the blinding sunlight.

It was morning, then. I had no recollection of the transition from evening to whatever time it was now, my last memory was of being at the campfire with Bobby Slayton... why couldn't I remember anything else?

The silent desolation of the beach resembled a post-apocalyptic scene after the cacophony of music, drunken squeals, bodies intertwined on the sand and dancing in the light of the bonfire at last night's party. The only signs left that anyone had been here were tyre tracks in the sand, a few piles of beer cans and the charred remains of the bonfire. There wasn't one other soul left passed out on the beach, sitting up bleary-eyed and head splitting. I was completely alone.

I looked down and was relieved to see my shorts and T-shirt were still in place, nothing ripped or bloodied. My flip-flops were missing, but that wasn't too concerning,

206

they were cheap and naked feet didn't scream sexual assault the way an absence of other clothes would. But why couldn't I remember anything? I would have sworn I barely had two full drinks, but the dryness of my mouth, the throbbing in my head and the complete black hole where the rest of the night was would suggest otherwise.

Pain washed over me again and I leaned forwards and vomited onto the sand. God, what a mess. I needed to get back to Holly's house and sort myself out, but I could barely move my arms, let alone stand up.

My bag. As soon as the thought occurred to me I began to panic. It wasn't on the sand next to me, so I had no idea where it could be. Which meant I had no idea where my phone or purse was.

Dread pounded in my chest. Panic had now taken hold of me and had started yelling a list of all the things that were very, very wrong about this situation. What had happened in those lost hours? I didn't just go from having a conversation with Bobby Slayton to passing out on the sand, and the realisation that I had been walking around, talking to people... and God knows what else... but now had no memory whatsoever – it was actually terrifying. I was completely alone on the Vineyard, I didn't have a best girlfriend I could call up to ask what the hell had happened last night, and clearly no one I could rely on to get me home safely. I had gone to the bonfire last night to discover more about the Slayton boys, to find out if they knew what had happened to Holly, and here I was not able to even look after myself. Disgust at myself made me want to throw up again. How could I be so stupid?

A picture of Bobby Slayton flashed in my mind, the last person I remembered being with, now he was nowhere to be seen.

I stood up as slowly as I could so as not to make my head pound any harder than it already was and my eyes scoured the sand for my belongings.

I found my flip-flops sticking up out of a mound of sand, made to look as though the person wearing them had been buried. Bending down to pick them up, I felt a sharp scratch inside my knickers – like a pointy label had slipped to a delicate place in-between my legs. I looked around; the beach was deserted and there was no one to see me. I reached inside my knickers to move the offending label and found my fingers closing around a small roll of what felt like paper. I pulled it out, puzzled. What the hell was it? Holding one end, I unrolled the paper, my heart picking up its pace as I read the words on it.

I could have screwed you at any time.

Heat flooded my cheeks and I sat down on the hard sand with a thump. Warm tears began to roll down my cheeks without any warning and within a minute I was sobbing uncontrollably. I had been so stupid thinking that I was in any way different to all the other people taken in by the Slayton brothers, or that I could somehow fly in like a white knight and save my sister. Well, if I ever had the delusion that I was in any way clever, or strong, or that anyone was shaking with fear at the thought of me coming for them, I knew now that I was very, very wrong. Tired, in pain and completely humiliated, I curled up on the sand and cried until I fell asleep once more.

Chapter Thirty-Seven

Claire

'Claire.'

I tried to open my eyes, but sand fell from my lashes into my eyes and mouth, making me splutter and cough. The whole side of my face was itchy and dry and when I tried to sit up, it just made things worse.

'Oh God,' the voice said, and a soft hand began to gently brush sand from the side of my face. All at once, I felt vulnerable, unable to see anything and at the mercy of this person. 'There, you should be able to open your eyes now.'

It was Gina's voice, I realised before I opened my eyes. No more sand fell into them, but my face was still unbearably itchy. The other side of it felt hot to the touch and I realised I was probably sunburned. How long had I been lying there? How many people had stepped over me or walked by me before Gina woke me up? I tried to look around, but the pain in my head and the sunlight piercing my eyes made me double over.

'Come on,' Gina said, and I felt her arm loop through mine. 'My car isn't far. I'll get you back to mine. I found your bag in the parking lot and came looking for you.'

Every inch of me felt as though it was screaming as Gina led me back to her car. My legs, my shoulders, my back – I felt as though I had been in a fight with Tyson Fury and then had the shit kicked out of me afterwards for good measure. Every step was agony. I'm not sure how I made it all the way to the car, but Gina opened the door and helped me onto the back seat where I slumped against the window. I was grateful that she wasn't trying to ask me questions; she just drove in silence for what felt like an hour before pulling up at a ramshackle house surrounded by trees.

'It's not much,' Gina admitted as she opened the door to help me out. 'And I've let it go a bit since Mom and Dad died. But it's somewhere to stay. And I don't get many visitors,' she added, her voice rueful.

I didn't have the energy to reply, and she guided me onto the wooden front porch with its peeling paint and split floorboards and opened the door.

Inside was cool and smelled fresh, despite the piles of junk scattered around – stacks of magazines and newspapers, cardboard boxes, bookcases overflowing with books. It looked as though someone was in the middle of unpacking, but every now and then had stopped to just tip a box on the floor. Despite the clutter, everywhere seemed clean, no dirty dishes on grimy surfaces or piles of actual rubbish.

Gina gave me an apologetic look. 'I've got a lot of sorting out still to do,' she said, although my mind wasn't working fast enough to decide if she meant from her parents leaving or Natalie's death, or that she'd started having a clear-out when a bomb had ripped through the house and she hadn't had a chance to right it yet. 'Can you manage the stairs?' she asked, and I nodded.

She led me through a maze of bin bags labelled 'charity' and to the staircase.

'The bathroom is this door,' she said, indicating to the door at the top of the stairs. 'And this is Nat— um, the spare room, you can get undressed in there. I'll grab you a clean towel and some loose clothes, some skin repair for that sunburn and a glass of water, and I'll be back up.'

'Thank you,' I said, and I realised that it was the first time I had used my voice since last night. It sounded broken and completely alien to me.

Gina held up a hand for me not to speak. 'And some warm milk,' she said, before disappearing back down the stairs.

I pushed open the door to the room she had gestured to and went over to the bed, gingerly lowering myself down. Somewhere in the back of my mind it registered that this had been the bedroom of a fifteen-year-old girl who went out to a party on this island and never came home. The walls were a pale lilac and there were squares of discoloration where it looked as though posters had once been tacked up. A few boxes sat piled up in the corner of the room – it hadn't been left a shrine, but it didn't exactly feel like a spare room either. It should have bothered me more than it did, but at the present moment all I wanted to do was lie down.

As I peeled off my T-shirt and shorts, parts of the last twelve hours edged their way back into my consciousness. Waking up on the bench, finding my flip-flops, not being able to find my bag – Gina said she'd found it, but I hadn't been in any fit state to check if everything was in it. I tried to think about what might be missing... my passport was at Holly's place, and the keys were thankfully in the lockbox on the wall, but my phone and purse were definitely in there. It would be a massive pain in the arse if I'd lost those.

And the last part, before I'd passed out again; the note I'd found rolled up inside my knickers. Had it been inserted inside me? Had Bobby Slayton pushed his little warning inside my private parts just to make his sick point?

Vomit surged up into my throat, but thankfully didn't come any further. I tried not to picture what might have happened, who might have been there and seen what he did to me. I tried not to picture Ryan and their friends laughing as Bobby wrote on the paper, then rolled it up, making lewd gestures as to where he should shove it so I got the point. Tears filled my eyes and I forced myself not to think about how many people had seen which parts of me. The whole thing was a big black hole where my memory should be but I had no doubt that Bobby was to blame. How else would I have blacked out after just one drink? Or had I decided to drink more? The whole evening was a black hole.

Gina tapped lightly on the door and I opened it so she could pass me the towel and the skin repair.

'I'll leave your drinks on the bedside table with some painkillers,' she said. 'I bought your bag up.'

'Thank you,' I whispered, the only thing I could manage without crying. When she left, I checked through my handbag – nothing seemed to be missing, thank God – and wrapped myself in the huge, fluffy towel and made my way across the small landing to the bathroom.

The bathroom was like the rest of the house, clean but in desperate need of some TLC. It was, I thought, what my mum used to call a 'fixer-upper'. A nice enough place that had just been gently neglected until it became almost easier to tear it down and start again. The shower started straight away though, and warmed up quickly. The pressure was low and it coughed and spluttered a bit but the hot water still felt amazing against my aching skin. It burned where it hit my face and I couldn't imagine how ridiculous I looked, like those drumstick sweets that were pink one side and white the other. Still, after ten minutes of standing under the hot spray, I was starting to feel half human again.

I dried myself off and, avoiding the mirror, went back to Natalie's bedroom. Gina had left a loose-fitting, light grey tracksuit on the bed. I'm sure she didn't have any idea how much it resembled the outfits you saw on English crime shows, the ones given to arrestees when their clothes were taken into evidence. Still, beggars couldn't be choosers and I put them on gratefully. I lathered my sore face in the cream she had left for me and took a swig of the water and two of the painkillers. They were an American brand I didn't recognise, but I didn't have the energy to check that they weren't going to make me grow an extra head. As long as it hurt less than the one I currently had, it was all good.

Getting into a stranger's bed and going to sleep in the middle of the day when my sister was still missing was the absolute last thing I wanted to do, but my body literally didn't feel as though it was giving me a choice. Every inch of me felt like a dead weight, I was absolutely exhausted. Whatever I'd been given the night before still hadn't made its way out of my system. I was feeling incredibly vulnerable and lost right now, and all I wanted to do was fly home to Jess and cry, I honestly didn't feel safe here.

I could just rest my eyes for an hour or so, nothing was going to happen in that time. Besides, if I was going to find Holly, I needed to be at the top of my game, and at the moment I didn't feel at the top of anything.

I lay back, closed my eyes and fell quickly and completely into a deep, dreamless sleep.

–

When I woke that evening, I was being shaken, not gently either, but urgently.

'Claire,' Gina's voice sounded desperate. 'Claire, wake up. You need to wake up. Something's going on, at the marina.' I opened my eyes and cringed against the light.

'What is it?'

Gina's face was distraught. 'There's something going on at the marina,' she repeated. 'People are saying they've found a body.'

Chapter Thirty-Eight

Claire

I was awake and out of bed in seconds, then sat back down with a thump. A body found in the marina. A body.

'I… Gina, I…' I was lost for words. If this was my sister, my world was over. I could hardly process the words, the thoughts just a jumble crashing together in my head.

Gina's face was ashen. She looked at me with nothing short of terror, and I realised that my face must have looked the same, the mirror image of this grief-stricken young woman. She knew exactly what this moment was, she had lived it five years before with her own baby sister, and now here she was, reliving it with me. I clung to her arm for comfort, for support, I don't know what for really, but she was the only person I had. It occurred to me that I had never really allowed myself to believe that anything bad had happened to Holly, I had run with the narrative that there would be a logical explanation to her disappearance if only I followed the clues and solved the mystery. Now, upon hearing those words… a body found… I could no longer pretend that it wasn't a possibility. That my sister might be gone forever.

I know that for some families of the missing, those who have been gone months or years, decades even, that the news of a body comes as a welcome relief. Finally they know what happened to their loved one and they can stop wondering, they have closure and their loved one is at peace. I was not ready for that. I absolutely did not crave closure, not unless it came in the form of my little sister knocking on my door with a tan and a pina colada to say that she'd been on a jaunt to Mexico. I was not ready to face that closure might mean identifying my beautiful sister in the county morgue.

'We should go,' Gina said, pulling a black T-shirt and some jeans from a wardrobe. 'Here, you can wear these.'

'Go?' I asked, stupidly. 'Where should we go?'

'To the marina,' she said, as if it were a day trip we'd planned all along. 'Come on.'

'No, no, no, no,' I said, shaking my head. 'I can't go there. I can't see… What if…?'

I couldn't even bring myself to say those words out loud. What if it's her? What if I see my sister being pulled from the water, bloated and hideous, her long blonde hair laced with seaweed, her body half eaten by crabs? The thought was in my mind now, and even if it wasn't Holly in that water, it would forever be seared into my brain.

'No, you're right,' Gina said, sitting down next to me on the bed. Her voice dropped quieter. 'No one should have to see that.'

It hadn't occurred to me that Gina might have been there when her own sister was found. 'Did you… I mean, were you…?'

She shook her head. 'No,' she said. 'It doesn't stop me imagining it though. My dad identified her. He said it was his job, but I always thought that he took it as his punishment – for not keeping her safe.'

'God, I'm so sorry,' I muttered. I looked at her, knowing that she knew exactly how I was feeling now, and that she could sense my terror.

She pulled me into the warmth of her chest and I folded against her as if I was a child, her arms enveloping me as the tears that had threatened me for days came at long last. I knew, in my heart of hearts, that Holly was gone. That I'd failed her. For the first time in eight months, I was glad my mum wasn't here to feel the deep, visceral pain that tore through my chest as I sobbed into Gina's shoulder, tears saturating the thin material of her cardigan. I didn't know how long she held me for, or how long I cried. All I knew was that when the phone call came I had wept myself numb.

Chapter Thirty-Nine

Claire

It was officer Derek Howes who made the call. I don't know if it should have been left to a more senior officer, or if he would get in trouble for breaking the news to me first, but I was glad it was him.

'Claire, I'm at the marina,' he started.

'I heard about what's happened,' I said, not able to bring myself to say the words 'found a body'. 'Is it her? Is that why you're calling me?'

'Officially, it's too soon to say,' he said, sounding like a police officer. Then his voice dropped and he sounded human again. 'But I saw the deceased, and I knew Holly. I'm so sorry, Claire.'

LIAR, I wanted to scream YOU STUPID LYING SON OF A BITCH. But Derek was none of those things. He was a good person, a nice guy and a decent police officer. He wouldn't have called me if he thought for a minute he might be wrong – he wouldn't have put anyone through that lightly.

'Are you with someone?' he asked, and I realised I hadn't said anything, I couldn't say anything. My throat felt as though it had closed up completely – I had no idea how I was still breathing when my heart was so surely dying. My entire body felt heavy, like I'd suddenly had dozens of weighted blankets draped across my shoulders. My arms, my fingers, everything began to go numb. Was I having a stroke? A heart attack? I didn't even feel any physical pain and I welcomed a heart attack if it could stop the emotional pain I was feeling.

I wasn't sure when Gina took the phone from my hand, but somewhere inside my head I heard her voice say that she thought I might be going into shock, should she take me to the emergency room? It sounded funny, a room for emergencies. Yes, this was an emergency, my baby sister was dead and I was never going to see her again. And the last words I ever said to her were to call her selfish. Her, Holly, selfish. When it was me who had been the selfish one, me who hadn't been able to bear the thought of being on my own. And now I was truly on my own. Was there a solution for that in the room for emergencies?

The next part of the day was shrouded in a haze. I remember Gina guiding me out to the car and doing my seat belt up. I remember thinking that it was stupid to do that because seat belts were for saving lives and if we crashed I didn't want to be saved, but I also didn't make any move to undo it, or mention this to Gina.

Holly was dead. Just like that. She had been alive, so completely and utterly alive and then... dead. Not like Mum whose steady decline had been soul-destroying but predictable, prepared for, and by the end a sweet relief. There was no relief in this, only cold, heartbreaking pain.

We didn't go to the emergency room, we drove straight to the police station. Derek apparently had arranged for his friend, a doctor, to meet us there, and I was taken to a light blue room with a painting of sunflowers on one wall and a painting of the Oak Bluffs lighthouse on the other. The officer who ushered us in brought us cups of scalding sugary tea – although I didn't remember being asked how I liked it, or even if I wanted it. I raised it to my lips and blew on it anyway.

Gina sat next to me on the sofa, watching me intently. Her face was a picture of concern and I thought that it must be because I still hadn't said one single word since the call from Derek. I opened my mouth to speak, but I had no idea what could be important enough so I closed it again and looked down at my hands clasping the mug.

'Isn't that hot?' Gina asked, and I noticed that she'd put her drink on the table in front of us. 'Mine's scalding.'

It was as though her saying it had broken some kind of spell, and the mug instantly began to burn in my hands. It happened so quickly that I almost dropped it. I slammed it down on the table, tea spilling over the sides, and Gina gasped.

'Don't worry, I got that.' Derek had been walking through the doorway at the exact moment I'd slammed the cup down, followed by a petite woman with huge glasses that made her look like her eyes were too wide for her face. As Derek stalked away, presumably to get cloths or blue roll, she crossed the room and sat opposite me.

'Derek tells me you've had a shock,' she said, her voice light and soft. It almost sounded as though she was whispering, and I knew that in normal circumstances it would irritate the hell out of me. Now though, when I felt like any loud noise might crack my skull in two, I appreciated it. She frowned. 'Have you burned your hands?'

I looked down at my angry red palms. 'It's fine,' I said, my voice cracking. I tried to clear my throat but couldn't seem to do it.

'Here.' She opened the bag that she'd set down beside her and handed me a tube of something out of it. 'Better rub this on them in case. They look a bit sore.'

I did as I was told, my movements automatic.

Derek returned with a huge roll of paper towel and cleaned up the spilt tea. He sat down next to the doctor and gave me the same look of concern as she and Gina had. All three faces stared at me like the three wise monkeys. I pictured them all lifting their hands and covering their eyes, mouth and ears in turn. It should have made me laugh, but it didn't. It would have made Holly laugh, I knew.

'Claire, the detectives on the case have asked me to come and speak to you before they have to interview you formally,' Derek said, leaning forwards to put his elbows on his knees. 'Just to check you're okay, and to ask if you're up to answering their questions.'

I stared at him for a second. 'It's definitely her then?' I asked eventually. 'You're totally sure? There couldn't be any mistake?'

'That's the other thing they've asked me to do,' Derek said. 'They need a formal identification. They don't want you to go and look at her,' he said quickly as he saw my body stiffen. 'She's been in the water a few days, by the looks of it. It's definitely the body of a young female, and I was able to make an initial identification, but if you'd consent to giving us a DNA sample, we can get a result quicker than applying to the UK for dental records.'

'Yes,' I said. 'Of course.'

'Thank you,' Derek replied. 'It's her though, Claire. I don't want you holding on to any hope.'

Hope. It felt like an alien word that didn't belong in my dictionary. What hope was there now?

'How did she...' I cleared my throat again, hoping that would help the words come out. 'How did she... die?'

Derek shook his head. 'I don't have any information at the moment. We've had to send her off the island for an autopsy – we don't have a coroner here.'

'But there will be an autopsy?' Gina demanded, with all the strength I wish I felt. 'There will be an investigation this time?'

Derek cringed at the words 'this time'.

'That's not up to me, Gina,' Derek said, not taking his eyes off me. 'But I won't stay quiet this time. Even if it costs me my job, I'll make my feelings known.'

I should have been touched at the idea that he would put his job on the line to make sure my sister saw justice, but at that moment justice was the furthest thing from my mind. It didn't occur to me to demand to know who was responsible, or vow to see them behind bars or make them pay. Nothing occurred to me except random thoughts about who would eat my egg whites, or about my sister's smile – not her photo smile, but the one she made when she was unexpectedly, genuinely tickled by something. My heart burst with pride whenever I made her smile that smile.

No, I didn't want justice, or revenge... I just wanted to curl up and die.

Chapter Forty

Claire

The call to Jess had been the hardest thing I'd ever had to do – harder than the day I'd called her to tell her to get to the hospital to say goodbye to Mum, and at the time I never thought I'd have to make a more difficult call than that one. She had screamed out in pure agony and I thanked God that Tom was close by to hold her as she sobbed. He sounded broken when he came on the line.

'Claire.' That one word held so much. Pain, despair, sorrow. 'I'll bring Jess to you straight away. She'll be okay, I promise.'

'Thank you,' I whispered. 'Please hurry.' I ached to see them both, to wrap my arms around my cousin and hold on to the last person I had left.

Two days later we received the confirmation that the body was Holly, and the preliminary autopsy. It showed that my baby sister had been strangled to death. There was evidence of blunt force trauma on the back of her head on the right-hand side, and her blood alcohol level was .18, twice the legal driving limit. Due to the time spent in the water, very little DNA was recovered, nothing under her fingernails, and there were no real signs of a struggle. There were no indications of sexual trauma, and when her body was recovered, she was still wearing her black dress and her underwear, even though they were degraded from the environment. Her feet were missing, and according to Derek it was hypothesised that the water had caused skin slippage to the point that whatever had been used to weigh her down had simply torn them away, allowing her body to surface. I found myself listening to the words as dispassionately as if it were one of the podcasts Holly would always listen to back home while she was doing her hair and make-up. It just didn't seem possible that he could be talking about my beautiful, young, vibrant sister – the idea that someone had put their hands around her neck and looked into her eyes as the life and light left them was unthinkable. So I didn't think about it. I pretended to listen to the details that Derek was reeling off – the detectives assigned to the case had clearly designated him as my liaison officer, but I wasn't ready to hear details about the investigation. I didn't want there to be an investigation, because I didn't want her to be dead.

I nodded in what I expected were the right places and I thanked him for his time. Then I rose from Gina's dining table, picked up the bottle of water she'd been forcing me to carry everywhere, and returned to her dead sister's bedroom. I put in my earbuds and pressed play on the podcast I'd been listening to – something about the royals. I couldn't remember the name, or even repeat a single thing they said, I just needed to block out the screaming inside my head that I had been hearing since Gina had uttered the words 'a body at the marina'.

I couldn't tell you how long I lay there, but it was long enough for Gina to leave a sandwich and a fruit platter outside the door. I ripped the sandwich apart to make it look as though I'd eaten some and tossed it out of the window for the birds. I took the half-empty plate back down and gave her a grateful smile.

'Thanks, Gina, I really appreciate it,' I said, and she looked relieved to see I'd eaten. It couldn't have been easy, taking in a complete stranger and then having to nurse that person through the worst grief they had ever experienced. I owed her a lot, and I was sure she could do with some time and space away from my all-consuming loss. 'I'm going to get some air,' I said, nodding towards the door. 'Do you mind?'

'Not at all,' she said, so quickly that I was sure she had been thinking the same. 'Um, do you want any company?'

'No, thanks, it's fine.' There wasn't anything I wanted to talk about and too much silence just felt weird. Then again, everything felt weird right now. Weird, and painful.

I sat on the beach wall watching people enjoying the beautiful weather as if someone amongst them hadn't had their entire life torn apart. It was quieter than it had been – news of a murder on the island had stunned the community, but it hadn't been enough to stop the holidaymakers enjoying their summer break. Life goes on.

I watched a girl, she looked about nine or ten, running into the surf, jumping the small waves as they broke against the shore. A group of four boys, maybe eleven or twelve years old, walked past and one of them made a comment, not loud enough for me to hear, but the girl obviously did because she straightened up, adjusted her swimsuit and made her way back up the beach to sit on her towel.

The apathy that had held me in its grip since my sister's body had been found shifted at the sight, anger on the girl's behalf slowly seeping in to take its place. Why should a girl so young have to learn how cruel boys could be, how they could make you feel worthless with one comment or a withering look? When would we be taken seriously? Would it be in my lifetime? Well, it wouldn't be in Holly's. How many times would this be allowed to happen? How many Natalies and Hollys would there be? Would I be hearing about another young woman dragged from the marina in five or six years' time?

I looked at the little girl's sad, confused face and I realised that it could be her. Holly could have been any young woman enjoying herself in a place where she should have been safe. We should be safe.

I closed my eyes and tipped my head back slightly, my face warmed by the sun. The smell of the sea and the screech of a seagull pulled me into a memory from just two days ago, although it already felt like another lifetime. A memory of waking on the beach, in pain and confused, not knowing if I had been the victim of a prank or a sexual assault. I'd done nothing to put myself in danger, I'd only had two drinks that night and I was in a public place. I should have been safe. And yet still danger found me. The same kind of danger that had found my sister.

I no longer felt the rush of humiliation at the thought of his fingers inside me as I lay passed out on the bench, neither did I care who else had watched him violate me, egged him on. I felt nothing for my own dignity, as I'd felt nothing for days, but it occurred to me then that he'd done that to me knowing my sister was dead. Bobby Slayton. He was the one I'd been with that night at the beach. Had he hurt Holly? I'd been so concentrated on Ryan but was I wrong, or were they both as evil as each other? I'd been telling myself that none of it mattered, Holly would still be dead whether her killer was brought to justice or not, but of course it mattered. I wanted whoever had done this to pay. Kennedy cousins or not, those Slayton boys had to be stopped.

Chapter Forty-One

Claire

I found Gina in her back garden, watching the waterfall.

'Natalie made Dad put this in,' she said, without turning to face me. 'She was going through a "spiritual" phase. Told us all she was converting to Buddhism. By the time Dad had finished creating her "zen garden", she was pretty much over it.'

I smiled, knowing all too well how younger sisters could be. 'Was your dad annoyed?'

Gina turned to face me, her cheeks wet with tears. 'No way. He'd have dug it all up and put it back the way it was if she'd asked him to.'

'Sounds like a typical little sister,' I said, moving to sit down next to her. 'May I?'

Gina nodded, and shifted over slightly.

'The pain is indescribable,' I said, tears welling up in my eyes. 'Does it get any easier at all? Because this is agony.'

Gina cleared her throat. Her huge brown eyes met mine and she sighed. 'It gets less intense, I think. Right now, it's hit you full force, and you feel like you can't breathe, like the pain is physical and it's gripping your chest and squeezing, and you aren't sure if you can bear it, or how you are going to live like this for the next week, let alone a year, or ten years. But the thing is, at the moment you don't need to live, you just need to survive. Just survive, and survive, until one day, for maybe just an hour, you live. You laugh at something, or you look forward to something. Then you feel the guilt. Guilt that you can still find humour in a world that Holly isn't in. Guilt that you get to appreciate the beauty of a sunset when she doesn't, or that you can share a drink or a meal with someone and not think of her for a given period of time.'

'And then?'

Gina shrugged. 'No idea. Because I'm stuck there, in the guilt stage. I need someone to blame for what happened to her. I thought I knew who was to blame...' She trailed off.

I was confused. Gina had been steadfast in her conviction that one of the Slaytons was responsible for Natalie's death. Was she saying now that she wasn't sure? I thought of the note I had been left and I shook my head. 'What do you mean, you thought? It has to have been Ryan. You saw him with my sister the night she disappeared. Don't tell me that you're giving up now. Your sister needs you. I need you.'

Gina stared into the flowing water, and a single tear rolled down her cheek. After a few minutes' complete silence, she nodded, and wiped the tear away. She took a deep breath. 'I know this has been the worst week of your life,' she said. 'It's been pretty tough on me too.'

'I know. I'm sorry.'

Gina shook her head. 'I'm not trying to make you feel bad. I'm just letting you know that I don't have much left in me. I've been so desperate to get justice for Natalie that I think I've lost sight of what justice is. The grief, the guilt, it's like it warps your perspective on everything. I don't know if I even trust my own judgement anymore. I don't know how much longer I can live with myself.'

I recognised myself in every word she spoke. The guilt I'd experienced over the way I'd spoken to Holly, about how I'd been so dismissive of Jess when she was worried about her, the way I'd left our last conversation. The loss I was feeling when I thought about the fact that I'd had the last conversation I was ever going to have with my sister without even knowing, we'd laughed our last laugh together, we'd shared our last pizza and cried at our last soppy film. The last time we sang to the radio at the top of our voices was the last time we'd ever sing together. The list went on and on. And that's how I knew that when Gina said she didn't know how much longer she could live with herself, I understood, but I never really believed that she meant that she was going to harm herself. Because like me she had made a promise to her sister to restore balance to the world. To get justice and to stop harm coming to another sister, or daughter. She hadn't been able to do it alone, and Holly was the price she had paid, but she wasn't on her own anymore.

'I need you,' I told her. 'And if you ever want to move past the guilt, then you need to make sure that no one else is ever hurt by either one of the Slayton brothers again. That's the only way we can truly show how much we loved our sisters. To make their legacy the safety of every other girl that would have fallen for their charms.'

Gina nodded, the life coming slowly back into her eyes.

'You're right,' she said, taking a deep breath. 'It was down to them. It was always down to them. And now it's down to us to stop them.' She looked at me. 'Don't let me give up, Claire. Don't let me forget who is really responsible.'

Chapter Forty-Two

Claire

We were almost at the house when I saw a familiar red truck in the rear-view mirror. I hadn't seen Bobby Slayton since the night of the party, the night he had given me his sick little warning.

Gina had spotted it as well, I heard her mutter a curse and the car sped up. The Slaytons' truck behind us matched our speed, then sped up a little more so the gap between us closed in even further. I thought back to my first day on the island, when the Slaytons and their friends had played chicken, nearly running me off the road in the process. I knew then that they were trouble. Why hadn't Holly?

'He's got some fucking nerve,' Gina spat, all her focus on the truck behind her. I almost warned her to keep her eyes on the road ahead, but my apathy for my own life hadn't subsided enough.

'Forget him,' I said quietly, but she wasn't listening. She slowed right down so that the truck was almost upon us, then sped up again. It felt so ridiculous, the idea of a tiny little car like this one taking on their beast of a truck, like a fly trying to knock down a bear.

'He thinks he rules this place,' she muttered. 'He thinks he can do whatever he wants, treat people however he wants…' She swung sharply to the left and slammed on her brakes, then, as Bobby's truck came speeding up alongside us, she turned the wheel to the right, ramming the side of the truck. I saw Bobby's mouth open in surprise and in the passenger seat Ryan stared at me.

Bobby slammed on his brakes and Gina did the same. They were in the middle of the road and I watched the door of Bobby's truck swing open and Bobby jump out and come striding towards us. Gina opened her door and got out, her face hard and defiant. It crossed my mind ever so briefly that she might have a gun. How easy it would be to take him out here, in the middle of the road, and make sure he never hurt another girl again. But that wouldn't be justice, and Gina would end up the one in prison and my sister would still be gone. What was Bobby Slayton's death going to change about that?

'What the fuck do you think you're playing at?' he yelled as they met like cowboys at high noon.

'You were the one driving like a fucking lunatic,' I think Gina replied, but I couldn't hear her as well as I'd heard Bobby.

Ryan had stayed in the truck, but when I climbed out of the car I saw him look at me in the wing mirror.

Bobby saw me and for a moment he looked almost nervous. I must have looked as bad as Gina kept telling me I did; dark circles under my eyes, no make-up, hair pulled back into a tight ponytail.

'I'm sorry about Holly,' he called over to me.

I glanced at Ryan, who closed his eyes and turned his head.

'Are you?'

His eyes widened slightly. 'Of course I am.' He dropped his voice and looked over at where Ryan was sitting, stony-faced, in the truck. 'We should talk some-where. Properly. Alone.'

I'd almost forgotten how handsome he was, how much he made you just want to believe every word he said, to gain his approval, earn a smile. Men who looked like him were so, so dangerous. And to a woman like Holly, young and idealistic, someone who believed in love and romance... he would have been lethal. Even now it was hard to deny him his request, even knowing what he had most likely done.

'You want me to give you the benefit of the doubt, right?' I said, as he held up his hands. Strong, masculine hands that had, in all probability, slipped inside my under-wear and pushed a rolled-up piece of paper into me. A warning. Hands that had— God, it made me retch just to think it. Had those hands strangled the life out of my sister? Had he been reeling me in all along, making me think he was in love with Holly when he was to blame for her death?

'I just want to talk to you.'

'Like we talked at the bonfire. When you drugged me and sexually assaulted me.'

Bobby's eyes widened instantly in shock.

My breath caught in my chest. Hell, he looked almost genuinely shocked. He glanced at Ryan again.

'I didn't do anything like that,' he said, looking from me to Gina and back at me again. 'Why would you say that? I don't understand – did she tell you I did that? Surely you can see how obsessed she is with me and my family?'

Gina flew forwards like a wild alley cat. I grabbed her arm; she was strong. 'If it wasn't for you, my sister would still be alive!'

233

Bobby exhaled and shook his head. 'I've told you a million times, Gina, I had nothing to do with what happened to your sister.'

'One of you had sex with her! She was fifteen years old!'

Bobby's expression darkened. 'I. Did. Not. Have. Sex. With. Your. Sister,' he said, anger punctuating his every word. 'She got into Ryan's car and Ryan took her home. I was with Harry and Nathan the whole time. Why would I lie?'

Gina looked unsettled, but before she could say any more, Bobby looked at me.

'Please,' he said, his eyes pleading. 'Just let's talk. Do you have a pen? I'll give you my number.'

'She doesn't want to listen to your lies and she doesn't need your number,' Gina spat, this time taking my arm.

I didn't move immediately, I just watched Bobby standing there and wondered why his brother hadn't even stepped out of the car.

'Please,' Bobby mouthed.

I hesitated, then turned to follow Gina back to her car, leaving him standing there, watching us drive away.

Chapter Forty-Three

Claire

Jess and Tom arrived on the Vineyard three days after Holly's body was recovered. Seeing them was a relief and a heartbreaking moment all at once. Suddenly, *my* world had collided with this strange new world and it rammed home that this was real. There would be no flying home to give them the good news that Holly was safe and fine.

I met them at the Vineyard Haven Airport on a beautifully warm day, sunlight beaming down on us as if the weather had no respect for our grief or loss. The brilliant blue sky cared little that our world was completely broken. Jess ran to embrace me the minute we caught sight of one another and to an outsider we could have been sisters escaping the nine-to-five for a summer of love. Until you saw the tears of grief and loss that streamed down our cheeks, and then Tom was upon us, holding us both tightly.

'I'm so sorry,' Jess whispered, over and over. The relief burst inside me at the sound of her voice, the smell of her hair, the scratchy feel of her familiar camel-coloured coat. Gina stood behind me; she had barely left my side for three days and I was more grateful than she'd ever know, but she hadn't known my sister, and although she had suffered her own loss, she had never suffered the grief of losing Holly. For that I needed Jess.

'What will we do?' I asked her, my eyes searching hers for the answers I desperately needed. 'What will we do without her?'

'Don't think about that,' Jess said, her eyes blazing furiously. 'First, we have to nail the motherfucker who did this.'

I didn't know if it was hearing my dainty blonde cousin say the word 'motherfucker' or if it was the fact that she was finally here and her fierce defiance against grief was exactly what I needed, but for the first time since the horrific discovery, I actually laughed. Gina was right, I felt awful immediately and my laughter died on my lips, transforming into more sobs as fast as it came.

Jess grabbed hold of the back of my head and held her forehead to mine. 'Laugh,' she said fiercely. 'Don't let yourself stop living. Holly would hate that so much.'

I pulled away and nodded, wiping salty tears from my face. 'This is Gina, who I told you about on the phone.'

Jess moved forwards to embrace Gina, who looked mildly surprised but hugged my cousin back as though they were long-lost friends. We were all united in this, in this awful experience, in the loss of someone so close to us, and now in the determination to bring Holly's killer to justice.

'I'm sorry for your loss,' Jess said to her when they broke apart.

'And me for yours,' Gina replied.

'We rented a place in West Tisbury,' Tom told me. 'We figured you might want to get out of town a bit.'

West Tisbury was far more rural than Edgartown and Oak Bluffs, the never-ending coastline replaced with rolling trees and grazing sheep. On the drive, Tom told us about an agricultural fair, art galleries and an annual film festival, but I tuned him out after a while. I texted Emmy to ask her to meet us at the rental house. I'd promised to keep her involved – she'd taken the discover of Holly's... of Holly really badly and I think it did her good to be around us.

West Tisbury was beautiful, much like every inch of the island that I'd seen so far. I wished more than anything that I'd come with Holly in the first place – although she'd never really made that seem like an option. She came here to find adventure and, even if just for the shortest time, that's what she'd done. She'd lived more here than she'd ever lived at home, and even though she'd paid the price, the thought that her last weeks had been spent here living her life to the fullest did bring me some peace.

Tom and Holly knew something about Natalie's death – they had read the official news reports from the time – but they had no idea about the unofficial story, about the underage boys who had driven away with Natalie, or about their connections to one of the most powerful families in the country.

'If you saw Ryan and Holly together on the night she was... on the night she went missing,' Jess asked when Gina had finished. 'Then why haven't you told the police? I know you said they didn't believe you about Natalie, but this is the second time – they'd have to believe you now.'

The five of us were around the dining-room table of the rental in West Tisbury. Me, Gina, Jess, Tom and Emmy.

Gina looked at me, embarrassment showing on her face.

'It's fine,' I told her. 'Jess is the last person to judge. She once called in a bomb scare to a restaurant to ruin her ex-boyfriend's new date.'

Jess scowled. 'Hey, there'll be another bus along in ten minutes if you want to get ready to throw me under that too.'

For just that second, it was like it had always been between us. Only usually Holly was sitting laughing with us too.

'Gina has been known to, um… make her feelings towards the Slaytons known, shall I say?'

Gina shrugged. 'You may as well pull the plaster off. I've basically stalked and harassed the Slaytons for five years.'

'With good reason,' I added. 'You were the only one who kept fighting for your sister. Now you have us.'

She looked at me with a gratitude I didn't deserve yet. Maybe if I got our baby sisters justice then I would.

'So the police are likely to think you're just making it up to frame Ryan,' Tom said.

'Which I'm not,' Gina put in.

'I really don't know how to ask this without causing massive offence,' Tom began. 'But how do we know you're not? If no one else saw them together…'

'I did,' Emmy said suddenly.

I turned to look at her. 'Wait, what?'

'I saw them getting into his truck. I didn't want to say anything before because at first I thought she was just going to come back and she'd be furious at me for getting her in trouble with Ryan. Then you showed up and I didn't know what to say, so I just said that I didn't see her with anyone.'

I clamped my back teeth together to try to stop myself from saying something I would regret. Even if Emmy had raised the alarm earlier, or told me the truth up front, I wouldn't have been able to save my sister, I was certain that she'd died on the night of the party, so I had to let go of the what ifs. Emmy had her reasons for not telling the truth, and although they didn't exactly make sense to me, I didn't want to alienate the one person who might be able to help us get justice. I took a deep breath. See, personal growth. If only I'd managed that before I spoke my last ever words to my sister.

'Would you tell the police this?' I asked, my voice even and calm.

Emmy nodded and relief flooded through me. I let out a sigh and Gina did the same.

'Then hopefully that will be enough to get a warrant to search his boat, or at least his truck,' I said. 'They might find something to prove she was in there.'

'I'll go to the station now,' Emmy said. 'Any longer and they'll wonder why I waited.'

As am I, I thought, but said nothing.

'I'll drop you off, I need to go to the supermarket,' Gina said. 'Do you guys want anything?'

I shook my head. 'Not for me, thanks. Jess and Tom will be needing some rest,' I said, noticing how shattered they looked and how relieved they were when I said that. They'd booked a rental with three rooms, but I had little doubt they would be staying in a room together. I was glad. For the first time in a long time, I wished I had a man to turn to myself, someone to give me some deeper comfort than a hug from Jess and Gina. Maybe Holly had been right about that too. 'I'm going to go for a walk.'

'I could at least use a shower,' Jess said. 'And a cup of tea. Would you mind grabbing us some milk please, Gina?'

Gina nodded and I gave both her and Emmy a hug as they left together. It occurred to me that I didn't know how well they knew one another — I hoped the car journey wouldn't be awkward.

I pulled on my trainers and left Tom and Jess to some time alone. If the police took Emmy seriously, things were about to start happening.

Chapter Forty-Four

Claire

Derek phoned me first thing the next morning with news. I knew instantly it must be about Emmy's statement because I'd never heard him sound so excited.

'We had a witness place Ryan and Holly together on the night of the party,' Derek said. 'She was seen getting into his truck. We just had a judge in Boston sign a probable cause search warrant – we have permission to search the truck.'

I blew out a sigh of relief. 'And the boat?'

Derek paused. 'Not yet. If we find evidence of her in his truck, then we might get the boat. We've got a dive team going out in the marina looking for other evidence. They're hoping to find—' He stopped short, as if remembering who he was talking to.

'You can say it, Derek, I'm not going to have another breakdown. They're hoping to find her feet.' I couldn't believe I was saying those words about my little sister, but Jess had been right when she'd said there would be a time to grieve, and a time to get justice. It was like that had opened up a space in my mind that I could shove all of my grief and hysteria into until the job was done.

'Well…' Derek faltered. 'Mostly we'd like to find what weighted them, and her, down. If it's an object from the

Slaytons' boat, then I really don't see how he can get out of it.'

There had been something niggling at me all night last night, after Gina had returned with some snacks and Jessica's milk, and she'd confirmed that she'd dropped Emmy off at the police station. Something about Emmy's story just didn't sit right, and it was now, hearing from Derek that reminded me what it was.

'Derek, do you know who the witness is who has placed Ryan and Holly together?' I asked him.

'No, not yet,' he said, confirming my suspicion. 'I just got word from one of the others about the PCSW. Why?'

I couldn't say why, not yet. And I wasn't sure what was going to happen when he found out. Because if the first story Emmy had told me – the one about how she had left Holly while she went off with Derek – was the truth, then Derek would know that Emmy couldn't have seen Holly get into Ryan's truck, because if she had, Derek would have seen it too. I didn't know why Emmy had changed her story now, or why she had decided to lie to place Ryan and Holly together, and I wouldn't like to bet that Derek was going to back her story up.

–

The search warrant on Ryan and Bobby's truck was executed at two p.m. on Saturday 19 July, less than two weeks after Officer Waylans had told me my sister was probably shacked up with some guy somewhere. I was fortunate enough to watch it all play out, thanks to Derek giving me the heads-up on when the police were planning to go into the garage Ryan had taken the truck to for repair after his run-in with Gina. They went in with a forensics team, Ryan and his father only turning up twenty minutes after they had started their search. The garage owner must have alerted them to what was going on, but thanks to the warrant, the police hadn't needed the owner of the truck present and by the time Ryan and his father – closely followed by their lawyer – showed up, the police had already taken away a full box of evidence. I hadn't been able to get close enough to see what was in it, but at one point there had been a flurry of activity, excited raised voices and a lot of talking into radios. It took all my restraint not to run under the cordon and risk arrest to see what was going on.

Please have something, I muttered, over and over. *Please have something.*

I'd listened to enough true crime podcasts to know that if Derek decided to dispute Emmy's claim that she saw Holly and Ryan leaving together, then this warrant would be overturned, and all the evidence gleaned from it would be inadmissible. Did that mean that if they got a warrant for the boat as a result of this search then that would crumble under cross-examination? None of it made Ryan Slayton innocent, but a good lawyer – and he would, of course, have a good lawyer – would have the trial thrown out in a heartbeat and Ryan would walk away a free man.

I had to know if Emmy had really seen them leave the party together, but part of me was too afraid to ask. If I found out that Emmy really was lying what difference would it make? Gina had definitely seen them together. So we weren't lying *exactly*, we were just lying about which one of them had seen Holly and Ryan together. And that was a small indiscretion compared to the lie after lie that the Slaytons had told. Every last one of them was to blame for my sister's death – if they hadn't protected one another so fiercely after what had happened to Gina's sister, then Ryan would already have been in prison and my sister would be alive. I wanted to hold every one of them to account, and perhaps there would come a day when the rest of the family would see themselves in court. Maybe it would be in a civil court, rather than a criminal one, but one way or another, I would have my pound of flesh. One way or another.

Chapter Forty-Five

BREAKING NEWS

Ryan Slayton, son of Laurence Slayton and nephew of Robert Kennedy Jr, was arrested today on suspicion of murdering twenty-two-year-old Brit, Holly Matthews in a shocking move that has stunned the residents of summer paradise, Martha's Vineyard. Matthews was found three weeks ago in the Oak Bluffs marina, her body believed to have been thrown into the water on the last night she was seen alive, based on accounts of a couple moored at Oak Bluffs who saw the boat belonging to the Slaytons leave the harbour and return a short while later in the early hours of the morning.

The Slaytons, who own a holiday home and have several boats moored on the island, are said to be 'shocked and disappointed' at the move by Oak Bluffs PD, which occurred in the early hours of this morning. Sources close to the family say that they are supporting Ryan 'one hundred per cent' and are sure that the misunderstanding will be rectified in due course. Vineyard PD, however, are confident in their arrest, citing in the probable cause affidavit 'substantial DNA evidence found on clothing believed to have been worn by the victim', as well as the 'fingerprints of the accused found on personal items belonging to the victim'. No more details have been released by the police at this stage, and the arrest warrant makes no mention that the police believe there was anyone else involved in Ms Matthews' death.

Chapter Forty-Six

Claire

Arrested.

I'd started running the weekend after my sister's body had been found. She would have found that hilarious – nothing short of the murder of a loved one could have forced me into running shoes and out of the house at five a.m. Before, if I'd been awake that early, it was because I hadn't been to sleep. The first time I'd pulled on a pair of Holly's trainers and run off in the direction of Lighthouse Beach, I'd felt as though my lungs might collapse, but it was good pain. Pain that made me feel alive. And it was focusing on that pain that took my mind off what was going on in real life, the waiting by the phone for news, the whispers and the rumours, the inquisitive looks, the pitying looks, the disdainful looks. Everyone on the island had an opinion about what had happened to my sister, and they weren't all entirely flattering. But that was the thing; I couldn't see those looks when my feet were pounding the street or the sand. It looked glamorous on TV, but running on sand was ten times harder than on the pavement.

It was ironic, then, that while I was avoiding sitting by the phone waiting for news, the news came in. Jess, Tom, Gina and Emmy were all in the front yard – Jesus, I was even starting to sound like an American – when I rocked up to Holly's house, sweating and panting. My face was bright red and I leaned over to catch my breath.

'What?' I gasped, straightening up and looking at each of them in turn. 'What is it?'

I knew it must be important, for all four of them to make the drive over here. Tom, Jess and I were still staying in West Tisbury. Jess had managed to arrange for a duty manager to look after the business, but I knew she needed to get back to it soon. I could see Gina's car and my rental car – which I'd driven over in – which meant that Gina had driven to West Tisbury to pick Tom and Jess up and come back to Edgartown to wait for me outside of Holly's apartment. I'd been there to check on the place and to finish packing up the rest of her things to have them sent home – the police had said they had everything they thought they needed.

'You tell her,' Jess said to Gina, a huge smile on her face. There was only one thing that would make her smile through her grief in that way…

'Ryan was arrested this morning,' Gina said, the words spilling out excitedly. 'Suspicion of murder. Murder, Claire. We did it.'

We had done very little, as a matter of fact. Emmy, of course, had done the most in making a witness statement to the police to say that she saw Ryan and Holly leaving the party together. A search of his truck had, according to Derek, revealed Ryan's red sweater – the idiot had been so arrogant in his belief that he was untouchable that he hadn't even bothered getting rid of it, instead stashing it under the passenger seat in a plastic bag. Forensics found Holly's hair, blood and trace evidence of Ryan's semen on the jumper.

Still, it felt very much like a victory. We had talked about when this might happen – if it ever did – and we knew that it was only the beginning. He would be held for questioning, then if he was charged there would be a trial. The Slaytons still had deep pockets and good lawyers and there was an awful lot of work to be done. But the detectives on the case had read the local feeling, and picked up on the interest of the media both here and back home in the UK, and they knew that if it had been easy to sweep Ryan's involvement in Natalie's murder under the carpet five years ago, it was not going to go so smoothly this time. The public wanted answers, and after the MeToo movement and all that had followed, the world was more willing to hold public figures and wealthy benefactors to account. Derek had introduced myself and the Holly Squad – yes, that was our silly little name for ourselves, Holly would have loved it and eye rolled in equal measure – to the detectives in charge and they had been doing everything they could to keep us informed without jeopardising the chance of a fair trial.

'How do you know?' I asked, my breathing returning back to normal after my run, but my heart still pounding from this new news.

'Derek called me,' Emmy said. 'He tried to call you but got no answer. He wanted us to hear from him before the news, but the press got hold of it almost instantly.'

'Good,' I said, my voice firm. 'Let everyone know. It gives them less hope of covering it up this time. I want everyone to know what he did to her.'

My voice sounded stronger than I felt. I knew the reaction to this would be huge, and I would have some work to do. In the three weeks since we had decided that justice for Holly, and hopefully for Natalie, was the only acceptable result, we'd been working on getting her name everywhere we possibly could. We'd made groups on social media, we'd tweeted and cheeped and neighed and whatever other noises we needed to make in order that everyone in the country and beyond knew my sister's name. I'd phoned and emailed every true crime podcast and given interview after interview, but never once had I been able to point the finger in the direction it deserved to go. Until there was an arrest, I hadn't been willing to jeopardise the police's case by pointing to Ryan. While he thought no one was looking his way, he would get sloppy and lazy. And he did, if that jumper was anything to go by.

'Here, look.' Jess handed me her phone and I scrolled down, reading the report of Ryan's arrest. I frowned. 'It says fingerprints on her personal items,' I said, re-reading the sentence several times.

'They found her phone,' Emmy said, her voice slightly squeaky with excitement. 'They found Holly's phone and it had Ryan's fingerprints on it. Derek said that is absolutely top secret,' she added.

I let out a breath. Blood, semen and fingerprints. The unholy trinity. What else could they possibly need?

'There's more,' Gina said, her voice level. 'They apparently have a couple who saw the Slaytons' boat go out into the marina in the early hours of Saturday morning. They didn't see who was driving it or what they were doing, but they said it only went about half an hour out then came back. And that morning, Ryan cleaned the deck.'

'Carl has testified to say that he saw Ryan cleaning the deck of his boat too,' Emmy added. 'And he said in his statement that the Slaytons absolutely never cleaned their own boat.'

That was that then. We had them.

So why was I still so unsure?

Chapter Forty-Seven

Claire

FOURTEEN MONTHS LATER

The last of the summer sun beat down on the back of my neck as I descended the steps of the small plane onto the asphalt. I saw the familiar face straight away, looking up at me, hand to her eyes as she shielded them from the sun.

'Claire!' Gina called, waving her arms back and forth. 'Jess!'

Jess let out a low whistle, and I immediately understood why. The transformation in Gina was astounding. Her long dark hair had a glossy, textured look now, and it had been cut into choppy layers around her face. A face which no longer looked drawn, waxen and pallid, but tanned, pink-cheeked and healthy. She had put on weight too, gentle curves where jutting pronounced hip bones had been the first time I'd met her.

'You look amazing,' I told her, pulling her into an embrace.

'So do you,' she said, and I knew what she was thinking. I looked sober, and healthy and I was. In the year that had followed Holly's death, I had quit my job at the bar and the lifestyle that went with it. I'd stopped drinking ever since the night at Left Fork and instead had thrown myself into renovating Mum's house for sale. I'd made such a decent amount on it that I'd been able to buy a second property for development and I was in the middle of flipping that. I hadn't bought myself another house to live in yet, I hadn't decided if I wanted to stay in one place or not. Instead I'd sold most of my possessions and rented a small but comfortable cottage.

'What about me?' Jess asked, pretending to pout.

'Terrible,' Gina said.

'Awful,' I agreed. We all burst out laughing, something Gina had promised I would do again one day, and she had been right. The guilt was still there sometimes – mostly that I couldn't have been this better version of myself for Holly rather than because of her death. But Jess reminded me daily that we owed it to both Holly and Mum to live life as much, and as well as we could.

Don't get me wrong, it had been a hellish year. After Ryan's arrest and subsequent charging, I'd decided to go home with Jess, knowing that I wouldn't be able to do any more until the trial, which wouldn't be for another year. Touching down on British soil without my sister, over a month after flying out to look for her was almost too much to bear. I'd broken down in the car on the way home, and again when I'd had to walk into my family home without my family. So many times over the past year, I'd wanted to hit the bottle and I knew that no one would blame me – I was supposed to fall apart after all, the worst thing that could happen to me had happened, it would be more unusual if I coped well and got on with my life. But I've never enjoyed doing what was expected of me, and if there was one thing I could give to Holly, and to Mum, it was to live the life they would have been proud of me for. So instead of reaching for the bottle, I reached for Holly's running shoes. They had become almost like my lucky charm, like my little sister was with me every time my foot hit the floor. And still, despite my sobriety and my work achievements, I would give it all back and be wasting away drunk in a bar just to speak to my sister one more time, just to tell her I was sorry for not supporting her, and I loved her more than she would ever know.

I couldn't turn back the clock and give her that, but I was going to try to give her the only thing I could now. Justice.

'Are you ready?' Gina asked, and I knew she didn't just mean for the short journey to her house, where we would be staying for a couple of nights. She meant for the trial, which started in Boston, in three days' time.

We could have gone straight to Boston, like Tom had done, but Jess and I had wanted to come back to the island, to feel near Holly. It was funny that I should feel closer to my sister in a place where we had never been together than I did anywhere in the UK.

I took a deep breath. 'Not really,' I admitted.

Ryan Slayton had continued to plead his innocence over the last year, but in the lead-up to the trial and without anything new to report, the news had become stale and then moved on. So far, there had been no problems with the warrants or probable cause documents and even though his lawyers had sought to have them overruled, Derek had assured us that wouldn't happen. No judge wants to overrule another judge's verdict without a damn good reason. With the trial starting, though, it would be hot news all over again, and I wasn't kidding myself that it would all be plain sailing.

'I had dinner with Emmy and Derek last week,' Gina said as we drove towards Oak Bluffs. I remembered the first time I had made this journey, irritated at my little sister for making me travel halfway across the world just to tell her to answer her phone. It hurt to think that she was already gone the first time I saw the beautiful Vineyard coastline, or smelt the sea air.

'How are they?' I asked.

'I think they're going to move in together after the trial,' Gina said. I smiled. Holly would have been so pleased for them. 'They would have loved to have met you here, but they went to Boston yesterday to prepare.'

To prepare to be the star witness for the prosecution, I thought. Even after all this time, with a year to reflect on the consequences of our actions, I couldn't bring myself to care that Emmy was going to lie under oath for us. We weren't framing an innocent man; we were making sure a guilty man saw justice. And it didn't just hinge on Emmy's testimony – there was the DNA evidence on Holly's bloodied clothes and his fingerprints on her phone – which I later discovered they had found buried on the edge of the Slayton property after a tip-off. Not to mention Carl's testimony that he had seen Ryan cleaning his boat the day after the party, and the couple who had seen him taking it out in the early hours.

There was a part of me, though, the smallest part, which still wondered how Derek felt about his girlfriend lying to the police. He must have known that she didn't see my sister and Ryan leave together, he was with Emmy after all. Had she convinced him that she'd seen them as he drove away from the bonfire? Had he chosen to believe the woman he was falling for? Or had Derek decided that the evidence was so strong that it was worth the smallest of lies?

One thing was certain, and it was the only thing that continued to plague my nightmares. If Derek Howes had an attack of conscience before Emmy took the witness stand, the whole house of cards would come toppling down and Ryan Slayton would get away with murder again.

Chapter Forty-Eight

Claire

I could say I don't know why I kept Bobby's number for that year, or why I dialled it that day, but I do. I needed answers, and I was certain Bobby could help me. Turned out, I was right, just not in the way I'd thought.

I'd imagined that he would have changed his number by now, after all the media circus that had surrounded his brother's arrest, so I was surprised when it rang, and even more surprised when he answered. It was Bobby's turn to be shocked though, when I told him who was calling.

'I'm in Boston,' he said. Of course he was – he was preparing for the trial. It only took me an hour and a half to get there on the ferry. Just ninety minutes after making the call, I was sitting on a park bench next to Bobby Slayton. He had on a baseball cap pulled down low and I wondered how much of his time he spent trying not to be recognised these days. His blue eyes didn't sparkle in the same way now either, he looked defeated, diminished.

'Why did you agree to meet me?' I asked.

'Curiosity,' he admitted. 'Why did you call me?'

I took a sip of the strong Boston coffee I'd picked up on the way and waited a minute to answer. 'I'm not convinced we have the whole truth,' I said eventually. Me having doubts didn't mean Ryan was innocent. He was, in all likelihood, as guilty as he looked. But if not, it was possible I was sitting next to a killer, baiting him.

'I didn't kill Holly, Claire.'

My breath froze in my chest. I hadn't expected him to come out with it so brazenly.

'Did Ryan?'

Bobby shook his head. He sat forwards on the bench, watching a jogger go by, then turned to me. 'I think so, yeah.'

Well, that was unexpected.

'Because of the evidence?' I asked.

'They have her blood and his semen on the jumper she was wearing. His fingerprints on her phone. The GPS data shows them on the boat together that night, and then Holly's phone going on and off near our house. It was buried on our property. How much more do you need?'

'More,' I whispered. Tears filled my eyes. Damn, I'd promised myself I wasn't going to cry. 'I don't know why, but it's not enough.'

'It's never going to be enough for you,' Bobby said. 'Because you want the unimaginable imagined. You want to know why her, why she went with him, why she had sex with him, why he killed her. Even if she'd woken up and said she was too drunk to consent, no one would have believed her. Ryan has got away with worse. So why did he feel he had to take her life? And to that I'd say because he could.'

It was a horrific thing to have to admit about your brother, and I watched the pain on his face as he said it.

'You said he'd got away with worse,' I commented, my voice gentle. 'Tell me, Bobby. Tell me what happened to Natalie.'

I thought he was going to get up and walk away, but he sat back on the bench and folded his arms across his chest, as though he wanted to keep the words in. He took a deep breath.

'Natalie had been drinking that night. Far too much. She was throwing herself at me – I was eighteen years old and I had plenty of girls my own age interested in me. I didn't need or want to be messing around with a fifteen-year-old, but she was determined. She said I'd been flirting with her all summer, when I thought I'd just been nice to some kid with a bit of a crush. She was getting louder and more insistent that I'd led her on – she was going to get me into trouble. I didn't want to be alone with her, so I put her in Ryan's car and told him to take her home, and I'd meet him back at ours. The lads were saying they would probably hook up and instead of going straight back to ours they followed them. I told them not to be assholes, that Ryan wouldn't take advantage of a kid like that, but, well, Ryan was just a kid himself, not quite seventeen yet. Sixteen-year-old boys are idiots, Claire, there's no excuse for it, but it's true. When we caught up to them, Ryan was pulled up on the side of the road, the passenger door was open and he was having sex with Natalie on the front seat.'

I swallowed hard. Finally, I was getting the truth and it hurt to hear it. What Bobby was describing, that was rape.

'What happened next?' I asked, almost not wanting to know.

'Natalie stood up and adjusted her dress, she looked fine. She wasn't upset or angry or anything, he hadn't been forcing her. She didn't even look as drunk as she had before, although she couldnt've sobered up that quickly, I guess. She asked if she could see him again and he said yes, he'd call her. I think he might have actually liked her. It would've been fine…' He tailed off, inspecting his hands intently.

'But?' I prompted.

'But then she called him Bobby. As soon as she did it, the lads burst out laughing at him and said she'd only screwed him because she thought he was me. I shoved them back into the car and told Ryan to get Natalie home quickly. We followed him most of the way, and he definitely went past the turn-off for the marina and towards her house. He met us back at the house and the next thing we knew the cops were turning up asking questions about Natalie.'

'And how did Ryan seem?'

'He didn't seem concerned that she wasn't at home, he said he'd dropped her there and she couldn't have got far. He looked genuine. I believed him at first. When she was found, the whole thing hit him quite badly.'

'At first?'

His jaw clenched and unclenched. 'I gave him the benefit of the doubt,' he said. 'But I think I always knew. He'd asked me about CCTV in the marina before her body showed up, and I found him googling GHB after death. Now, after Holly…' Bobby sighed. 'He's my brother, Claire, and I love him. But your sister was beautiful, funny and sweet. I barely knew her, but I know she didn't deserve what happened.'

'Neither did Natalie,' I said, my voice harsher than I intended it to be.

He shook his head quickly. 'I didn't mean it like that. But I feel responsible for what happened to Holly. If I'd told the police, or Mum and Dad my suspicions about Ryan...'

'They'd still have covered it up,' I said. I wasn't sure why I was trying to make him feel better. Not for the first time, I found myself wanting to believe that he was a good person. He was handsome and charming, and the way he spoke about my sister, I wanted to believe that all that was true and that he wasn't just playing me to try to win me over.

'The bonfire party, on the beach. You drugged me. You...' I still couldn't bring myself to say the words, but I had to see his reaction. 'You left me a note. In my underwear.'

He looked genuinely surprised now – probably the most genuine I'd seen him look. 'I have no idea what you're talking about,' he said, looking me in the face. 'You barely drank anything that night. We didn't even stay that late. You said you were going to get something to eat and I dropped you at Remmy's to get take-out. It was a couple of minutes from where you were staying, and you said you'd walk back.'

I tried to pull back the memory of that night, but there was just nothing. Bobby's story sounded so plausible, but I hadn't imagined waking up on the beach, or the horrible warning that had awaited me. If not Bobby, then who?

'You could ask Carl,' Bobby said suddenly. 'Him and Stacy were there when I dropped you off, getting food.'

Chapter Forty-Nine

Claire

I left the park as a swirling bag of emotions, drained from the hour I'd spent talking to Bobby. I'd told Jess I was going for a swim – it was easier to fake than running, all it took was a bottle of water to wet my hair and swimsuit and shove my damp suit and towel on the back seat of the rental for her to spot. Besides, Jess had no reason to think I'd lie to her. Tom might be a bit savvier – he was still having his steak every Wednesday.

I knew I should leave things alone. Ryan was going to trial in a couple of days and he was going to say that he was innocent. The jury would either believe him or not, but there was nothing I could do to change any of that. If I started telling people now that I'd suddenly had a change of heart and had doubts, they'd think I was as crazy as they'd all branded Gina. Gina who had finally been vindicated in her years of insisting Natalie's death was no accident. People were already comparing Ryan to Ted Bundy, purely because of how sweet and wholesome-looking he was, how charming. Imagine the headlines: Killer charms victim's sister into thinking he's innocent.

But it wasn't in my nature to leave well enough alone – it never had been.

I'd learned from keeping in touch with Derek, Emmy and Gina the last fourteen months that Carl had quit as harbour master and taken up renovating furniture from his home workshop in Oak Bluffs. I guess two murdered girls in five years can make you lose your love for a place. My sister's death had hit the island hard – I think that everyone wanted to believe it was Ryan because he wasn't a local, and that lent a degree of separation to what he'd done, but at the same time the Slayton family were so well known, so ingrained in the culture of the island, that the separation was in name only, all for show. It had rocked the entire community of Oak Bluffs, and the shockwaves had been felt over the other towns too.

Carl's home was on Ocean Avenue, in a row of colourful houses that looked as though they had been designed on The Sims, all facing a beautiful expanse of shoreline.

Carl answered the door almost immediately. He looked exactly the same as he had a year before, except a little thinner perhaps, and his jaw was covered in stubble. It actually suited him.

'Claire,' he said, holding out his hand. I admit to being a bit surprised at the warmth of his greeting – he'd been one of the more hostile locals when I had been searching for Holly. What he said next went a way to explain why. 'I'm glad to see you. I always felt bad about how we didn't believe anything had happened to Holly. I wished I'd been more help. Stacy didn't want anyone to know about the fight they'd had – she was embarrassed enough at the way she'd behaved – but it didn't seem strange to us that she hadn't turned up for work. We weren't expecting her to, in all honesty.'

'It's fine,' I said, waving a hand. 'It wouldn't have made much difference; the police are certain that Ryan Slayton killed her the night of the bonfire.'

I watched his reaction closely, but it wasn't any different to anybody else's when Ryan was mentioned. A scowl.

'I had them put new cameras in at the marina before I quit,' he said, rubbing a hand over his face. He shrugged. 'Some people didn't like their privacy being invaded, but there weren't any real complaints, just a few mutterings. And when Ryan Slayton goes to prison for life we'll all feel a little safer.'

'I actually came to ask you something about Bobby Slayton,' I said, and he instantly looked suspicious. I'd seen what the internet sleuths had been saying about Carl, and they hadn't been kind. There were a lot of people who had never been near the Vineyard, never met anyone involved and never heard my sister's name before she was murdered who thought they knew the facts of her murder better than the police did. Carl was justified in being suspicious – although the feeling on the island, where it mattered, was that Ryan was guilty and Bobby had covered it up.

'I barely know him,' he said, and I knew that if he hadn't felt guilty about the way he treated me last year he'd have stopped talking and clammed up by now. I wondered where his guard-dog wife was, but maybe she cared less about who he chatted to now he wasn't surrounded by girls in bikinis.

'I know. It was actually about whether you saw him drop me off at Remmy's when I was on the island last year. He said you were there with Stacy. I appreciate it was a long time ago...'

'I remember,' he said. 'I remember because we were avoiding you like the plague. Stacy was worried when you said that Holly hadn't been answering calls, and she thought we were going to get blamed if something had happened. Between us, I always thought she might have suspected that I did follow Holly that night. I didn't, of course,' he added quickly.

'So you saw him drop me off? And leave?' I asked, my thoughts working to understand what this meant. If Bobby had dropped me off just fine, how did I end up back on the beach with no memory and that awful note?

'Yep. I said to Stacy that it hadn't taken long for him to charm you. You didn't see us, just got your food and went.'

'And I left alone?'

'You left alone,' he said. 'But you got picked up by a car just down the street.'

Chapter Fifty

Holly

THAT NIGHT

Holly tried to scream as the figure pulled her into the long grass and spun her around. She realised it was Bobby a second before he slipped a hand behind her neck and covered his mouth with hers. His lips were warm and tasted of whisky and peppermint. Still, when they broke apart, she smacked his arm.

'What the fuck, Bobby?' she hissed. 'Was that supposed to be sexy? You scared the life out of me.'

'Who did you think it was?' he asked, his eyes wide. 'I thought you'd know it was me. I found your bag.' He held out her handbag and she snatched it away from him, her heart still thumping uncomfortably.

She probably would have recognised his voice if she hadn't been so damn tense. She couldn't stop thinking about what Emmy had told her about Ryan driving away with a young girl who had ended up dead. What part had Bobby played? Were both Slayton boys rotten to the core, or were they innocent, tarnished by being in the wrong place at the wrong time? Holly looked at Bobby's beautiful face and couldn't believe someone who looked so perfect would need to resort to taking advantage of underage girls. And Ryan... well, Ryan had yet to try anything other than over-the-clothes action with her – he'd been the perfect gentleman, and she'd been alone with him, if he'd wanted to do anything to her he'd have had the chance. Even now, if Bobby wanted to hurt her, there wasn't a chance anyone would hear her scream over the music, the fire, the delighted shrieks of drunken teens and twenty-somethings chasing each other around on the beach, and yet she didn't feel afraid. She just couldn't bring herself to think of Bobby – or Ryan for that matter – as dangerous rapists and killers.

Bobby stepped towards her and put a hand against her cheek. Even in the faint glow of the moonlight, she could see the concerned look on his face. 'Hey, are you okay?'

She looked him in the eyes and she wanted to trust him. The attraction she had to Bobby was undeniable – more than anything she'd felt for any of the boys back home – and as much as she'd thought Ryan was the right choice, now all she could do was wonder what it would be like to spend the night in Bobby's arms, to wake up next to him in the morning. The idea made her stomach flutter and she heard her mother's voice telling her to live without regrets. She'd known Ryan a few weeks, he'd be over her as soon as the next summer blonde arrived on the island. It wasn't like it had been true love.

'Hey, come here.' Bobby pulled her into his arms. His chest was warm and solid, it felt safe and he smelled like woodsmoke and alcohol. She let herself stand there for a moment and sink into his embrace. That was the one thing she missed most about home, the calming power of one of her sister's hugs.

Bobby lifted her chin and pressed his lips to hers once more, but this time his kiss was tender and gentle. She kissed him back without thinking, without overanalysing or trying to decide if it was the right thing, and before she knew it, she was lost in him, in the smell of him, the warmth of him, the feel of him. She was drowning, and there was no pulling her to safety.

When they parted, she could see the dark glint of his eyes in the pale glow of the moon. They were filled with lust and longing, as she was sure hers were too. She knew that this was it: she was in too deep to stop this now and whatever was going to happen was written in the stars as surely as if she'd uncapped the pen herself.

'Let's go back to mine,' she said, placing her hand on his chest. 'Where it's just the two of us.'

Bobby's eyes widened slightly and he no longer had the look of an arrogant rich kid, he looked like any other twenty-something who couldn't believe his luck. Then his face fell slightly and he leaned forwards to kiss her once again. When he pulled away, he shook his head slightly.

'I can't believe I'm going to say this, but I can't.'

Holly's face flushed with humiliation. After all that he was rejecting her?

'Honestly, I want to,' he said quickly, seeing her expression. 'But you've had a lot to drink, and I don't want you to wake up tomorrow thinking I took advantage of you. I wasn't lying when I said I really like you, Holly. When we spend the night together, I want to be sure you're going to wake up with no regrets.'

Holly tried to rearrange her features into a less disappointed expression. 'I… um… you're right, I guess. I should tell Ryan too – should I?'

Bobby nodded. 'Not tonight though, not while he's… while you're tired. Think about it in the morning.' He took her hands. 'We can go away for a few days if you want, take the boat. Just you and me. I can show you Boston, then we can fly to New York, I can take you to Hollywood?'

Holly laughed. 'Calm down, rich boy.' She grinned. 'But I'd like to go sailing with you, start slow?'

Bobby grinned back. 'Sure, sorry.'

'Okay, in the morning.' Holly nodded. 'I'll call you.'

'Are you going to get home okay? You will go straight home, won't you? Now?'

'Sure, Emmy and Derek are waiting for me.'

Bobby looked in the direction of the bonfire and nodded. 'You can get to the car park quicker through that way,' he said pointing. 'You don't need to go back to the bonfire.' He leaned forwards and kissed her again. It was exciting, exhilarating, dangerous. No matter how much she'd had to drink, Holly was certain she would call Bobby in the morning. The promise of adventure outweighed any fear she had of getting her heart broken.

'See you tomorrow,' she promised.

He held up a hand and disappeared through the long grass towards the beach.

Holly took a deep breath and headed in the direction Bobby had indicated. He was right, in the darkness she hadn't realised they were so close to the car park. Her relief was short-lived when she realised there were only six cars in the car park and none of them were Derek's.

Chapter Fifty-One

Claire

Carl had given me the description of the car. It made no sense, and yet it almost made perfect sense. I drove along the coast to Edgartown, my mind feeling like it was made of rice pudding. I hadn't been this way since I'd moved out of Holly's rental last year, my entire body had wracked with sobs as Holly's tearful landlords Sheila and Hank had helped me pack away my sister's things to be mailed home. Complete strangers who had been present for the darkest moments of my life. We had kept in touch; they had sent me photos of a beautiful memorial garden that had been set up for Holly in Oak Bluffs and I had arranged for flowers to be delivered for their anniversary. I would forever be linked to this place by my sister's death, and yet I couldn't bring myself to hate the island. It was a place of beauty, and kindness, and one dark act wouldn't change that. The community had found a way through the notoriety and handled it with respect and dignity. I wondered if one day I could convince Tom and Jess to set up home here. They were the only family I had left and I wouldn't dream of leaving them, but I could imagine them living on Martha's Vineyard, and I could certainly picture myself growing old here. It was like Holly had given me this place as a final gift.

Edgartown hadn't changed, except we were here off season this year, so it was quieter and a lot of the bars and cafes were closed for the year. It still looked picturesque, Fourth of July decorations still adorned some of the windows and patriotic flags still swayed in the gentle breeze.

I don't know what I was hoping to achieve by going to the Slayton mansion. The place was empty – according to Derek, the family hadn't been back here this summer, not since Ryan's arrest last year. They had stood by him, getting him the best lawyer money could buy and were protesting his innocence loudly – just from the sanctuary of their home in Boston instead of their holiday home on the island. I didn't blame them in the slightest. Everyone knew who they were, there wasn't exactly anywhere for them to hide from their own notoriety.

The gardener must have remained in employment, because the lawns were still trimmed, the bushes shaped, the flowers in bloom. I wondered which flower bed my sister's phone had been buried in.

'They aren't there, so get your goddamn picture and get lost!' a sharp voice called to me. I turned to see an elderly woman in the garden of the house next door. 'I got you on camera!' she shouted.

'I'm not a journalist,' I called over, starting to walk towards her. These expensive houses were spaced so far apart that it felt as if neighbours were in a different postcode. Sorry – zip code. 'And I'm not here to steal anything.'

She lifted her sunglasses up on to her head as I reached her. She was in her sixties or thereabouts, with a smart trouser suit and a silk scarf round her neck. She had on gardening gloves and I realised that this must be how rich people dressed to prune their petunias.'

'Who are you then?' she said, in a voice that insinuated that if she didn't know my face then it mustn't be worth knowing. Still, she didn't exactly look unfriendly, more just pompous.

'My name is Claire Matthews,' I said, holding up my hand in a half wave. I didn't think she looked like she'd want to shake it.

Her eyes widened ever so slightly in recognition, but she had been raised too well to show genuine shock. 'Oh, my dear, I'm so sorry about your poor sister,' she said, her tone immediately softening. I supposed she'd had enough of ghouls and reporters interrupting her gardening time. 'I was away last summer so I wasn't here when that boy was arrested, thank the lord. Is there something I can do for you?'

I started to shake my head, but then had a thought.

'Did you say I was on camera?' I asked.

'Well yes, but...' She looked embarrassed. 'Obviously I'm not going to report you to the police. It's just that the place has been inundated with damn journalists since it happened, and this week, with the trial...' She tailed off.

'Oh no, I don't blame you,' I said. 'It must be the opposite of why you chose to live here. I was just wondering, have you had the cameras put in recently?'

She shook her head. 'My grandson put them in a few years ago now. To be honest, I don't entirely know how they work. He says it's all on the laptop and I should just let it do its thing.'

They were probably the kind that taped over themselves after a week, I thought, trying not to get my hopes up. The police surely would have checked them anyway.

I wasn't going to find anything that a trained detective wouldn't. Still...

'Did you say you were away last summer?' I asked.

She smiled. 'Oh yes. My sister had these tickets for a cruise for her and her husband, but she found out a week before that he had been sleeping with their gardener's wife – I suppose he knew when her husband would be out because he was doing their garden so he—'

I was almost disappointed to have to cut her off. 'Sorry, but did the police ever ask for these tapes?'

She frowned. 'No. They rang me when I was on the cruise, but I just said I hadn't seen anything because we were in the middle of the Mediterranean Sea and the day it happened—'

'Is there any chance I would be able to take a look, please?' I'd never been able to quite nail the Bo Peep, little girl lost, victim face, but to my surprise she motioned me towards the front door.

'Of course you can,' she said, pulling off her gardening gloves. 'I'll get Pippa to put the kettle on and I can finish telling you all about it.'

-

The filing system for the camera set-up was so simple that it took longer to boil the kettle than it did to find the file I was looking for. Bobby's neighbour, who had introduced herself as Margaret, hadn't been lying when she'd said she was just leaving it to itself. The laptop had a TB of memory and as far as I could see she'd never deleted a single file. Each twenty-four-hour time period was in a folder of its own marked with the date, and inside each folder were six MP4 files, one for each camera. Once I'd identified the number of the camera that looked directly over the Slaytons' garden – Omega 78573 – and the seven-date period that the phone could have been hidden, I was left with 168 hours of footage. It was unlikely that anyone had put the phone there in the day, so that left roughly 56 hours to start on.

Margaret had gone to follow up on the tea, so I dragged the files into a WeTransfer and emailed them to myself using two different email addresses. I'd always been of the mind that it was easier to ask forgiveness than permission.

When Margaret came back with the tea, I didn't have the heart to refuse – Pippa had gone to the trouble after all. So we drank our tea while she told me all about her cruise and her philandering brother-in-law. Then she started on the exploits of the Slayton brothers and how she'd always known they would come to trouble, all the drinking and partying they did over there while their parents were swanning off to galas and charity evenings. When we finished our drink, she apologised that her cameras hadn't been of any help after all.

–

'What are we looking for?' Jess hissed, as I sat in the back garden of the same West Tisbury rental we'd had just over a year ago. The weather had cooled quickly and I had a shawl over my shoulders and a mug of hot chocolate in one hand, the other clicking forwards in fifteen-second increments.

'Someone going into the garden in the middle of the night, preferably with a spade and a mobile phone,' I replied. I hadn't told her yet about the car Carl had seen me get into the night of the bonfire – mainly because it might not have meant what I thought it meant, but also because I hadn't actually told Jess everything that had happened that night. It wasn't anything I could take to the police, or even Derek, so there was little point until I had something more concrete.

We found it on the third night after Holly's body had been found. When I had just moved out of Gina's house to stay with Jessica and Tom in West Tisbury.

'There,' Jess said, jabbing a finger at the screen. 'Someone there!'

I watched as the someone scanned a torch over the lawn of the Slayton house. Only the back of their head was visible as they disappeared into the garden. We watched, too afraid to skip forwards in case we missed something. After about ten minutes, the figure emerged, walking towards the camera this time, their face fully visible in the night vision.

'Holy shit,' Jessica whispered. 'Gina.'

Chapter Fifty-Two

Holly

THAT NIGHT

TWO HOURS BEFORE

'Hey, there you are!' The voice came from behind her and she froze, knowing exactly who it was. Darkness swam around her as she tried to remember why she had been avoiding Ryan Slayton – something Emmy had told her? But that seemed forever ago now – the night had been split into before her conversation with Bobby and after, and all she could grasp was that she was supposed to be going home with Emmy, and Emmy wasn't here.

'Ryan. Where have you been?' She spun around and plastered on a smile. 'I wanted to say goodbye, but I couldn't find you.'

'Well, I'm here now,' he said, moving closer to her in the darkness. There was one solitary street lamp providing the small, dirt-track car park with the dimmest of light. Why did his words sound like a threat? Why was her heart pounding a hole in her chest at the sight of him? Was it because she had just seconds ago left his brother's embrace? Or something else – something she should be able to remember but couldn't?

She had never felt nervous around Ryan before, she was sure of that. He always treated her with respect – so much so that she'd allowed herself to fall for his much less respectful and far more arrogant brother.

That was probably it. She was nervous and guilty about her feelings for Bobby, but Ryan didn't need to know that. She didn't have anything to worry about, she just had to get home and clear her head.

'How are you getting home?' he asked, concern in his voice.

'I was supposed to be going with Emmy,' she replied, looking around. 'But I think she's gone without me, so I guess I'll walk.'

Left Fork, as the locals knew it, was less than fifteen minutes' walk from her apartment, and in the daytime the thought of walking that far would have been welcome – Holly had never been the type to get a taxi when the distance was walkable – but in the dark, after six hours of drinking, it felt like a ten-mile hike.

'I'll drive you,' Ryan offered immediately. When he saw her expression, he held up the can in his hand to show her it was a Coke. 'I've hardly had anything to drink, don't worry. I'd like to see you get home okay.'

Holly took a deep breath, and looked between Ryan and the truck. She'd been in that truck dozens of times with him, why was she so reluctant now? She grasped for a memory that she felt was just at the edge of her consciousness, but it slipped away again.

'It's okay, you don't have to leave on my account. I can walk…' She didn't even sound convincing to herself.

Ryan waved away her weak protest with his hand. 'Honestly, I'm bored of this party anyway. I only wanted to come to apologise to you for me having to help my mum all night. Let me make it up to you by making sure you get home okay.'

Holly considered. He looked sweet and genuine – the same Ryan she had known for weeks. And she really needed her bed.

'Sure, thanks,' she said, following him to his car.

'Do you want a Coke?' Ryan asked as he helped her clip her seat belt in.

Holly noticed that her mouth was dry and her tongue was furry. A Coke sounded heavenly.

Ryan opened the can and handed it to her. She drank greedily until the fizz took her breath away.

'Wow, I guess I needed that.' She tipped the can in a 'thank you' and Ryan put the car in drive. He pulled out of the car park and turned right. Five minutes and she'd be home and in bed. She leaned her head back on the headrest and closed her eyes, just for a minute.

She re-opened her eyes just as the *Jaws* bridge came in to view. It was a beautiful view in the daytime, but at night the water was an infinite mass of inky black – impossible to tell where it ended and the night sky began. There was something else wrong with the picture. What was it? And then she realised.

Jaws bridge was in the wrong direction. Ryan wasn't taking her home.

Chapter Fifty-Three

Holly

Holly tried to sit up, but her head felt too heavy for her neck.

'Where going?' she asked, her tongue and lips struggling to form the words properly. 'Home.'

Ryan turned to look at her, confusion on his face. 'You asked to see the boat,' he said, continuing to drive straight on.

Had she? She remembered something about the boat, and being excited, but it was so hard to focus. She didn't want to see the boat now, she wanted to go home, but she didn't have the energy to argue. She was finding it hard to think right now.

Holly could barely keep her eyes open as Ryan pulled into the marina. When he opened the passenger door, he took her arm and helped her out. Her legs buckled slightly and Ryan held around her waist, gripping onto her tightly as she swayed.

The boat. She was on the boat, wasn't she? They passed a kitchen area, seats, a TV, then a bedroom. Ryan helped her sit down on the bed and Holly resisted the urge to lie down and go to sleep. How had she got this drunk? She hadn't felt this bad at the beach – had she? A bit dazed and dizzy, but nothing like this. She didn't understand what was going on.

'Do you like it?' Ryan asked, gesturing around.

Holly nodded. Did her head move? She wasn't entirely sure.

'It's gorgeous,' she managed to say.

She must have said it out loud because Ryan smiled.

'You're gorgeous,' he said, reaching out and hooking his hands under the red hooded jumper she was still wearing over her dress. He began to lift it over her chest and she tried to lift her arms to help him. She was definitely hot. Why was it so hot in here? Her arms felt like lead, but Ryan pulled the jumper up gently and her arms went with it. She was still sitting up straight – she couldn't be that drunk, could she? She'd seen girls in college get fall-down drunk, but she hadn't fallen down yet. Maybe she was okay. She just felt so confused. Maybe if she could get some water.

She asked Ryan, but maybe she didn't say it out loud because he didn't seem to register that she'd spoken. He was leaning towards her now, like he had on their dates. He was going to kiss her. Did she want him to kiss her? She had wanted him to at the beach, on their picnic. Why didn't she want him to now? He was her boyfriend, wasn't he? Yes, she'd been dating Ryan for what – weeks? A memory tugged at her mind, something she couldn't quite grasp hold of. His lips touched her and it was fine – there was nothing to worry about, was there? They were going out together, they had done this before. He wasn't a stranger. So why did it feel like she was doing something wrong?

She closed her eyes and tried to enjoy the feel of his lips on hers. This time, though, it felt different to before.

His tongue rammed into her mouth almost angrily and his mouth felt like it might leave a bruise on her lips. She tried to pull away, but his hand was behind her head, holding her to him. This didn't feel right.

Holly managed to jerk herself backwards, falling back onto the bed. Ryan looked surprised and then concerned, his face swam over hers in a dizzy blur.

'What's wrong?' he asked, in his familiar gentle tone. Then he frowned. 'Isn't that how Bobby does it?'

Bobby. Those words were tinged with anger and Holly began to remember. Something about Bobby… that was why she didn't want to kiss Ryan, and that was why he was mad at her. Wasn't he? Wasn't it? God, if only everything wasn't so fuzzy. Maybe Ryan would let her sleep here, on the boat, until this fuzziness went away and she could think straight. He was nice, Ryan, and he was gentle and kind. He would let her stay until she felt well.

'I waited for you to be ready,' he was saying, his voice still sounding angry. 'I wasn't some pushy asshole like my brother. I was a gentleman, I treated you with respect. When all you really wanted was for someone to lean you over the bannister in an expensive house and shove their way into your pants.'

Holly could barely understand what he was saying. None of this made sense. Was he still talking to her? Was there someone else in the room? She tried to sit up, but Ryan was pulling at the spaghetti straps of her dress, yanking them down until one of them snapped. Holly gasped out. He pushed up the fabric of her dress.

'I always get it wrong,' he said, his voice no longer sounding like his own. 'Bobby keeps telling me that nice guys finish last, that girls want a man who shows them what he wants. I told him he was wrong about you. Then

I saw you on the balcony at the party. He didn't ask your permission then, didn't take you out and treat you like a lady. He came up behind you and treated you like a whore and you closed your eyes and took it like a virgin on prom night. And that's when I knew he was right. You don't want to be wined and dined, you want to be treated like a dirty little bad girl, don't you?'

Holly tried to shake her head – no. She did shake her head, she was sure she did. His hand was on her throat, her words wouldn't come out, but surely he could see this wasn't what she wanted? Had she told him that this was what she wanted? In her drunken state, had she made him think that she wanted him to do this to her? She must have, that's what he was saying. That he'd seen her with Bobby and now he knew what she wanted. Maybe he was right. Maybe she had made him think that. After all, he was a good guy, a nice guy. This had to be a misunderstanding, all a mistake.

–

Holly didn't know how long she'd been lying there, but Ryan was snoring gently and she felt like maybe she'd been asleep too. The blackness outside the window had given way to a dark grey, but it was still the middle of the night.

Everything hurt, but she managed to move to the edge of the bed, and to swing her legs over. She pulled herself to a sitting position and immediately vomited onto the bedroom carpet. The noise made Ryan stir, and Holly let out a squeak. He opened his eyes and looked at her.

'Jesus, look at the state of you,' he said, his voice croaky and harsh, so unlike the Ryan she knew. 'I don't know what either of us saw in you. I suppose you think you're going to run back to Bobby now, are you? You think he'll want you after you've just fucked me?' he scoffed. Holly hung her head as more vomit stung her throat. 'Well he won't. He won't want my sloppy seconds. My brother's only interested if he can steal my toys before I've played with them.' He leaned over the side of the bed and reached into the jeans he had been wearing the night before. He pulled out his wallet and tossed a pile of twenty-dollar bills at her. 'I had a good time, thanks. Let me know if you want to do it again sometime.'

Tears stung Holly's eyes and she turned away so that he couldn't see how much his words had stung her. She probably deserved it. She was the one who had kissed the brother of the guy she was seeing. How had she managed to make such bad choices?

Being sick had made her feel slightly more human – or at least like she might be able to stand up. Whatever Ryan had given her – and she was sure now he'd given her something – couldn't have been too long-lasting. Her knees buckled slightly when she got to her feet, but she didn't fall – she wasn't going to fall. She stumbled from the room without looking back, and she was certain she heard Ryan snoring again before she'd even made it up the stairs.

Chapter Fifty-Four

Claire

Oak Bluffs PD still looked like an upscale home with a white picket fence. Brenda greeted me with a warm smile. Of course the police all knew I was back on the island for the trial.

'Good to see you, Brenda,' I said. 'Is Officer Howe around?'

Derek appeared in the doorway before Brenda could even reply. 'Claire, I thought I heard your voice. I've been trying to get hold of you, did you turn your phone off?'

'Yes,' I said, lowering my voice so Brenda couldn't hear. 'I didn't want Gina to be able to get hold of me.'

'Gina?' Derek looked confused and concerned. 'Is everything okay? Should I call Emmy?'

'No,' I snapped, then felt guilty for my tone. 'We need to talk to you. Please. Just you. Somewhere private.'

Derek held up his hands. 'Okay, sure. You're freaking me out a bit though. Where are Jess and Tom?'

'In the car.'

'There's a room back here we can use.' Derek led me through the back of the station to a small room with just a table and chairs and motioned for me to sit down. Then he looked at me expectantly. The truth was, I had no idea how to approach what I wanted to say to him – that I

284

suspected that Gina had planted evidence in the Slaytons' garden. I took out my laptop where I'd saved the CCTV footage.

'Tell me what you see,' I said, watching his face as he studied the screen.

'I see someone with their hood up walking across a lawn,' he said with a frown.

I leaned over and skipped forwards nine minutes. 'Wait,' I instructed.

'Okay,' he said, when the figure emerged. 'I see Gina walking across a lawn.'

I let out a breath. At least we hadn't been imagining that it was her. 'That's the Slaytons' lawn,' I said.

He scowled. 'Is she still stalking that family? She's going to get the whole freaking case thrown out. Isn't a murder conviction good enough for her?'

'That's not recent,' I told him. 'It was three nights after my sister's body was found.'

Derek seemed to lose his tan instantly. 'What?'

'Just before you found Holly's phone in that garden.'

I watched him realise the full implications of what he'd seen.

'She's been obsessed with the Slaytons since Natalie died.' I realised my stomach was churning. I wanted to be sick. 'She was following their truck the night of the bonfire. She saw them together, not Emmy.'

Derek didn't look surprised, but of course he didn't.

'Which you already knew,' I said.

Derek nodded. 'I was with Emmy, I knew there was no way she could have seen Ryan and Holly leave together because they were both still at the bonfire when we left. But she told me that Gina had seen him, and she was worried that no one would believe her. After how we'd failed Gina with Natalie...'

'You felt like you owed her justice,' I finished.

He sighed. 'I believed that she'd seen them. I justified it to myself that it wasn't a complete lie, it was just Emmy reporting it instead of Gina.'

'He might have been there,' I said. 'Otherwise why would Holly have been there? What we didn't consider was that Gina saying she saw Ryan at the crime scene put her there too. She could have just as easily hurt Holly and planted her phone in the Slaytons' garden. I'd wager she called in the tip-off that it was there.'

'But why would Gina have a reason to hurt Holly?' Derek asked, shaking his head.

'I think we know the motive,' I said, acceptance and shock washing over me in alternate waves. 'Obsession. Gina was obsessed with getting justice for what happened to Natalie. And I think she killed my sister to get it.'

Chapter Fifty-Five

Holly

There was a pool of light on the horizon, but the sun was yet to rise as Holly managed to reach the entrance to the marina. She considered just sitting down there and waiting for someone to help her, but although she had pulled Ryan's jumper back on to hide her ripped dress, there was vomit in her hair and she stank of alcohol. Ryan had been right, she must look like a complete state. She couldn't let anyone see her like this — it was just too humiliating.

It was only now that it occurred to her that she had no way of getting home, and the thought of walking back to Edgartown with a hangover beating against the inside of her skull and only high heels to wear on her feet was enough to make her consider going back into the boat and taking the money Ryan had thrown at her. Usually at a time like this, she would have called Claire to come to her rescue, or perhaps Jess. And just like that she was craving her sister's voice, the comforting feel of one of her hugs, a dropped kiss on the top of her head. She knew how upset Claire had been at her going away, her sister had made that very clear, but Holly also knew that the reason Claire was so upset was that the distance between them so soon after Mum had left was so hard for her. Holly had been Claire's anchor in the storm and she'd pulled it up without a second thought to how that would impact her older sister. She had a real urge to apologise, to hear her sister's voice, to bridge that gap just a little.

She pulled out her mobile phone – it would be five a.m. in the UK but that wouldn't matter to Claire. She was the one person in Holly's life who had little use for a watch, except to know when to show up to work. It was funny how Claire was more of a free spirit than she realised. Perhaps Holly would suggest they took the next trip together, invest in a camper van and go off exploring the world in their mum's memory.

The phone went straight to answer phone, no signal. Probably for the best, if Claire had been working she might only have got in a few hours ago. Still, Holly was sure she'd call her back later and they could talk properly, without the anger that had marred their last interaction. It would all work out, she was sure of it. She would call Emmy for help now, and just pretend she'd had enough to drink. Then, when she had showered and slept, she would pack her stuff and buy a plane ticket home. She had no job anymore, and lord knows what Ryan was going to tell everyone about what just happened. Bobby was going to hate her... there was nothing here for her anymore.

'Are you okay?'

The voice shocked her so much that Holly almost screamed. It had been the last thing she'd expected, lost in her thoughts on the edge of the marina. She turned around to see a woman, maybe early thirties, standing on the other side of the gate. She was petite, with dark hair and sad eyes. She looked tired, not just because it was late but like her very bones were tired. Almost like she was done with this life altogether. Holly wondered for a second if she had come here to commit suicide.

She took a deep breath. 'Actually, I had a little too much to drink and I didn't bring any money out because I was at a bonfire and—'

'You're here with Ryan Slayton,' the woman said, and Holly winced at hearing his name out loud. Yes, she definitely had to go back to a place where their family name meant nothing. 'I saw you get off his boat.'

'Please don't tell anyone that,' Holly pleaded. Her throat was raw from the drink and whatever Ryan had spiked her with and she just wanted to stop using it and cry. 'I was really drunk, and I'd prefer no one knew.'

'Why not? I've seen you with him before. Did he do something to you?'

'Have you been watching us?' Holly asked, fear beginning to build in her chest. 'Nothing happened to me. Why would you ask that?'

'It's not the first time,' the woman said, taking a step closer.

Holly swayed as she tried to step back. Oh dear God, she was going to be sick again.

'He's done this before. To my sister, Natalie.'

Natalie. Holly felt as though she knew that name, as if she had heard it recently.

'I don't know what you're talking about,' Holly said.

'If he hurt you, you have to go to the police,' the woman said, taking Holly's arm.

Holly pulled away, grabbing onto one of the thick guard ropes at the edge of the dock for support.

'He didn't...' Holly stopped, unable to admit or deny what had happened. She barely knew what had happened herself. Mostly, everything of the night was a blur and she just wanted to forget it had ever happened and get away from this place. 'Leave me alone.'

'No, please,' the woman said, her eyes wild and crazy now. 'Please, you have to tell them. Natalie is never going to get justice unless other people come forward. Those boys are bad news, everyone knows it, but because they're rich and good-looking the whole fucking island falls to their knees when they walk by.'

She grabbed at Holly's arm again. Holly was unable to believe this was actually happening. She couldn't deal with this now, and if this mad woman didn't stop screaming people were going to start coming out of their boats. Why was she following her around in the middle of the night anyway, and why did she still have her fingers gripped around the crook of Holly's elbow?

'Get off,' she said, anger and frustration in her voice. For a frail-looking woman there was a surprising amount of strength in her grip. 'I'll scream.' She almost choked on the words, but she said them anyway, just to get her off. 'Ryan's still in the boat.'

At the mention of Ryan's name, the woman's face darkened. Holly tried to take the opportunity to catch her off guard and shoved into her, knocking her off balance. The woman shrieked and stumbled backwards, and Holly stumbled towards the gate, trying to pull it open before this crazy psychopath could stop her again. The woman recovered too quickly, though, and launched herself at Holly, grabbing her jumper and pulling her backwards.

'I'm trying to help you!' the woman shouted. 'Why won't you just listen to me?'

'Get off me!' Holly tried to scream, but her throat was still too raw. She stumbled along the dock, her legs giving way completely now. She had no energy left.

The woman let go abruptly and Holly fell backwards, her head smacking against one of the metal poles used to rope off the edge of the water. Holly sat there stunned. She lifted a hand to her head, where blood was matting her blonde hair. She looked from the blood on her fingers back to the woman who was staring at her in dismay.

'Oh God, I'm so sorry,' the woman started to say.

Holly opened her bag to get her phone out.

'What are you doing?' the woman said, making a grab for Holly's bag and missing. She grabbed a fistful of Holly's hair and yanked her backwards. Holly flew back onto the deck, her eyes wide in surprise. Then she began to scream.

The woman shoved a hand over Holly's mouth, climbing on top of her to press down with all her weight. Holly tried to bite her fingers, but she wrapped her free hand around Holly's throat and began to squeeze. Holly tried to gasp for air, but it was impossible; the grip on her throat was too tight. When Holly stopped screaming, the woman put her other hand around her throat and squeezed harder. And harder.

Holly had always thought that at the moment of your death you saw your entire life flash before your eyes. The reality was, in the six minutes it took for the life to be squeezed from her, the only thought she had was that she didn't want to die.

Chapter Fifty-Six

Gina

Gina stared at the lifeless girl underneath her, unable to register what had just happened. Had the girl attacked her? Or had she struck first? It already all felt like such a blur. All she could picture in her mind was this girl refusing to help her get justice for her sister. She was just like the others, covering for that son of a bitch, when Gina could see what he had done to her. She knew what the Slaytons were capable of, what would it take for them to be brought to justice?

What are you *capable of?* her own voice in her head asked.

She gave the girl a small shake, then harder, but she was floppy and unresponsive. She was dead – Gina had killed her.

Gina struggled to catch her breath. She tried to pull in air, but it was like her lungs were sealed up. She sucked breaths in greedily, but it did no good, she knew she was hyperventilating, but she didn't know how to stop herself. What had she done? What had she done? This girl had a family, like Natalie, and now even if Gina didn't suffocate, she was going to go to prison, even though no one went to prison for what had happened to Natalie.

But they could now, the same little voice said. *One death can be covered up, but two? They'll have to listen to you if another girl is dead.*

Her breathing began to slow, breaths becoming easier to take now. All wasn't lost. This could even be a good thing.

Gina knew she didn't have long to sort this mess out. At any moment, someone could just walk off their boat and see her here, her life would be over in seconds. Natalie would never get the justice she deserved.

She looked around at the other boats on the dock, her eyes landing on the Slaytons' luxury Azimut. She knew Ryan Slayton was on board – the question was, was he sleeping? And would Gina have the strength to pull this girl up onto the boat without alerting anyone's attention?

She knew she had to try. This girl had had sex with Ryan – if she were found dead on his boat, then there would be no way it could be swept under the rug this time. And maybe she could only get one of them. Bobby would get away scot-free for his part in what had happened to her sister, but the ringleader, and in Gina's opinion the most dangerous – Ryan – would be taken care of. Behind bars, no matter how good his lawyer was.

It took every ounce of strength she had to drag the lifeless body to the boat. She had pulled Holly's jumper off and tied it around the wound in her head to stop any kind of bloody drag marks and she winced at every thump the girl's body made as she pulled it onto the deck of the Slaytons' boat, but she managed it. She dragged it over to the stairs leading down below deck and left it there, untying the jumper and pulling it out from under the girl's head. She checked around for anyone who might have seen what was happening, then gingerly slid the girl's handbag strap from under her body as well. Finally, although she wasn't quite sure what she was going to do with them, she pulled a handful of bloodied blonde hairs from the girl's head and wrapped them in the jumper. Then she put the hood of her own jumper up and, clutching the red hoodie and black handbag she ran back to her car without stopping to look back.

–

It almost felt impossible that no police cars had surrounded her home by the next morning. Gina hadn't been able to sleep a single minute since she'd arrived home and she was almost certain she would never close her eyes again without seeing the face of that poor girl lying underneath her. She had just sat at her kitchen table, waiting for the police to come. She was glad, for the first time in five years, that none of her family were around to see what was about to happen to her. Someone would have seen her dragging the body onto the Slaytons' boat, or maybe Carl had reinstalled the cameras in the marina after a spate of burglaries, or the Slaytons had cameras on their boat – there were a million ways she could be caught for what she'd done and that was without her DNA all over the body, which it was bound to be.

When the police hadn't come for her by ten a.m., Gina calmly went upstairs and stripped all her clothes off, putting them into a plastic bag, and had a long, scalding-hot shower. She washed her hair, then dried, put on a fresh outfit and took the bag of clothes she had been wearing the night before and tipped them into her father's metal burning bin in the back garden, covering them with lighter fluid and setting them on fire. When it was roaring, she went back inside and put on a pair of dishwashing gloves, then took the girl's handbag and jumper out of her car. The handful of bloodied long blonde hair was still wrapped carefully inside the jumper. Gina transferred them to a ziplock bag and folded the jumper up into another plastic bag, tying the top tightly. She knew she should burn these things too, but she was bolstered by the fact that the police hadn't arrived yet – someone surely must have found the body. Perhaps no one had seen her, maybe the police really were going to focus on Ryan Slayton. And if she could give them an extra push in the right direction, she fully intended to do so.

She waited until noon but still she'd heard absolutely nothing about a body being found on a boat in the harbour. On an island as small as the Vineyard, news like that would travel in minutes, it would be on the news, talked about on Facebook, she would probably have heard the sirens of the emergency response even. When she could stand it no longer, she got into her car and drove to the marina. It was bustling, as was usual for a day in July, but there was no sense of urgency, no sign of crowds around the part of the dock the Slaytons' boat was docked at, and no police.

She parked up and wandered down to where the boat was docked – it looked the same as it had the night before, with one noticeable difference – there was no dead body on the deck.

'Hey, Gina.' A voice she knew all too well by now startled her. Ryan Slayton was leaning over the edge of the boat. 'Everything okay?'

He spoke to her as if the last five years hadn't happened, as if she'd never accused him of killing her sister, as if he hadn't woken that morning to find a dead girl on his deck. Gina knew in that moment that this was one of the most evil men she had ever laid eyes on, and that one way or another she was going to finish him.

Chapter Fifty-Seven

Gina

The jumper was easier than she'd expected. After she'd crashed into the side of their beloved truck, she'd known that the Slaytons would take it to Kieran Fairstein to be fixed. That was the benefit of five summers of watching, five summers of waiting, she knew them like no one else did, not even their own mother, probably. She'd seen the revolving door of girls in and out of Ryan's life – she'd even warned a few of them away, the same as she'd done to Holly, but she'd had to stop that once he'd got wind of what she'd done and had her tyres slashed every time she'd replaced them for a month.

So the truck had been taken to Kieran's. And all Gina had had to do was to wait until Kieran went for lunch, leaving the garage wide open, and shove the jumper she had taken from Holly under the passenger seat. Perhaps in places where cars were stolen if the garages were left unattended it would have been harder, but in all honesty in a place like Martha's Vineyard there were a million times you could open the door of someone's car or truck without them noticing.

She had never really expected it all to work, if she was honest. She'd expected to be caught or for the forensics team to realise that the jumper had been planted, but she barely cared anymore. This was her last roll of the dice, the last chance she was going to have to get justice for her sister, she truly believed that now. It had been five years and Natalie's case had been deemed accidental, never to be reopened. Perhaps now, given what had happened to Holly, it would be. Gina thought of the Drew Peterson case, and how the police were unable to prove he had murdered his wife, but the investigation had caused the reopening of his first wife's suicide and Peterson was currently in prison for her murder.

Gina pictured the look on Ryan Slayton's face when the jury said the word 'guilty'. Would he know she had been the one to make it happen? There seemed no sweeter justice than Ryan going to prison for a murder he didn't actually commit, after the smug way he had evaded justice for the last five years.

But she was getting ahead of herself, she thought, slipping on her gloves and opening Holly's handbag. There was still work to be done.

Chapter Fifty-Eight

Gina

She waited, watching for the exact moment that he approached his usual spot and saw it, wedged in the crevice of the beach chair. This had all come down to timing and luck – it might have been a complete waste of time if Ryan had chosen somewhere else to sit that day or if someone had made it to the seat before him. She was sure there was enough evidence without the fingerprints on the phone, but surely it was better to have too much evidence than not enough. Especially as Ryan had taken care of Holly's body so swiftly. Gina hadn't given him nearly enough credit in that respect – he had woken up earlier than she had expected and on finding Holly's body he'd just dealt with it. Did he think that maybe he had killed her? The smug look he'd given her when she'd seen him the next day had made her think that he knew she had something to do with it, but Ryan very often looked smug in her presence. Well, not for much longer.

The phone had rung almost continuously for two days – it had started with Bobby the next morning, then someone called Jess, a few calls from Emmy, one from Holly's mum who she'd jokingly saved under 'Pain in the ass mum' and, tellingly, a few calls and messages from Ryan. He was clever, obviously he was trying to account for the fact that Holly's phone might be found, and he didn't want his to be the only number that hadn't called her. Gina used the phone to text Jess back, and Bobby – when it was found, it would be clear that Ryan was setting up his alibi and hopefully it would stall any of them raising the alarm about Holly's disappearance until the sea had washed away any of the physical evidence Gina might have left behind.

It seemed like luck was on her side for the first time in five years. All of the bad luck that had occurred to get Ryan off the hook for her sister's murder seemed to have been reversed as, just as planned, he grabbed the phone, looked at it and upon seeing that it was out of battery he'd gestured to a waiter and slung it onto his tray, muttering something she couldn't quite hear. She waited ten minutes until the waiter had returned with the tray and approached the bar.

'Excuse me?' she'd called in her most breathless, ditsy golly-gosh-I'm-so-silly voice. 'I think I left my phone on one of the sun loungers.'

'Yeah,' the bartender said, barely throwing her a look. 'We just had it handed over. It's on that tray.'

'Thank you so much,' Gina smiled, picking the phone up with the sleeve of her kaftan and quickly tipping it into the plastic ziplock bag hidden inside her beach bag. 'You're a star.'

'No problem,' the bartender said, holding up a hand. Gina would bet he couldn't pick her out of a line-up five minutes after she left. Not being a tanned curvaceous blonde did have its advantages sometimes.

She'd gone in the middle of the night to the Slaytons' place, parking far enough away that the headlights of her car wouldn't be spotted but close enough to make a fairly quick getaway if needed. She chose a spot that bordered the property, under a particularly sturdy-looking conifer, and began to dig into the ground with her gloved hands. Once the hole was deep enough, she took the ziplock bag out of her handbag and tossed it into the hole, covering it back up again. In a couple of days, she would call in an anonymous tip, hopefully long enough for Ryan and the bartender to have forgotten the stray phone they had found at the beach club.

As it happened, the police didn't break the news of the phone to Ryan until his lawyer got the discovery file ready for his trial, and by then it was as if the beach club and the days before his arrest had never even existed.

Chapter Fifty-Nine

Gina

She'd kept it together well so far, but it was getting harder every day. Seeing Claire's pain, watching her go through what she herself had gone through… it was harder than she had thought it would be. She told herself over and over that Holly's death had been an accident, and the only way for her death not to have been worthless was if she used it to get justice for Natalie. That was what this was all about, after all. Justice for her baby sister. Besides, Claire would have understood. She was willing to let Emmy lie to get a search warrant of Bobby and Ryan's truck, after all. Sure, she'd pretended to believe her, but Gina could see straight away that Emmy was lying and she could see that Claire knew it.

'Why are you doing this?' Gina asked her when they were on their way to the police station together. 'Why are you lying about seeing Ryan and Holly together that night?'

Emmy's eyes widened in shock, then she started to cry. 'Because I lied to Claire when she came to see me to ask if I knew where Holly was,' she admitted. 'I told her that Holly had told me to go, and that she wanted to stay with Ryan. The truth was, she had wanted to get away from Ryan, and Derek and I were supposed to be taking her back to mine. But she left her bag on the sand and went back for it. She told me to go and tell Derek to wait for her. We waited for like ten minutes, and Derek had to start his night shift in half an hour and we wanted to...' She looked embarrassed. 'I told him Holly had probably changed her mind and to go on without her. And if I'd waited maybe just five more minutes for her, perhaps she would still be alive.'

Gina let out a breath, stunned at this admission. 'So you trust me that I saw Holly and Ryan together?'

Emmy looked confused. 'Why wouldn't I?'

Gina laughed. 'Oh I don't know, maybe because everyone on this island thinks I'm totally crazy? And that I've had it in for Ryan for five years?'

'I don't think you're crazy,' Emmy whispered and Gina felt a huge rush of gratitude. 'But I do have something to admit to you. I was there on the night that your sister got into the car with Ryan. And I did nothing.'

'Lots of people were there, Emmy,' Gina said. 'And I'll admit I spent a long time wishing that one of them had stopped her, noticed that she'd had too much to drink or called me. But how can I hold it against you when I was the one who should have been looking out for her? I was her big sister. You guys were only a couple of years older, and drinking yourselves.'

'I've tried to tell myself that so many times,' Emmy admitted. 'But I know that I felt like something was wrong at the time and I don't think anything anyone can say will convince me that it wasn't my fault. One word from me was all it would have taken – the people there were locals, they were my friends. If one of us had acted...' She trailed off. 'I've waited five years for a chance to redeem myself for letting your sister get in that car and when the chance

303

came along to do the right thing, it took ten minutes of waiting for Holly for my resolve to break and for me to drive off with Derek. A second chance to be the person that if anyone asked, I would say I was in an instant, and I blew it.'

Gina was silent for a minute. She understood everything Emmy was saying. Gina had wondered so many times why people's actions didn't always align with who they wanted to be, but the reality was that in so many situations, you only got a split second to react. One split second to make the decision that would define who you were, versus who you thought you were.

'What you don't realise,' Gina found herself saying, 'is that even if you had made the right decision, if you'd waited for Holly and taken her home and the next morning you'd both woken up safe in your beds, you never would have known that that was your second chance. No one would have told you what a difference you made in the timeline of her life that night. Do you know what that means?'

Emmy shook her head.

'That means you've probably had your second-chance moment a hundred times over since Natalie died,' Gina said. 'You've probably made the right decision and done the right thing so many times, but you would never have known it. And Ryan Slayton has been on a hundred nights out that didn't end in murder. But the one time your bad decision meets his opportunity to be the predator we know he is, and bam! Our lives are altered forever. No one can make the right decision every time, Emmy. It's just that most people have the luxury of making their mistakes away from the evil that lives inside Ryan Slayton. He's the one to blame for this, not you.'

Emmy took a deep breath and nodded. 'You're right,' she said, 'I know you are. But someone needs to make sure that no one ever has to suffer at his hands again.'

Gina smiled and took Emmy by the shoulders. 'And that,' she said, 'is exactly what we're going to do.'

Chapter Sixty

Claire

I told Derek about how I'd been seen getting into Gina's car the night I'd ended up drugged and on the beach, and how I was almost certain she had followed me to the bonfire and spiked my beer when I'd stupidly left it unattended in the dunes. Then she'd come to my 'rescue' and let me believe that it was Bobby Slayton who was responsible. She hated those boys and she was determined to convince everyone, including me, that they were evil. And maybe they were. Bobby had told me that he and my sister were going to be together after the bonfire, and yet she'd been at the marina with Ryan that very night. What had changed her mind? A can of Coke with my sister's saliva on was found in the truck, but any traces of a date rape drug would be long gone. I'd discovered that GHB can be out of a person's system as quickly as two to three hours. Ryan might have started what happened that night but there was more to the story.

'You really think she did all this, don't you?' Derek asked, rubbing a hand across his face.

'How else would she have my sister's phone?' I asked him. 'I'd have said she was just trying to frame Slayton because she was sure he was guilty, but how would she have got hold of Holly's phone if she hadn't had anything to do with her death? Ryan wouldn't just have handed it over to her. And of course she managed to avoid admitting to anyone other than me that she'd ever been anywhere near the crime scene.'

'Which I let her do,' Derek said, shaking his head. 'I still don't know that we've got enough to go to the Chief. Ryan's trial is in a couple of days.'

'It's reasonable doubt, Derek. It's enough.'

Derek looked pained. His phone rang and he glanced at the screen. 'Emmy,' he said.

When Derek answered the phone, I could hear Emmy's hysterical voice on the other end. I looked at him quiz-zically.

'Calm down,' he instructed. 'Where? What makes you think that? Shit, okay, I'm with Claire, we're on our way.'

He hung up the phone and looked at me. 'Emmy's just seen Gina driving like a maniac towards Oak Bluffs. Gina left Emmy a message saying she's sorry for getting her involved in her lies, and not to look for her.'

'Oh Jesus,' I said, jumping up.

'I'll take a squad car on blues,' he called. 'Don't kill yourself getting there – I'll handle it.'

I ran across the street and pulled open the passenger door of my car.

'Tom, we have to go to Oak Bluffs.'

'What the hell is going on?' Jess demanded.

'I think Gina knows we're onto her,' I said. 'She's sent a message apologising to Emmy for getting her involved in her lie and not to look for her.'

'Oh God,' Tom said, putting the car into drive. 'How does she know?'

'Ummmm…' Jess looked grave.

'What?' I asked, trying not to snap at her. 'What did you do?'

'I didn't mean to.' Jess pulled a face. 'She called me and I said we were at the police station talking to Derek. Then she asked why you'd been to see Carl, then at the Slaytons' neighbour's house. I panicked and hung up.'

'She's been following me,' I said, gripping on to the seat belt as Tom took a corner at high speed. 'Jesus, Tom.'

'Sorry,' he said, easing off slightly.

'We're twenty minutes away. Anything could happen,' I said, resisting the urge to call Derek to find out what was going on. Derek would be driving so fast that even on handsfree he'd be distracted.

'Call Emmy,' Jess suggested, leaning between the two seats. Tom slammed on the brakes for a crossing and she jammed against the seat belt. 'Fuck!'

'Sorry.'

Emmy's phone rang and rang. Voicemail.

Then, still in my hand, my phone rang. Gina's name flashed on my screen and my heart seemed to stop.

'Gina, where are you?' I tried to sound calm – maybe we'd got the wrong end of the stick. 'Can you meet me somewhere please?'

'There's no point,' Gina said. Her voice had a slightly manic, high-pitched tone to it. 'I think you suspect why. I thought I could live with it because Natalie would finally have justice, but I can't stop thinking about...' A sob, and then silence.

'Gina,' I said, my tone urgent. 'Gina where are you?'

There was a long silence. 'You have to know this,' she said. She sounded calmer for a second, like she was trying to hold it together to give me this important message. 'I saw what he did to her that night.'

'Ryan,' I said. It wasn't a question.

'Yes. He didn't kill her, Claire, but he's still evil. You didn't see the state she was in when she got off that boat. Her dress was ripped, there was sick in her hair. She'd obviously been crying and she could barely stand. She did not look like a girl who had just had joyous consensual sex with the love of her life. I'd bet my own life that he drugged her, Claire, or that she was so drunk she wasn't able to consent. He did it to Natalie and he did the same thing to your sister.'

I noticed that Gina hadn't said my sister's name. I wondered if I could ever remember her saying Holly's name.

'He'll do it again, Claire. Ask Emmy what he said to her the morning Natalie was missing. Ask her.'

The phone went dead. I tried Emmy's number again, and again, and again. Just as I was about to give up, she answered.

'Claire?' she sounded distraught.

'Where are you?' I asked. She was outside, it didn't sound like she was driving.

'I'm at the ferry. Her car is at the side of the road, but I can't see her. I don't know what to do!'

'Derek will be there any minute,' I said, knowing that Derek was at least ten minutes away even if he broke every speed limit on the island. 'Listen, Emmy, what did Ryan Slayton say to you on the morning Natalie was missing?'

'Didn't Gina tell you? God Claire, it's the whole reason I was convinced he was guilty. Although obviously no one believed me, or said I was mistaken. I told Holly the night of the bonfire, that's why I wanted her to come home. After Natalie went missing but before her body was found he told me that she'd been a silly little girl who had only

309

been with him to make his brother jealous, and if anything bad had happened to her at the marina, then it was her own fault.'

'So how did he know she was in the marina,' I said, letting out a breath. I thought about my sister, wanting to get home and sleep off a hangover, excited about what might happen with Bobby, feeling guilty at the thought of leaving Ryan. Giving him the benefit of the doubt like she always did with everyone, getting in his truck for a lift home. Did he know about Bobby? Is that why there was a can of soda with Holly's saliva on in the truck – had he drugged her?

'Can you see Gina anywhere?' I asked Emmy.

I pictured Emmy looking around frantically. 'Oh shit,' she said, as I heard a horn sound in the background.

'What? What was that? Emmy?'

'The ferry. It's leaving now. If you wanted to end it all... you could jump.'

–

When we pulled into the car park of the ferry terminal, we could only just see the ferry in the distance. Derek had arrived before us, but not in time to make it onto the ferry. He'd been greeted by a hysterical Emmy who was sitting on the floor now, her head in her hands. Derek radioed for police in Nantucket, where the latest ferry was headed, but anything could have happened by then. The new harbour master radioed the ferry to send someone to look for Gina, but a thirty-something woman with brown hair doesn't exactly stand out. The only hope was that the ferry was too busy for her to be able to jump without anyone noticing.

Derek's phone began to ring and we all held our breath as he answered it. 'Okay, thank you. Okay. Yes, thank you.'

He hung up and looked at us, his face grim.

'There's been a report of a woman in the water. They've launched a rescue effort.'

Epilogue

One year later

We take turns in laying the flowers down at the memorial, Jess, Tom, Emmy, Derek and I. There is a bunch from Hank and Sheila, another from the women at the cafe opposite the marina and dozens of bouquets from names I don't recognise. People behind us line up to pay their respects. Martha's Vineyard had taken my sister and Natalie Burton into their hearts, and I have taken the island into mine. The sun is setting over the sea against a beautiful slash of purple, magenta and orange sky. When darkness fell, we would light our candles and there would be music and dancing, food and celebrating. We already knew that this would become an annual pilgrimage to the place my sister spent her last weeks, and rather than resenting our presence as a reminder of a time the locals would rather forget, we had been treated with respect and understanding.

The tragedy of Gina Burton not being able to deal with her sister's death any longer and trying to take her own life still looms large over the island. Some people think it was because she had done what she vowed to do and had nothing to live for any longer. Some people believe it's because she couldn't bear the possibility of Ryan Slayton walking free so she wanted to end it before the verdict. Only Derek, Emmy, Tom, Jess and I know the truth. At least as much of it as we could work out. Gina saw that Ryan had taken advantage of my sister that night and there had been an argument, we'll never really know what Gina's intentions were or why my sister died. I try not to hate Gina. I'm allowing myself to believe she was clearly ill, her obsession with the Slayton family a disease like the cancer that had stolen my mother, driven by the death of her own sister, but it's almost impossible not to feel hatred for the person responsible for the senseless loss we've suffered.

I don't think even Holly was a good enough person to forgive Gina for what she's done, but I think she'd agree with the decision we made between us to let Ryan Slayton go to jail for her murder. That way Natalie gets the justice she deserves. It was talking to Bobby that made me realise that Ryan may not have killed my sister, but he had taken the life of another young girl and that couldn't go unpunished.

Gina was pulled from the water that day in time to save her life, but she had been under water long enough to cause damage to her brainstem. Now she is locked in a body that can never hurt anyone again, with nothing but time to think about what she's done, the pain she's caused us. Some would say a fate worse than death or prison. I call it poetic justice for the week I spent believing my sister might still be alive. Just like the photo I had sent to the hospital of Holly at the beach; I chose it carefully, Holly's expression almost judging. The nurse promised to put it on Gina's bedside table; she didn't speak much English and didn't seem to know who the girl was when I took it in. Perhaps someone will notice and decide it would be kinder if she didn't have to stare blankly ahead at her victim every day for the rest of her miserable existence. Perhaps they won't.

Acknowledgements

My first thanks (despite the fact that she's read the book fifty times by now and probably won't read it at this stage) goes to my amazing agent, Laetitia. Thanks for sticking with me. Also Ciara McEllin, sorry I'm so slow at tax forms, and Rachel Richardson who makes sure my books get to readers all around the world.

To everyone at Canelo—what an awesome bunch. Honestly, you all rock. Alicia Pountney, Katy Loftus, Francesca Riccardi, Kate Shepherd, Nicola Piggott, Thanhmai Bui-Van, Claudine Sagoe, Hannah Bond and Jade Craddock.

Thanks to Kelly Lacey and her team of awesome book bloggers, the work you do is just phenomenal and it's a pleasure to work with you. I'm pleased to call so many bloggers my friends, writing has opened me up to a community of the most amazing book people.

Thanks as always to the people who read my books when there are so many cool TikTok videos they could be watching, washing up they could be doing and family they should be feeding—one takeaway won't kill them.

Lastly but never least, to my friends and family who are the most supportive people I could ever have hoped to collect around me. As you grow older you realise that the circle around you gets smaller, but stronger. And to the loves of my life, my two boys who are growing into the most wonderful young people—know that I am very proud of you and I hope you never read this because mum's books are off limits—and Ash, I'm sorry about deadline week (again) and will always be grateful for your support.